War for the Sundered Crown

The Sundered Crown Saga Book Two

M.S. Olney

Copyright © 2015 by M.S.Olney

All rights reserved.

No portion of this book may be reproduced in any form without written permission from the publisher or author, except as permitted by U.S. copyright law.

PROLOGUE

"Asphodel, Sword of righteousness I cast thee from the grasp of mortals for no man should wield thy power"– The Champion Alectae, following the murder of King Marcus, the Mighty, the second year after the fall of the Golden Empire

*

The night embraced the King's Spire, a monolith of power and opulence that pierced the starlit sky. Legends whispered of its impregnability, a fortress never breached, safeguarding the realm's most precious treasures. Yet, to the shadowy guild known as the Fleetfoots, such tales were but challenges whispered in the dark. For the right price, they claimed, no wall stood too tall, no vault too secure. Among them moved a thief, a phantom draped in silence, whose very breath seemed a secret kept from the night itself.

The thief approached the Spire, his figure melting into the contours of darkness. He was a wraith on a mission fueled by the lure of gold and the thrill of an impossible challenge. The Hall of Treasures within was his target, a vault of legendary wealth, rumored to house an object of unfathomable value and power. This night, it called to him, whispering promises of fortune and fame.

He surveyed the daunting structure, its walls stretching skyward, bathed in the ethereal glow of the moon. Undeterred, the thief withdrew a rope, its fibers woven by the finest craftsmen for strength and silence. A grappling hook, meticulously crafted, gleamed at its end. With a fluid motion, he retrieved a crossbow, its compact form sliding from its holster with practiced ease. He aimed aloft, where the shadows of the Hall's highest windows beckoned invitingly. With a deep breath and a steady hand, he loosed the bolt. It sliced through the night, a fleeting whisper before the hook found its mark, securing itself with a muted clink against the ancient stone. The sound, a potential alarm, faded unanswered into the night.

The thief allowed himself a momentary smile. The walls may be unyielding, the doors insurmountable, but he had no intention of engaging them directly. His eyes were fixed upon the stained glass windows adorning the Hall's upper reaches, their vibrant hues a stark contrast to the darkened world below. They were a vulnerability, a flaw in the fortress's armor, and his gateway.

He tested the rope with a cautious pull, ensuring its steadfast hold. Then, with the grace of a creature born to the shadows, he began his ascent. Each movement was deliberate, a symphony of muscle and intent, as he scaled the Spire's flank. Upon reaching the window, he paused, a sentinel listening for any hint of discovery. The night held its breath with him, offering only the soft caress of the wind as company.

The thief withdrew his knife, its blade a marvel of craftsmanship, inlaid with diamonds that caught the moon's gaze. With precision born of countless nights such as this, he cut a circular section from the glass, working around the leaded contours with delicate care. The piece came away silently, eased onto the roof tiles by steady hands. He slipped through the opening, a shadow passing into the heart of the Spire.

Inside, he found himself within the rafters of the Hall, a vantage point overlooking a sanctuary of wealth. Below him, the vault stretched out, a grandiose expanse of marble and gold. It was a testament to the kingdom's power, each surface catching the moonlight in a display of splendor. Yet, for all its beauty, it was merely a backdrop to the pedestals scattered throughout the room, each a sentinel guarding treasures untold.

The thief descended, his rope a silent conduit between the heights and the trove below. His landing was a soft whisper against the cool marble. Before him, the pedestals stood vigil, each crowned with glass domes that shimmered in the ethereal light. He moved among them, a specter haunting the edges of opulence, his eyes scanning for his quarry.

Jewels sparkled, ancient tomes whispered secrets bound in leather and gold, artifacts from realms distant and time-worn rested within their protective covers. Each was a fortune in its own right, a king's ransom waiting to be claimed. But the thief's gaze passed over them, drawn inexorably to the center of the Hall.

There, upon a pedestal swathed in red velvet, sat a stone. It was simple, unadorned, a slate piece amidst a sea of splendor. Yet, its unassuming appearance belied its value. His employer, a shadow as enigmatic as he, had promised wealth beyond imagining for its safe retrieval. It was not for him to question why; the allure of the reward was enough.

With a steady hand, he breached the glass dome, the barrier between him and his goal. The stone felt almost warm to the touch as he slipped it into a hidden pocket within his tunic. With the prize secured, he retraced his steps, ascending once more to the roof. The rope, his faithful ally, was retracted and cast down into the courtyard below in preparation for his descent.

As he maneuvered down the Spire's exterior, the thief remained vigilant, a part of the night itself. His movements were careful, calculated to avoid the slightest sound that might betray him. He reached the ground, the soft earth a welcome contrast to the cold stone above. The rope was gathered and stowed, its purpose served.

He moved away from the Spire, his form a wisp of shadow dissolving into the darkness. If fortune favored him, the guards would continue their rounds, oblivious to the breach in their fortress until the morning light revealed the unfathomable truth. The thief allowed himself the ghost of a smile, if fortune smiled upon him, the Spire's inhabitants would remain blissfully unaware of his visit until the stone's absence was discovered at dawn's first light.

A tall figure, shrouded in a cloak as black as the void, waited at the desolate crossroads just beyond the bustling city. The capital, a labyrinth of light and shadow, had offered its own challenge, but the thief, a master of his craft, had navigated its streets and alleys with the ease of a wisp of smoke. It took him an hour to extricate himself from the city's embrace, an hour during which the thrill of his recent conquest kept his spirits high. Humming a tune of victory and freedom, he ambled down the moonlit road, his way lit by a flickering lantern.

As the cloaked figure loomed into view, a momentary flicker of uncertainty passed through the thief. The crossroads, a place of ancient pacts and whispered legends, held an eerie stillness. The cloaked figure stood as if carved from the night itself, an ominous statue awaiting the thief's approach.

"Do you have it?" The figure's voice sliced through the silence, a whisper yet carrying an undercurrent of threat that made the air around seem colder.

The thief, masking his sudden unease with bravado, produced the stone from his tunic. "I do indeed, friend," he declared with a smugness that his rapidly growing apprehension did not feel. "Surprisingly easy, despite all the tales surrounding the Hall of Treasures."

The figure extended a hand, enveloped in the shadow of its cloak, and took the stone. As it examined the object, a chuckle, devoid of any warmth, escaped its lips. The sound was like the crackling of dry leaves, a prelude to some unseen horror.

The thief's heart, which had been a drum of triumph, now beat a rhythm of dread. "Er... so where's my pay?" he asked, the words catching slightly in his throat as the sinister aura of the figure seemed to tighten around him.

The chuckle ceased abruptly. "Here is your pay," the figure responded. With a snap of its fingers, the shadows at the edge of the crossroads stirred.

From the darkness emerged figures clad in cloaks of crimson, like fresh blood spilled on the night. Silent as ghosts, they converged on the thief, their hands brandishing knives that gleamed with a sinister intent. The thief's scream was a strangled thing, cut short as the blades found their mark, plunging into his flesh with ruthless efficiency.

As the life bled out of him, the thief's vision blurred, his thoughts fragmenting into chaos and pain. The last thing he saw was the cloaked figure standing over him, a smile playing on its lips, a smile that spoke of malevolent satisfaction.

"You have doomed all the world, thief," it whispered, its voice a serenade of coming darkness. "And its fall shall be glorious to behold."

The night at the crossroads returned to silence, the shadows reclaiming their own as the cloaked figures vanished as mysteriously as they had appeared.

In the distance, the city slept on, unaware that its fate had been irrevocably altered, and dark tides were on the horizon.

CHAPTER ONE.

The girl whimpered as the jeering crowd roared with hatred. Men, women and even the children she had grown up with. All were there; all had hate in their eyes and vile words spewing from their mouths. She cried out as strong hands shoved her forward; the force of the blow sending her crashing to the mud. The street wound its way through the village and led to an ominous wooden scaffold. The girl's white dress was now covered with mud and filth.

"Keep moving, witch," the guardsman growled. With one hand, he violently grabbed the girl's golden hair and hauled her back to her feet. In his other hand, he held a long spear, which he used to shove back those in the crowd who drew too close. Behind him were a dozen other guards, each escorting a similarly terrified prisoner.

Rotten fruit and excrement flew from the screaming crowd and pelted the pitiful prisoners. Some tried to shield their faces; others simply accepted the extra insult. Finally, the sad procession reached the scaffold. A dozen nooses hung from the wooden frame.

The guards roughly shoved their charges into place behind each of the hoops. One terrified man pleaded with the baying crowd. Another pissed himself. Fear was evident all around. Once all the prisoners were lined up and stood on square wooden blocks, a large man with a black hood upon his head stepped up onto the scaffold. At seeing the executioner, the crowd's cries grew more excited; they knew that death was fast approaching.

The hangman stood silent. He raised his arms to the sky to quiet the crowd. The guards formed a line in front of the gallows, their spears pointed outwards towards the increasingly excited mob. A tall man adorned in a long leather coat and purple trousers stepped forward from the sidelines. His long gaunt face was fixed with a long bony nose, thin lips and cruel grey eyes. A wicked smile creased his lips as he stared at the pitiful prisoners. The magistrate had long ruled the village with an iron fist.

"Behold! Here stand those who have deceived us all," the magistrate shouted above the roars of the crowd. "These wretches who made you believe that they were just like us. These villains have broken the sacred law; they have hidden their wicked powers from us and the eyes of Niveren. Magic users brought doom upon Eclin; they brought doom upon the world!

"Under the laws of our king, Alderlade the First, you are all sentenced to die!"

The man gestured to the hangman. The prisoners screamed in terror as one by one the hooded man kicked away the blocks. The first to die was the blond girl; the snap of her neck could be heard above the crowd's shouts. As the executioner reached his last victim, the yells had stopped. The horror of it all had finally sunk into the minds of the villagers.

Women wept while the men stared on, white faced and ashamed.

The final prisoner stared out over the crowd, his shoulder length black hair hanging loose over both his shoulders and the rope about his neck. A scar ran down his right cheek. His brown eyes stared at the crowd. To the people's surprise, the man chuckled.

CHAPTER ONE.

"Something funny, worm?" the magistrate snarled.

The condemned man's chuckle turned into a mocking laugh. He turned his fierce gaze upon the magistrate.

"You're all going to die, you fool. Whilst you wasted time arresting magic users, the Fell Beasts that I have spent the past week hunting have entered your village. You have condemned me, Ferran of Blackmoor, the only man who can save you from death. I find that ironic and amusing."

A scream came from the rear of the crowd. Another sounded, and then another. Soon the villagers began to push and surge forward towards the scaffold. Over the sounds of panic came unearthly roars. The magistrate's face drained of colour.

"Cut me free, you fool, or this whole village will be destroyed!" Ferran snapped. "And bring me the items you stole from me. I'm going to need them to save your wretched hides."

The magistrate stared in horror as a pack of snarling beasts appeared down the muddy street. Squat, brown creatures stalked their way towards the scaffold. Their long talons held an assortment of iron weapons, and saliva dripped from their fang-filled jaws. Upon their heads, the creatures wore material stained with the blood of their victims. This bloody trophy gave them their name: redcaps.

The magistrate bellowed at the hangman, who was holding an axe in his large hands. The man's fear was evident even through his thick black executioner's hood.

"Free him! Cut him down hurry!" the magistrate yelled, his voice filling with panic. One of the goblin-like creatures had cornered a petrified woman against the scaffold and was advancing menacingly towards her.

The hangman swung his axe, the blade slicing clean through the rope tied above Ferran's head.

Ferran sighed in relief as the pressure eased about his neck. Angrily, he removed the knotted material from his throat and threw it to the ground.

"My affects if you please, Magistrate," he demanded, holding his hand out to the terrified man.

"Here, take your things! If you get rid of these beasts, I will spare you, I promise!" the magistrate pleaded as he handed Ferran a sack containing his valuables.

Ferran tipped the contents of the sack onto the ground, sighing in relief as he saw the hilt of his tourmaline sword. The magic item was the weapon of all Nightblades. When inactive, it looked just like the hilt of an ordinary sword; but activated by the power of a Nightblade, a bright blade of pure magic burst into life. It was a weapon made to fight dark magic, and nothing was darker than the Fell Beasts of the Void.

The hangman turned and fled, pushing the magistrate to the ground in the process. The tall man scrambled about in the mud in a desperate attempt to regain his footing. But before he could regain his balance, a snarling redcap leapt onto his back. The magistrate screamed as the beast plunged its dagger-like teeth deep into his neck.

Ferran simply watched. As far as he was concerned, the magistrate was getting what he deserved. He was the murderer of innocent men, women, and children. He was a man who ordered the deaths of people simply because they were different.

After a brief struggle, the magistrate's pitiful cries stopped, and the redcaps started gorging themselves on his flesh. Slowly, Ferran moved away from the horrific scene and jumped from the scaffold. There were too many redcaps for him to fight alone. This village was doomed, but he was not sad to see it so.

Using the skills of his trade, he snuck out of the village, doing his best to ignore the pitiful screams of the folk who had moments before been lusting for his death.

He ran from the chaotic scene, jumping over a low fence to reach the open fields beyond.

Ferran refused to look back. The smell of smoke drifted on the breeze as the monsters torched the doomed village.

CHAPTER TWO.

Sunguard

Luxon watched the bustling city below. The people looked like ants as they scurried back and forth, and from his high vantage point from the top of the King's Spire they even looked the same size as the tiny tenacious insects. He had only visited the rebuilt palace twice in the past five years – once to visit the king, and the other at the behest of Caldaria's grand master.

During his first visit, the Spire had only been half-complete, and on his second the final additions had been hastily made. The Spire towered over Sunguard and offered spectacular views of the huge city below, and the expanse of countryside outside the high walls. On the horizon, he could just make out the outline of the distant seaport of Kingsford. If he stood on a balcony on the opposite side of the tower, he would have been able to see the clear calm waters of the Ridder River. He stepped back from the railing he was leaning on and stretched his back. He had been waiting for over an hour and his patience was wearing thin.

"You sure you don't want some of this pie?"

Luxon smiled as he turned and walked back inside. On one of the waiting room's ornately decorated chairs sat his best friend. Yepert had grown taller in the past few years, but his waistline was still wide. Food would always be his passion.

"Maybe later," Luxon replied as he sat down on another of the room's dozen or so pieces of furniture.

"You would have thought the council would offer you some respect and not keep us waiting for so long," Yepert said through mouthfuls of blueberry pie. His mouth was already covered in the blue fruit's juices. "I mean you're a wizard and the hero of Eclin."

Luxon ran a hand through his sandy blond hair and blew a raspberry in exasperation.

"Only a few people call me that, Yepert," he sighed. "Most just blame me for what happened. If it weren't for me there would be no dragons terrorising the Western lands or Fell Beasts marauding unchecked throughout the realm."

For a moment in time, Luxon had been hailed a hero for his actions at Eclin. Together with his friends and the brave men of Balnor, he had defeated the dark wizard Danon and saved the boy who now sat upon Delfinnia's throne. It had not taken long however before his name was used with scorn and anger. The tear, which had opened upon Luxon and Danon's escape from the Void, had unleashed countless Fell Beasts and other long forgotten horrors onto the world.

He was snapped out of his thoughts by his friend.

"Lux, you okay?" Yepert asked.

Luxon looked down. His right hand was shaking uncontrollably. He grabbed it with his left and willed it to be still.

Not now! he thought.

"I'm fine …"

Yepert looked at him, unconvinced.

"It's just stress …" he added.

"What's happening out there is not your fault," Yepert said. "The whole mess could have been cleared up if the council had allowed the mages to leave Caldaria and aid the Nightblades in hunting down the Fell Beasts."

Luxon's hand stopped shaking. He was about to offer a retort, when a tall woman wearing a blue velvet dress approached them. She was one of the city's noblewoman, charged with overseeing the kingdom's administration and civic affairs. The sapphire pendant around her delicate neck was the badge of her office. She was young, no older than twenty at a guess. She smiled politely at the two magic users. Luxon frowned slightly – he could see in the woman's eyes that she was nervous around them.

"The council will see you now, Master Edioz," the woman said. "I'm afraid your friend will have to stay outside however as the barons … well, the barons aren't comfortable having two spell casters in the chamber at once."

Her eyes moved quickly between the two young men. Yepert wore the long blue cloak of a mage, whereas Luxon wore green, the colour of a wizard. The cloak had been dusty and in need of repair when the mages finally found it hidden away in Caldaria's stores. With no wizard seen in the kingdom for a century, the etiquette of how to treat Luxon had been confused at best.

Yepert rolled his eyes and muttered under his breath.

"You go on ahead, Luxon; I'll just sit here and finish my pie. Wouldn't want my mighty powers to scare those brave lordlings too much now, would we?" He flashed the woman a smile before settling back into his pie.

The noblewoman bowed slightly, an uncertain look on her face.

"If you would follow me," she said before hurriedly leaving the waiting room.

Luxon took a deep breath and followed her out of the room. The woman led him along a corridor that spiralled upwards. Lining the marble walls were large arched windows, which offered more stunning views of the city below. As they went higher, Luxon could see as far as the distant Eclin Mountains to the northeast. Memories of the terrible battle in the now destroyed city of Eclin flashed into his mind: the bodies scorched by dragon fire, and those rendered asunder by the claws of the undead. He shook his head to get the memories out of his mind. Since that day, whenever he found himself alone, a dark mood would threaten to overwhelm him. It was at those times that memories of his time trapped in the Void would try and surface in his mind.

"Everything alright?" said the woman with a look of genuine concern, and perhaps a little fear, on her face.

Luxon looked down and noticed that he was gripping the marble handrail that ran along the corridor's side. His knuckles were white. Slowly he opened his hand and stared at it for a moment.

"Master Edioz?"

He looked at the woman. For a brief moment, she looked like his mother, before her features reverted to those of his now ashen-faced guide.

"I'm fine. I'm sorry ... please lead the way," he said, giving her a poor attempt at a smile. Hesitantly, she turned away and continued up the corridor.

Do they really fear us that much? Luxon thought. He had heard the stories filtering in from across the kingdom of magic users being attacked. Now that he had witnessed the looks of fear and mistrust for himself, he knew that the stories were likely to be true.

Finally, they reached the tower's highest level. A large foyer was decorated with statues and exquisite pieces of art. The stained glass windows on this floor were taller than a man. Images of Delfinnia's kings and heroes adorned the panes.

The noblewoman stopped in front of a pair of large oak doors. Two members of the King's Legion stood guard on either side, their silver armour contrasting with the purple of their tunics. At their hips hung short stabbing swords, and in their hands, they held a long spear and large oval shields adorned with a silver background and the image of a golden sword – the badge of King Alderlade.

They, too, gave Luxon an unpleasant look as they opened the doors. The woman bowed politely before hurrying off back down the spiralled corridor.

Luxon braced himself, held his head and walked into the council chamber. A large circular table made of serpentine was in the centre of the oval room. Twelve high backed chairs were placed around its circumference. To Luxon's surprise, only two of the chairs were occupied.

Why the long wait if there is no one here to see me? he thought in annoyance.

His nerves eased slightly as he recognised one of the men, who were in the middle of a heated debate. Of the child king there was no sign. The men stopped their hushed argument as they noticed Luxon standing in the doorway.

The elder of the two stood and walked over to Luxon. He still moved with a limp. A broad smile was on Davik's face, but his eyes gave away his tiredness. The man had fought at Eclin and had held the title of King's Regent for the last five years. His rule had been anything but easy, for dealing with the aftermath of Danon's return had tipped the realm into chaos.

"It is so good to see you, my lad. I apologise for making you wait for so long. I trust you and Yepert are well?"

Luxon smiled back; there was no fear or distrust in Davik's eyes. The other man in the room however regarded him with barely concealed loathing. The man stood and cleared his throat.

"Introduce us, Davik. Long have I wanted to meet the wielder responsible for the kingdom's woes."

Davik frowned. "Sorry," he mouthed to Luxon. Reluctantly he gestured to the man.

"Luxon Edioz. This is Ricard, the Baron of Champia."

Ricard was a tall man. He wore a tunic of black felt lined with gold. His grey eyes shone with intelligence and his neatly trimmed short black hair and beard made him look dashing. The Baron of Champia was the king's uncle and was well renowned for his prowess on the battlefield. His hatred for magic users was also famous.

"I have told you time and again, Ricard, that Luxon was not responsible for the destruction of Eclin and all that has followed," Davik added angrily. "If anything, he could help us."

Ricard scoffed.

"Davik, your fondness for wielders is well known, but even you cannot deny that since that day, this realm has been in chaos,' Ricard replied shortly. The baron pointed at Luxon. "This boy may be a wizard, but the realm would be a far better place without his kind constantly endangering us all. Danon is free because of him."

Davik shook his head in exasperation. Luxon felt an anger rise in his chest. He knotted his hands into fists; it took all his willpower stay in control.

"Sadly, I have pressing business elsewhere, so I will leave you two in peace," Ricard said. "I'm sure we will meet again … wizard." With a mocking bow, he turned on his heel and left the chamber.

"I am sorry, Luxon,' Davik said, gesturing to one of the vacant seats.

Luxon sighed and sat down. "I had no idea how bad things were getting outside of Caldaria," he said sadly. "I've lost count of the number of people who have looked at me and Yepert with fear in their eyes."

Davik sat heavily in one of the other chairs. He reached into his tunic and pulled out an envelope, which he then slid across the table's shiny surface.

"It's worse than you know. This arrived this morning penned by the hand of our mutual friend Ferran of Blackmoor. I fear that magic users will not be safe. Attacks have increased, and now even Nightblades are feeling the wrath of the mob. Luckily, Ferran escaped, but the village of Resden was lost to Fell Beasts."

Luxon's stomach knotted as he read the letter.

Davik rubbed his eyes with his fingertips. His time as regent had been a disaster. It had been a role he had never wanted and one that he was never trained to do. He was a warrior; he preferred a straight fight to all the intrigues of politics. Ricard, however, was better at the game of kingship;

Davik could feel his grip on the council slipping through his fingers. Even the eight-year-old king was falling away from his influence.

"I may be losing control, but at least I can offer you some positive news," he said with a weary smile, "and tell you why I summoned you to the capital."

Luxon put down the letter. Excitement filled him.

"Do you have news?" he asked, some enthusiasm returning to his voice. He had lost hope of finding his mother.

Naively, he had hoped to find her after the crowning of the king, but he had quickly discovered that she had hidden her trail well. Luxon's mother had been a source of mystery throughout his life. She had answers to questions he had to know.

"A strange woman was spotted at the gates of the fortress of the Watchers. The woman apparently wanted to pass through the gates and enter the Great Plains. The King's Legion commander on duty tried to stop her. She ... resisted."

"Magic?" Luxon asked.

Davik nodded in the affirmative.

"Six legionaries were left unconscious but unharmed, and the fortress gates had been forced open. The commander sent riders out to find her, but after a few hours of searching they were forced to turn back after coming under attack by one the plains tribes."

Luxon sat back in his chair and stroked his chin.

"What makes you think it was my mother? Perhaps it was a witch fleeing persecution or perhaps a rogue mage?" His mind raced. Why would his mother have travelled so far to the southwest? Why now?

"The commander said she had an emblem on a broche about her neck. He drew a sketch …"

Davik pulled another piece of paper from his tunic pocket and passed it to the wizard. On it was a rough drawing of a golden serpent upon a blue background.

"The sigil of the Diasect!" Luxon's blue eyes widened as he recognised the image.

He quickly stood from his chair; the paper gripped tightly in his hand. After years of dead ends, now he had a solid lead. Finally, he had a place to start. He would travel to the Watchers, he would traverse the vast Great Plains, and he would find his mother and get the answers he sought. Davik stood, too, and held his hand up.

"Before you go, Luxon I must ask something of you. Do you remember the sigil stone we retrieved in Eclin?"

Luxon paused. The last time he had seen the stone was on the day of the king's coronation. When he had touched it, visions of war and a sword shining brightly in the darkness had burned into his mind.

"I do," he answered warily. The visions still appeared in his dreams.

"King Alderlade wants answers," Davik said pacing the room nervously. "I want answers. According to Esma, his guardian, his highness dreams every night of the stone. In fact, he dreams of it so often that he rarely sleeps through the night. She grows concerned about his health.

"I have caught him staring at it for hours in the royal vaults. Whatever it is, its grip over the boy seems to be growing stronger."

"Perhaps my mother will have some answers," Luxon said thoughtfully. "From what I've learned in my research of the sigil stone, the Diasect was charged with hiding it away."

The answers they both sought were with his mother. Now all he had to do was find her, and that would not be easy.

CHAPTER THREE.

City of Kingsford

Sophia Cunning pulled the hood of her cloak tighter around her head. The marching soldiers ignoring her as they passed. Quickly, she moved from the doorway and crossed the narrow cobbled street to hide once again in the shadows of an alleyway. She narrowed her eyes as the man she had been tailing appeared in the inn's doorway. She could tell he was worse for wear from drink as he staggered slightly and gripped the doorway with a shaky hand to stop himself from falling over. In the distance, the sounds from the docklands carried on the breeze. Ships bells tolled out to warn each other of their presence in the misty darkness.

The man was dressed in a smart red velvet tunic and white breeches. A white cape, which reached his knees, hung from his broad shoulders. Around his waist was a leather belt complete with a sword in its scabbard.

Cautiously, he walked down the path leading away from the inn and into the street. At this time of night there was little in the way of traffic; only a group of pedlars and their pony were visible. A laughing band of drunken sailors staggered past Sophia's hiding place. One of the inebriated men vomited, causing his friends to bellow with laughter and mock him mercilessly. All the while, Sophia kept her gaze fixed on her target. Slowly, he staggered off down the street, Sophia close behind. She kept to the shadows as she stalked him. Side streets and dimly lit doorways were her friends.

She followed him for a few streets until he reached a narrow crossroads. Silently, she slipped into a doorway and once more waited. To her mild surprise, the man went from acting like a drunkard to someone who had never touched a drop of ale in his life.

"Where are you, Sintinius?" the man whispered into the darkness. "My master has little patience for your games and neither do I."

A quiet mocking laughter came from the shadows.

"So, the baron sends you to do his dirty work, does he? I had hoped to meet him face to face. We have much to discuss."

A thin tall man stepped out from a nearby doorway into the clearing of the crossroads. He wore a long black cloak similar to the one Sophia wore, and his features were hidden by a thick hood. Out of the shadow cast by the material, two white dots were visible. Sophia stifled a gasp as she realised that what she was seeing was a pair of eyes.

The smartly dressed man coughed nervously before holding his head high.

"Lord Accadus could not leave Retbit safely," the man said in a shaky voice. "The King's Legion would have had him arrested as soon he set foot outside of his lands. There is a war on, you know."

He was clearly nervous around Sintinius, and Sophia could not blame him. Just looking at the strange tall figure with the white shining eyes was making even her uncomfortable, and she had hunted witches and Fell Beasts.

"I do not care if Accadus is afraid for his safety," Sintinius replied dismissively. "I sailed all the way from Sarpia for this little meeting."

Accadus's man shifted uncomfortably under that unblinking gaze.

"Tell your master that my forces are ready, we only await his signal. I trust that he will keep to his end of the bargain. I do not take treachery lightly and my people have become accustomed to –" Sintinius paused before sniffing the air. "You were followed, you fool," he snapped.

He raised his arm and pointed back down the street, straight at Sophia.

Accadus's man spun around and drew his sword. Just as he was about to advance upon Sophia, the strange tall man behind him dashed forward. A vicious looking dagger sliced through the man's throat. It happened so fast that not even a gargled scream emanated from his ruined oesophagus.

Sophia tried to run but Sintinius moved faster. He caught her nimbly by the hair, causing her to scream in pain, and threw her to the stony ground. He placed a boot onto her back to keep her pinned to the floor.

"You will regret this. I cannot allow you to live," he hissed into her ear.

Sophia tried to struggle, but his grip was too strong. She reached into her cloak pocket with a free hand and fingered the hilt of the dagger tucked inside. Sintinius grip lessened slightly as he raised his own blade high to deliver a killing blow. Sophia took her chance, drew her dagger, and stabbed its point deep into her attacker's leg. The pressure eased slightly as Sintinius reeled backwards.

Sophia scrambled to her feet, shrugging off the cloak still trapped under her attacker's foot. She reached into a pouch at her waist and threw a smoke bomb at her feet. The dark vapour enveloped them both. By the time it had cleared, Sophia was gone.

Sintinius stared at the now empty alleyway. His eyes narrowed into slits. On the floor and still under his boot was the woman's cloak.

He picked it up and sniffed it. He breathed in the woman's perfumed aroma and put the scent into his memory. Accadus had sent a fool to do his work and now their plans were at risk, something that he could not allow. Sintinius stalked down the street towards the city's docks. He would sail to Retbit and see the baron in person. As he walked, four cloaked figures silently fell into step with him.

"Take this," he commanded. "Find the woman who it belongs to and silence her." He gave the cloak to one of the figures.

"Your will be done, eminence," they replied as one before drifting back into the shadows.

Sophia ran as fast as she could through Kingsford's streets. She could feel strange eyes upon her, and she shook her head angrily. The strange man's creepy white eyes had spooked her greatly. She kept running until she had crossed most of the city. Finally, she came to a halt outside of the tavern in which she had taken up lodgings. Her breaths came in ragged gasps. If the man were not alone then the city gates would now be watched for her presence. She glanced around the empty streets for any sign of pursuit before taking a deep breath and entering the brightly lit tavern. It was past midnight and most of the patrons had staggered off to their beds or to their homes. Only the tavern keeper was awake and active.

The barman looked up from cleaning glasses when he noticed her standing in the doorway.

"Rough night?" he asked. Her hair was ruffled, and several small cuts were on her cheek from where she had hit the ground.

She walked through the tavern, carefully stepping over the tavern owner's dog, which was snoring happily next to the fireplace.

"You have no idea," Sophia replied before heading up the small flight stairs that led to her room.

CHAPTER FOUR.

The King's Road

Luxon enjoyed the quiet. It set his mind at ease and allowed him to think. He was sat under a tall oak tree, which stood in a small clearing at the side of the King's Road. In the distance stood the city of Sunguard, its high towers gleaming in the sunlight. He was glad to have left the capital. The hushed tones and unfriendly looks from its citizens had been unnerving, to say the least. The trip had been worth his unease, however, as he now had something to go on. He would find his mother, not for any childish need, but to set his own mind at ease. To all appearances, Luxon looked like any normal nineteen year old. His shoulders had broadened, his voice was deeper, and sandy coloured stubble now grew on his strong chin. To those that knew him well, however, his eyes belied the truth. His body may have been young, but his soul was old. His imprisonment in the Void had felt like an eternity. For every hour that had passed in the real world, a year had passed in the Void. He had only been trapped there for two weeks, but to him it had felt like centuries.

In the years since his return from that foul place, he had been plagued by nightmares and strange fits in which he lost control of his power.

Now he and Yepert were travelling back north to the mage realm of Caldaria. He would need the advice of his mentor – the city's grand master – before he rushed off after his mother's trail. As tempting as it was, he had made a life for himself in the city. Hannah would be waiting for him, as would his other friends.

He smiled as Yepert returned from his visit to the nearby roadside inn. As usual, his best friend was singing a song from his homeland; they never failed to make him chuckle.

"The silly old fishwife leapt from her stool as the mermaid ran into view la le la le lo ... fancy an apple?" Yepert threw Luxon a green variety of the fruit.

He caught the apple easily and took a large bite out of it. The tangy juices sated some of the thirst he was feeling.

"Any trouble in the inn?" he asked, standing up and patting the dust from his trousers.

"Nope. I didn't wear my mages cloak. I did hear an interesting conversation between the inn owner and a traveller."

Luxon raised an eyebrow.

"Do tell," he said.

Yepert shrugged his shoulders as he devoured his apple.

"The traveller was saying how he spotted strange folk landing on the Marble Shore. He said that the ships were in the shape of serpents. They were not of Yundol or Delfin design. He then went on to describe his bowel movements and – whoa, that guy has some issues."

CHAPTER FOUR. 31

Luxon looked away and watched the distant horizon to the south. Black ominous clouds were forming, and he could make out the bright flickering of lightning. A storm was coming from the south. The visions of the men in strange armour and serpents flashed in his mind.

"You alright, Lux?" Yepert asked in concern.

Luxon shook his head as though to clear it. He smiled at his friend weakly. The sense of dread in his gut was growing by the hour. Something was coming, something that promised to bring pain with it.

"We should hurry and get back on the road," he replied weakly. "I don't like the look of those storm clouds."

As night fell, the two men spurred their horses into a gallop. They had tarried on the road for too long and when the light fades, horrors emerge from the blackness. The storm Luxon had spotted earlier in the day had now struck with ferocity. Heavy rain hammered down upon the stone of the road, and howling winds caused the trees lining its sides to creak and groan.

"We must reach the safety of a rune stone," Luxon shouted to his friend.

He had the hood of his cloak pulled close to his face in an attempt to shield it from the wind and rain. He was soaked through as the material offered little in the way of protection from the water. Just as he about to tell Yepert to keep moving, he spotted a shape moving in the tree line. He paused and gestured to Yepert to stay still.

The two looked at each other in concern. Lightning flashed, illuminating the trees. Yepert cried out as he recognised the things watching them. The creatures had squat bodies lined with nasty looking black spines, which ran down their backs. Narrow yellow eyes were offset by a tiny nose and mouths filled with needle-like teeth.

They were Fell Beasts of the Void. Pucks, to be precise. Countless numbers of the deadly creatures had escaped the Void at Eclin. Their numbers had multiplied over the years, so much so that the King's Legion and the Nightblades had struggled to protect the realm's roadways.

Slowly, Luxon reached for the staff tied to his saddle. Yepert, likewise, reached into his sodden cloak for the short sword that hung from his waist.

A tense silence fell as the mages and pucks watched the other. A loud, violent thunderclap shattered the stillness. With a chorus of high-pitched screeches, the pucks burst from the tree line to launch themselves at the magic users.

Yepert yelled out in fear, but Luxon whipped his staff, Dragasdol, from his saddle. With a flick of the wizard's wrist, the leaping pucks were blasted in all directions by magic.

"Ride, Yepert, ride!" Luxon yelled as he kicked his heels into the flanks of his horse.

He shot off up the road, his friend close behind. He dared look over his shoulder and instantly regretted doing so. Dozens of the Fell Beasts were gaining fast. Some ran on all fours, whilst other pursued them by swinging from tree to tree.

Yepert cast a spell of his own. The trees full of pucks burst into flames, roasting several the vicious little creatures. Luxon reigned in his horse to face their attackers. He spied a large rock lying in a small clearing at the roadside. A snide smile creased his lips. Once again, he raised his staff. He focused on the rock and pulled it backwards. The rock shook before it ripped from the earth.

"Let's do some bowling, shall we," he muttered under his breath.

He swept his staff through the air above the road. As the pucks drew within striking distance, he jolted his arm backwards. The heavy rock flew across the road, striking a dozen pucks and sending the small creatures scattering like bowling pins in all directions.

Luxon could not help but yell out in triumph. His joy was short-lived, however, when an ear-splitting roar came from the dark sky. The pucks skidded to a halt, their eyes growing wide with fear.

"Luxon, what is happening?" Yepert cried out.

It took all of Luxon's skill to keep his horse under control. A second roar and the sound of massive leathery wings flapping drew closer. Luxon cried out when a flash of lightening illuminated the beast flying towards him.

"Dragon!" He shouted, turning his horse and spurring it into a gallop up the road, Yepert close behind.

The massive winged serpent rapidly gained ground upon the terrified horses. The animals panted in haggard breaths and foam came from their mouths.

Luxon glanced over his shoulder and swore under his breath. An orange flame was building within the dragon's throat. He could see that the beast was black, its scales were torn, and a vicious wound ran from its jaw to the top of its skull. Its eyes glowed yellow in the darkness. The dragon dove lower until its massive claws raked the treetops. Wood and leaves were sent flying in all directions as the trees toppled like dominoes. Another lightening flash revealed its sheer size. It was larger than a castle, with wings that stretched across the sky. Luxon yelled for Yepert to go faster, but he knew it was no use. Desperately, he tried to make out the terrain. With a free hand, he summoned a ball of magical light into existence and threw it with all his strength. The bright ball of energy flew for several meters before exploding in a blinding flash. The surrounding countryside was revealed for a dozen miles all around. A pained roar let Luxon knew that the beast rapidly gaining upon them had been blinded momentarily by the spell.

"Over there, head to the valley!" he shouted to Yepert.

Off the main road was a dip which led down into a narrow valley of stone. Yepert nodded in acknowledgement before violently yanking the reigns of his steed to turn towards it. Luxon did likewise. He cried out as searing heat threatened to overwhelm him. The dragon had unleashed its fire, vaporising the stone of the road and engulfing the vegetation in flames.

Just as he thought the fire would reach him, his horse entered the valley. The dragon fire dissipated. With a frustrated roar, the monster pulled up to circle the skies above the valley.

Luxon slowed his horse. His hair was wet with sweat and his cloak steamed from the closeness of the dragon fire.

"We're trapped," Yepert, cried pointing to the far end of the valley. Sure enough the terrain beyond was impassable; a wide crevice lay at the far end.

Luxon wracked his brains, desperate to remember where they were. A mental image of the King's Road came to his mind's eye. He sighed as he realised that they were close to the Ridder lands. The land to the west was riddled with deep valleys and canyons carved out by the fast flowing waters of the Ridder River. They were still half a day's ride from Caldaria and safety.

"Perhaps it will lose interest." Yepert offered hopefully. The dragon's roars however put paid to that. The beast was hovering over the valley; it was only a matter of time before it tried to get at them. Luxon closed his eyes. At Eclin, he had defeated a dragon, now to save himself and his friend he would have to face one yet again. He remembered the silver scaled Umbaroth and his promise.

For the first time in countless ages, my kind is back where it belongs. Many of my kin will be lost and confused. I must find them and keep them safe. I will find us a home, one where we can fly in the blue freely and without fear.

What had happened to Umbaroth? Five years had gone by, and there had been no sighting of the silver dragon. At first, it seemed as though he had kept to his promise, but then something changed. Dragons had returned to Delfinnia and destruction had come with them.

"Stay here and get behind those rocks," Luxon told Yepert, pointing to an outcropping. If something went wrong, he hoped the stone would offer his friend some protection from dragon fire. Yepert nodded, a look of concern on his face as he took hold of the reins of Luxon's horse. Luxon took a deep breath and slid from his saddle. The weight of his staff offered him some reassurance.

"Good luck," Yepert said as he led the two hoses behind the outcropping. "You're going to need it."

The storm had eased slightly as it moved off towards the east. The heavy rain had turned into a light shower and the wind had turned from a gale into a harsh breeze. Once again, Luxon summoned a ball of mage light into being and stuck it onto the top of Dragasdol. Cautiously he made his way down the valley. The ground was uneven and covered in small sharp stones. Eventually, he reached the valley's end. Luxon peered over the edge of the pitch-black crevice. He shivered as the thought of tumbling into the gaping maw popped into his head. The dragon was circling in the skies above, the sound of its leathery wings flapping giving away its position. Luxon took a deep breath.

"Come and get me, dragon!" he yelled. His voice echoed off the hills. Within seconds, the dragon replied with an excited roar as it dove towards its prey. Luxon jumped backwards when the massive beast flew past the crevice. It circled in a wide arc before landing surprisingly gracefully on the opposite side of the gap.

The dragon watched Luxon with curious eyes.

"You do not run, mortal?" it growled in a voice that sounded like thunder.

Luxon puffed out his chest holding his head high.

"I am Luxon Edioz, wizard and friend of the Dragon King Umbaroth. Who are you?"

The dragon's yellow eyes widened upon hearing the words. Its massive forklike tongue flicked out to smell the air, to smell the strange man who claimed to be a wizard.

"I am Sarkin. I have heard your name, wizard. You were the one that set us free." The beast's eyes narrowed, and its tail shook violently, setting off a rockslide on the hill upon which it sat.

Luxon stepped back to avoid being hit by falling stones. Once the rock fall had ended, he raised his staff into the air and aimed it at the dragon.

"Why have you and your kin returned here? Why are you harming the people of these lands?" Something was not right, Luxon could sense it.

CHAPTER FOUR.

The dragon flicked its tail again before leaning across the crevasse. Its massive head came within an arm's length of Luxon, who had to use all his courage to not turn tail and flee. It was so close that he could clearly smell the dragon's breath. It smelt like sulphur mixed with roasted pork.

"We are here to reclaim our lands," the dragon roared. "We were here long before you. The Great Drakis will make you all our prey to hunt and devour as we please. Now, wizard ... get inside my tummy for I am hungry!"

Luxon leapt backwards just as the beast's head darted forward, its jaws open and wide. Using magic, he propelled himself out the way of the dragon's snapping teeth.

Sarkin reared upwards until he towered over the valley. An orange glow formed in his belly before moving rapidly up his body and into his throat. Luxon was ready. He braced himself and thrust his staff into the ground. The dragon unleashed his fire. The searing heat lashed downwards towards the wizard, but the flames never reached him. Instead, they dissipated harmlessly as Luxon's magical shield absorbed the energy. The dragon roared in disbelief and fury.

With a flick of Luxon's free hand, the hundreds of sharp loose stones which covered the valley floor began to shift and move until they hovered in the air.

"This is your last chance, Sarkin. Leave this place and never return or I will destroy you. Tell me of Umbaroth – does he live?"

Sarkin hissed in response. His huge wings opened to balance himself as, with a massive talon, he ripped a boulder from the hillside upon which he sat. Luxon narrowed his eyes and focused on the rock. He clenched his hand into a fist and the rock exploded into tiny fragments.

The dragon roared in surprise and pain as its talon was hit by the shattered rock. Quickly, Luxon thrust his staff forward, sending the hundreds of sharp stones shooting towards Sarkin's exposed wings. The deadly projectiles slammed into the soft leather, shredding them in the process. With its wings damaged, the dragon lost its balance. With a panicked shout, the huge creature toppled into the deep crevice.

Luxon had to steady himself as the beast bounced and crashed off the valley's sides. With every impact, the ground shook.

"Are you alright?" Yepert called from behind him.

"I'm fine. We should be safe –" Before he could finish his reply, a clawed hand dug itself into the ground in front of him. The dragon was climbing. Luxon was about to run, but Sarkin's head came back into view. Once more, Luxon held his ground and pointed Dragasdol.

"Impressive, wizard,' the beast growled in pain. 'For your courage, I will tell you what you wish to know,"

Luxon lowered his staff in surprise. He had expected the dragon to try to eat him again.

"In exchange, I ask that you mend my wings with your magic."

"Do you promise to never return to Delfinnia and to not harm the people?" Luxon asked.

The dragon rolled its eyes.

"Fine. I promise. You Delfinnians are all bone anyway."

Satisfied with the dragon's answer, Luxon told the dragon to meet them back on the road. He would need plenty of open space if he were going to aid the huge beast.

CHAPTER FOUR.

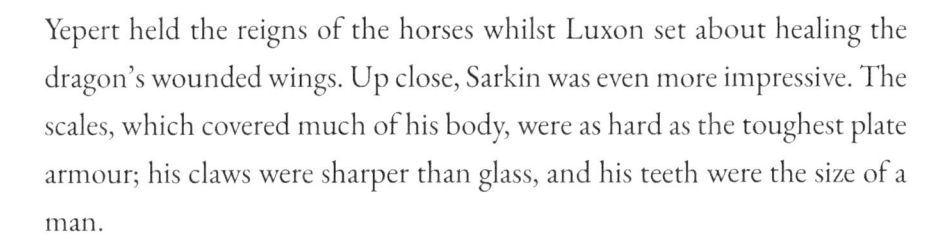

Yepert held the reigns of the horses whilst Luxon set about healing the dragon's wounded wings. Up close, Sarkin was even more impressive. The scales, which covered much of his body, were as hard as the toughest plate armour; his claws were sharper than glass, and his teeth were the size of a man.

In the east, the sun was beginning to rise above the distant mountains, its warm light chasing away the dark of night.

Luxon stood underneath one of Sarkin's wings. With his hands pressed against the leathery skin, he focused with all his might. A bright white light emanated from his hands. Healing magic took a lot of concentration at the best of times; with a dragon towering over him, it was more than a little daunting. Slowly, the damaged skin began to close and the tiny stones which had embedded themselves within began to drop out of the wounds and fall like hail onto the grass.

It took him a full hour to finish the task but finally, with a satisfied sigh, he stepped back and admired his work. The dragon, too, seemed relieved as it stretched its wings and checked them over carefully.

"Perhaps Umbaroth spoke truth, when he said that not all of your kind are foes of the dragons," Sarkin muttered in gratitude. "Your kindness and forgiveness will not be forgotten."

Luxon stepped back and placed his hands on his hips

"I have held my side of the bargain. Now, tell me of Umbaroth and tell me why the dragons are attacking the Western lands."

Sarkin nodded, his huge head before sitting back onto his haunches. Luxon tried not to smile, as the sight of the fearsome beast reminded him of an obedient dog waiting for its master to throw a stick and play fetch.

"Umbaroth was usurped by Drakis, a dragon who was an enemy to the world of men before we were banished by the gods into the Void. With our freedom, Drakis and others refused to listen to Umbaroth's message of peace. For a time, we were free to fly in the blue without fear in a land far across the sea. But that all changed when men came. They hunted us and took our kin away."

Sadness entered Sarkin's voice. "The first baby dragon born in thousands of years was taken by them: loaded into their wooden ships and taken from us. Drakis blamed the men of this land for the attacks. In their anger, other dragons joined him and turned away from Umbaroth. There was a battle, and Drakis emerged the victor. He sent others and me here to search for the baby and to learn of its fate. Umbaroth, shamed in defeat, was exiled. To where, I do not know."

Luxon stepped forward and placed a hand upon the dragon's snout. He rubbed it reassuringly.

"I had no idea. I will investigate this. I promise you. I am a friend to the dragons, to Umbaroth. Return to your kind and tell them that Luxon the wizard is helping. Tell them to halt their attacks until I have answers,"

Sarkin lifted his head and flapped his wings. With a flap, he lifted off the ground to hover.

"I will do my best, wizard, but I cannot make any promises," the dragon said, before it flew off into the brightening sky.

CHAPTER FIVE.

The Marble Shore

Kaiden sighed contently as he watched the sun dipping below the horizon. The clear shimmering Marble Sea was the colour of fire as the last of the light danced and flickered over its surface. A warm breeze ruffled his hair and he breathed it in. The scent of desert sand filled his nostrils; the southerly wind was blowing from the hot land of Yundol, which was located far across the water.

He smiled as soft hands wrapped themselves about his waist. Alira's warmth pressed into his back as she hugged him tightly.

"Dinner will be ready soon," she said, nibbling her husband's ear. "It is so beautiful here. I love it."

Kaiden turned and lifted his wife off her feet. Playfully, she struggled before sinking happily into his strong grip. The five years since Eclin had been the best years of his life. He had married the woman of his dreams, had a child and lived in peace. Since Eclin, he had not wielded a sword and he was glad not to.

"I am starved," he said, his stomach growling. "The new crops should be ready for harvesting by the end of the month, and I think I will ask some of the lads from the village to help with the task." Alira's long blonde hair lifted in the breeze, tickling his face. With his wife on his back, he walked back up the hill towards their small cottage.

The cottage was sat on the top of a hill which overlooked a valley and the coast. To the north was a hundred miles of farmland, pockmarked here and there by small settlements and homesteads. To the east was the vast Fell Forest, which stretched all the way from Marble Shore to Retbit. Nestled amongst the other hills was the village of Seawatch. In Kaiden's youth, his father had been lord of the land but nowadays the baron of Kingsford ruled the Marble Shore.

After the horror of Danon and the destruction of his order, Kaiden had made a vow to Niveren to live a life of peace, and with Alira at his side he kept that promise.

"Tamlin came by the house earlier," Alira said. "He said that tales of those strange ships landing down the coast were still being told. Apparently, just two nights ago, a dozen more were sighted rounding Estran's Point."

Kaiden chuckled. "Tamlin is always telling tales. He is the biggest gossip in the kingdom. Do you remember last year when he said he saw a sea serpent whilst on one of his fishing trips? Turned out it was nothing but a piece of driftwood."

Alira laughed at the memory. "We spent a whole day in that blasted boat until we convinced him of the truth," she chuckled.

Her laughs stopped, and Kaiden slowed to a stop as they crested the hill. In the distance, a plume of black smoke was rising into the sky. Kaiden lowered his wife from his back and held her hand tightly. As he focused, he realised that there were more plumes on the horizon, a dozen in all. The husband and wife glanced at each other before breaking into a run. Their house was just round the bend; if trouble was coming their way, they had time to escape it.

Kaiden sighed in relief as they arrived at their thatched cottage. Sitting on the doorstep was Tamlin, and on his lap, giggling, was Kaiden and Alira's daughter, Ilene. The middle-aged angler looked up and gave them a serious look.

"By the look on your faces I'm guessing you've spotted the smoke," he said. "I told ye there was weird folk abroad. I dashed up here to check on you and found little Ilene here on her lonesome, so I thought I'd best stay and wait for ye to come home."

Alira opened her arms as her daughter toddled towards her. She scooped her up and kissed the child's forehead.

Kaiden shook the old angler's hand. "Thank you, Tamlin. When did you spot the smoke?" He reached above the cottage's doorframe and took a key from its hiding spot.

"I saw the first around an hour ago, far to the east. Then the others appeared, one after the other. Could it be Yundol raiders?"

"I hope to Niveren it isn't," Alira whispered. Ilene was fast asleep her golden hair intertwined with her mother's; her face pressed into her parent's neck. The child was snoring softly.

Kaiden unlocked the cottage's door and led the way inside. The house was not very large. The ground floor was an open space comprised of a kitchen and living area. A ladder led up to the roof space and the bedrooms. Alira climbed up to the higher floor and set about putting Ilene down for her evening nap. Kaiden and Tamlin, meanwhile, sat down in front of the open fireplace.

"I doubt it is the Yundols," Kaiden said. "I remember their last invasion. I was just a boy when they landed. The fighting cost my father his life, but we drove them back into the sea. It was a hard, long fight, but we smashed them."

Kaiden's mind drifted back to his childhood and the dark memories it brought with it. He had held his father in his arms, as he died, the sounds of battle raging all around. It had been the day when he had first taken up arms.

"Aye," Tamlin said. "I had doubts myself. The ships I saw were not of Yundol make. If anything, they reminded me of the stories my grandfather used to tell. He used to talk of the men of Sarpi, the men who wore strange armour and sailed serpent ships ... the men whose eyes glittered in the darkness."

Kaiden nodded. He was deep in thought. He, too, remembered the stories of the Sarpi. Once they had been masters of a vast Empire far across the ocean. Then Danon had come, and his rule of darkness brought down all the ancient empires of man. The Sarpi had not been heard from ever since those days. Even during the time of the Golden Empire, they had only been a myth. After all that he had witnessed at Eclin five years before, he could not help but think that Danon's return and the Sarpi were connected.

"Well I best not keep you," Tamlin said. He stood up and stretched. "I'll head back to the village and see what news I can gather. Goodbye, Alira, goodbye little one," he called to the roof space.

Both men smiled when a giggly "goodbye" responded. Kaiden waved his friend farewell. He stood in the cottage's doorway and frowned. His gaze drifted over to the nearby stable house. He waited for Tamlin to disappear down the hill before crossing over to the wooden structure. Inside, he was greeted by a welcoming snicker from Herald, his trusty horse. The white animal was old now, and past his prime as a warhorse. These days, Kaiden just used him for easy farm work; in the old beast's retirement, it should not have to work too hard after all. He affectionately stroked the horse's grey mussel.

"I had hoped that I would never have to do this again, my old friend," he sighed reluctantly. The horse licked him in the face. Kaiden chuckled as he entered Heralds' pen. At the back was a long oak chest hidden amongst the straw. Kneeling in the hay, he unlatched it and lifted the lid. Inside was his sword, sheathed in its blue and gold scabbard. He picked up the weapon and reverently pulled the sword from its sheathe. The silver blade was polished to a bright shine, and the seven-pointed gold star engraved on the pommel glistened. The weight felt good and familiar.

"I pray to Niveren that I will not need to use you," he whispered.

Quickly, he closed the chest and hurried out of the stable, the sword tucked inside his tunic. If Alira saw him with it, she would only worry.

Kaiden could not sleep; but it wasn't the sound of the sea or the night's heat that had woken him. It was a feeling of dread. The sight of the distant smoke plumes had him worried. He slid out of bed, being careful not to disturb Alira who was snoring happily. Ilene too was sound asleep in her little bed, which lay close to the door. Tiptoeing to the room's door, he took the tunic hanging from the peg and put it on before slipping out of the room and onto the landing. He climbed down the ladder, which led to the ground floor. Once at the bottom, he tilted his head in order to listen.

A clink sounded from outside the cottage. Cautiously, he moved towards the front door and stopped. Only the sound of the nearby sea lapping gently against the sandy shore could be heard. Nonetheless, Kaiden could not shake the sense that something was wrong. He walked to the fireplace and reached up into the chimneystack. He sighed in relief as his fingers grazed the hilt of his sword. After he had brought the weapon inside from the stables, he had hidden it inside the chimney.

He took the sword and unsheathed it from its scabbard, before returning to the door.

As quietly as he could, he unlatched it and slowly opened it. Cool night air drifted into the cottage. He sniffed it. The sense of unease deepened; the tinge of smoke entered his nostrils.

Another clink sounded nearby. Kaiden raised his sword and settled into a defensive stance.

"Who's out there?" he called out into the darkness.

He flinched as a loud crash came from the stables. The sound of Herald in distress made Kaiden break into a run. Within moments, he reached the outbuilding and kicked open the door. Herald was pacing his stall nervously, his eyes wide with fear. Kaiden narrowed his eyes; in the dark he could see little.

"Easy boy," he said soothingly to the horse. With his sword, he swept the straw laid on the stable floor. It was deep enough for a man to hide beneath.

He spun around with a shout as the stable door slammed shut. He dashed over to it and tried to pull it open. It would not budge. He pressed his head against the wood and heard someone sliding a metallic object through the door's latch. Panic filled him. Alira and his child were in danger; he had to escape!

'Alira!' he bellowed in panic. He took a step back before savagely kicking the stable door.

The wood rocked with the impacts, but it would not budge. A scream sounded from outside, followed by another. Kaiden roared in frustration. He kicked the door repeatedly until sweat poured into his eyes and his breaths came in ragged gasps. The sounds of struggle could be heard, and shouts followed.

A bright light flashed quickly, followed by an agonised scream. Kaiden closed his eyes. Alira had used her magic. He just hoped that her untrained power would be enough to protect their child.

"Leave her alone!" Ilene cried. The little girl must be terrified. His daughter's cry spurred him into action. With his sword, he began to hack savagely at the wood until the sharp blade pierced the door. Now it was weakened, he rained blow after blow with his weapon. The wood cracked. He tossed aside his now blunted sword and ripped the door apart with his bare hands. Splinters bit into his skin but he ignored the pain.

He could now see outside.

A group of four men stood outside the cottage. Lying in a smoking heap was another, a victim of Alira's magical fire. In their hands were deadly two-handed curved swords of the like Kaiden had never seen before.

They all wore dark cloaks over a suit of scaled armour, which glinted in the moonlight, but their most striking feature was their eyes. They shone silver in the darkness. Kaiden cried out as one of the strange attackers struck Alira, sending her sprawling onto the ground.

"Take the child and the mage. They will fetch a good price," hissed the biggest of the four.

"What of him?" asked another, one slightly shorter and more muscular.

The leader turned to glare at Kaiden who could only stare back in frustration. He looked down and saw the metal rod, which had been used to secure the stable door. He reached through the hole he created and tried to remove the metal. It would not budge.

"We have tarried here for too long as it is," the leader replied. "Leave him. He is helpless."

Kaiden raged at the strange men, but his angry shouts soon turned into desperate sobs as his unconscious wife and screaming child were dragged off into the night.

The sun peeked over the eastern horizon, lighting up the sea with a dazzling array of colour. The sky itself turned from darkness to a fiery red.

To any observer, the sight would have inspired or promoted the thought that the day ahead would be a good one. Kaiden did not notice the sight. He was asleep, his eyes red and sore from the tears he had shed. He was exhausted by his efforts to escape the stable.

His hands were bloody from his attempts to rip his way through the stubborn wood, and by his side laid his broken sword. The blade had snapped as he savagely hacked away at the metal object barring the door. Finally, he had collapsed to fall into a deep sleep.

Kaiden moaned as Herald licked his master's face. The horse's muzzle was soft and damp. With a groan, Kaiden opened his sore eyes. For a moment, he had thought that it had all been some terrible nightmare, in which he had dreamed of his wife and child being stolen from him. When he realised it was real, he sobbed. He pushed Herald's muzzle out of his face and absent-mindedly stroked his loyal steed.

"Ahoy there!" came a voice from outside the stable. Kaiden scrambled to his feet and ran to the door. He cried out in relief as he recognised Tamlin cautiously approaching the house.

"Tamlin! By Niveren, it is good to see you. Please get me out of here!"

The old man jumped in surprise, and his thick grey eyebrows rose on his wrinkled head as he spotted Kaiden's predicament. Tamlin scurried over to the stable. He tried to move the metal barring the door but could not. He gripped the object with two hands and heaved, but again it would not budge.

"I can't move it!" Tamlin said scratching his head. "It doesn't look heavy; it doesn't feel heavy and yet I cannot move it."

Kaiden frowned and leant out of the hole in the wooden door. Now that the sun was casting his light, he could see the object which was barring the stable doors. It was a simple metal rod, dull grey in colour. The light caught the object for a brief second, and a kaleidoscope of gold lines flashed upon its surface. They were runes, Kaiden realised.

"The rod is magical in nature," he whispered. Tamlin had his hands on his hips. His old and worn cloak was smeared with dirt and the old man's face was covered in what looked like soot.

Before Kaiden could ask why, the old man disappeared from view. He heard Tamlin rooting around for something.

"Aha!"

Tamlin came back into view. In his hands was the heavy sledgehammer that Kaiden had used the previous day to break up some rocks for the path he was planning on making.

"Stand back, lad!"

Kaiden did as he was told.

The old man raised the hammer high above his head with a grunt. Tamlin may have looked old but he was far stronger than many expected. His years of swimming and fishing kept him in good shape.

With a shout, Tamlin swung the hammer with all his might. The heavy head smashed into the metal rod. It did not break.

"Son of a …" the angler muttered. He shrugged his shoulders and took a deep breath before swinging the hammer for a second time. This time when the hammer struck, a satisfying cracking sound came from the rod.

Swearing, Tamlin delivered another three blows before the strange rod finally cracked in two. The old man cackled and wiped the sweat from his brow.

Kaiden pushed open the door and fell to his knees.

Tamlin caught him before he fell on his face.

"By Niveren, what happened here, lad? Where is Alira and the little one?"

"They're gone," Kaiden wept. "Men took them, men whose eyes shone in the darkness." The old man held his young friend tightly as he sobbed.

Finally, he eased Kaiden's grip and knelt before him.

"They weren't the only ones, lad. The village … the village was destroyed last night. I saw the flames and heard the screams from my hut on the beach." He looked away. "I am afraid to say that I hid when I saw the men with the eyes. They must have come from further up the coast. Those smoke plumes were other villages put to the sword."

"You said others had been taken, Tamlin," Kaiden said, staggering to his feet. "How many?"

"A dozen at least – men, women and children. It is the strangest thing, though. They killed some folk, spared others and only took a few."

Kaiden rubbed his eyes tiredly. He spotted a bucket of water next to the small stone well in the centre of the courtyard. He strode over to it and dunked his head into the cool water. He shook his head, sending spray everywhere. The coldness of the liquid cleared some of the weariness from his body and sharpened his mind. Clenching his fists, Kaiden went back inside the stable. He took a saddle off the rack on the wall and set about preparing Herald for travel.

"You're going after them," Tamlin said. It sounded like he already knew the answer.

Kaiden pulled the harness tightly around the horse's muzzle and checked the animal's hooves.

"They have, what, a few hours head start at best? With prisoners in tow, they will not be moving at speed." He climbed into the saddle. Herald's ears perked up and he stamped his feet in excitement.

"Good luck, my friend. Be careful," Tamlin said as Kaiden kicked his heels into Herald's flanks and bolted from the stable.

The wind whistled through Kaiden's black hair as he galloped along the cliff tops. He had been riding hard for the past half hour and already Herald was panting heavily in exhaustion. The aging horse would need to rest soon or risk injury. He was riding east along the Marble Shore, the long golden beaches and turquoise waters passing quickly by beneath him. He had passed through a small hamlet and found its cottages in ruins and the bodies of half dozen villagers lying face down in the dirt. He was on the right trail, but he knew that his old horse would not be able to take him further, not at top speed at any rate.

With a roar of frustration, he pulled back on the reigns to slow Herald to a trot. The horse's breaths were ragged but slowed.

"It's not your fault, boy," he said soothingly into Herald's twitching ear. "I should have protected them."

The sun was rising higher in the eastern horizon and already the day promised to be a hot one. Temperatures on the Marble Shore could rise to unbearable levels – another obstacle to his pursuit. He looked out to sea and frowned. Four black dots were visible on the horizon. As he focused, he could see that they were ships, serpent-shaped ships. He swore before spurring Herald into a gallop once again. He made his way down the cliff side road and towards the village of Seaedge. As he got closer, he could see that it, too, was on fire. A thick black plume of smoke was rising high into the air. As he rode into the village, he saw a number of people rushing about with buckets of water.

"Hail there," one of the villagers said as he spotted Kaiden. He was a man with a ragged face and spindly arms, an old angler, no doubt.

"What business do you have here? If you're looking for fish, well as you can see there isn't any." The man chuckled to himself. Kaiden arched an eyebrow. For someone whose home had probably just been destroyed, the man was in surprisingly good spirits.

"I'm not here for fish," Kaiden said as he slid out of the saddle. "I am in pursuit of men dragging prisoners with them. Was it they that burnt the village?" He led Herald over to one of the fire-fighters buckets and the horse greedily began to drink.

"Aye, the Sarpi were here. Their ships came at first light. At first, they looked as though they were wanting to trade. We even offered them food and drink, and they paid in coin. They soon turned aggressive though when others reached the village from the road. There must've been fifty of them, and with them they had double that number of folks in chains."

"What happened then?" Kaiden asked. "I passed through a hamlet back yonder. No one was left alive." He ran his hand through Herald's mane and petted the horse gently. Herald looked up in surprise as a cry came from the village square and a wooden house collapsed with a crashing of timbers.

"If they weren't in such a hurry," the man said, "then things could have been a lot worse here."

Kaiden looked at the man questioningly.

"Why were they in a hurry?"

The man was about to reply when the low tone of a horn sounded from the cliffs above. Marching rapidly down the road was a cohort of a hundred legionaries, their silver breastplates glinting in the sunlight.

"That's why," the man said simply with a shrug of his shoulders. With a nod, he scurried off to join other villagers tackling a blaze.

Kaiden waited for the soldiers to reach the village. As soon as they arrived, the cohort's commander began to bellow orders to his men to assist in tackling the flames.

"Get those fires out, you gits. Blast it all – we were too late again."

Kaiden walked towards the commander. Perhaps the soldier had some idea as to where the raiders would be heading.

"I thought we had them this time," the commander growled. He was a tall muscular man with cropped greying hair. Kaiden guessed that he was around forty is age.

"Do you know who they are? My wife and child ..."

The commander jumped and swore loudly as he noticed Kaiden standing close by. He regarded him with a look of suspicion before taking off his plumed helmet.

"Niveren be damned, but I think they are Sarpi. Me and my men have been trying to catch the bastards in the act, as it were. Twenty coastal settlements on Delfinnia's south coast have been attacked over the past month. At first, we thought they were Yundol marauders or pirates, but the testimony of survivors suggested the Sarpi. They described men with eyes that shone in the dark."

"Do you know where they could be heading?" Kaiden asked hopefully.

The commander shook his head slowly and grimaced.

"If you're thinking of going after them, do not. One of our ships tailed them earlier in the month. Looked like they had set sail from the city of Stormglade. Either they took it, or the Merchant King has gone mad."

Kaiden looked to the horizon. The city of Stormglade had been built in the early days of the Kingdom of Delfinnia. Three hundred years ago, it had fallen to a rebellion, and ever since it had been run by the self-styled Merchant Kings. In truth, they were nothing more than pirates, and a thorn in the realms side.

"I recognise that look, friend," the commander said. "Seriously, heed my words. Do not go there. The garrison at the Watchers will turn you away and even if you did make it through, you'd have to contend with the tribes that roam the Great Plains."

"I could go by sea," Kaiden replied.

The soldier chuckled and shook his head.

"No, you can't. We received orders from Sunguard. No civilian ships can sail past the White Crag. Pirates and those raiders infest the seas beyond. They have had the navy stretched thin the past few weeks. I even heard they sunk a convoy sailing from Blackmoor in the North West."

Kaiden kicked the ground in frustration. He wanted to pursue his family, but the commander was right. He did not even have a sword, let alone a way to reach Stormglade. He swore under his breath and ran his hands through his long black hair. He looked to the north. He had allies there

– powerful ones. Perhaps they would help him save his family. After a few seconds, he firmed his jaw and nodded thanks to the commander. He leapt into Herald's saddle and spurred the horse into a trot.

He would head north to Caldaria and his friends.

CHAPTER SIX.

Caldaria

Caldaria's crystal towers glinted in the sunlight. The scene always made Luxon smile. In the city, he felt safe, and the world's many woes could be forgotten. He breathed in the air, noticing the freshness that the onset of winter often brought with it.

He and Yepert rode their horses towards the bridge leading to the gateway of the city. The place was thronging with people.

"What's with all the people?" Yepert asked.

Luxon shrugged his shoulders.

Men and women were accompanied by children; each had a look of desperation on their faces. Some pulled carts laden with valuables behind them; others had no possessions. But all looked afraid.

"They look like refugees to me," Luxon said. Since the battle of Eclin, large parts of the north had fallen to marauding Fell Beasts, or to the mountain tribes that had begun to swarm south. The Legion and Rangers did their best to protect the people, but they were undermanned and overstretched.

Luxon groaned as people in the crowd spotted him. Some pointed and whispered to their friends as they recognised his wizard robes and the staff strapped to his back. Some glared in anger, whilst others had hope etched on their miserable faces.

"The wizard! The wizard is here!" cried a woman. More people turned to look at him, and an excited babbling built up amongst the crowd.

Yepert glanced nervously at his friend and brought his horse in closer, his hand drifting to the dagger tucked into the belt of his robe. The crowd pressed closer, and Luxon's horse shifted nervously. To his amazement, some people reached out to touch him.

"You will save us, won't you?" pleaded a young woman no older than himself. "The Fell Beasts burned our village and forced us to flee. We came here because of you. You have the power to save us."

Luxon stared at the girl. These people saw him as some sort of saviour – a stark contrast to those he had encountered in the capital and in the south. He was about to say something when the banging of drums caused the crowd to part. Luxon looked up to see three riders dressed in black push their way through the masses. He sighed in relief as he recognised the Nightblade Welsly and two of his companions.

"Move aside, people,' Welsly bellowed. 'Let the wizard and his friend through."

At the end of the bridge, the huge crystal doors of the gatehouse opened, and out marched fifty more black-clad Nightblades. They pushed the crowd apart to clear a route into the city.

"I will do what I can for you," Luxon told the girl before Welsly took hold of his mount's reigns and led the way towards the gates. The Nightblade glanced over his shoulder and smirked.

"I bet you weren't expecting a welcome home like that?" he said over the noise.

"I'm glad you were here," Luxon answered wiping his brow with the back of his hand. The encounter had spooked him. "Why are these people here? I would have thought Caldaria would be the last place folk would come in times of need, what with the Privy Council doing all it can to spread distrust of magic users."

Welsly nodded. "A lot of folk from the eastern lands know the truth, and the Baron of Balnor has done all he can to dispel the slanders. These people believe that the mages can protect them from the Fell Beasts."

"Has it really gotten that bad?" Yepert chimed in from behind them.

"It has. Three days ago, Fell Beasts attacked Balnor itself and ravaged their way through a large swath of land. It took the might of the fourth and eighth legions to check them. The Nightblades took a beating in the battle, so we have been recalled to Caldaria to regather our strength," Welsly explained.

More hands reached out for Luxon, but the Nightblades shoved the people back.

"Looks like you two had a tough couple of days yourself," Welsly said with a raised eyebrow. If anyone held a mirror up to Luxon and Yepert, they would have seen that their faces were covered in dirt and soot.

"Yeah ... we had a bit of a run in with a dragon near the Great Wood," Yepert answered. "I could kill for a bath."

"Nothing serious I hope?"

Luxon let out an exasperated sigh.

"Probably. It's just one of many things I need to discuss with Grand Master Thanos."

Luxon sighed happily, as he sank into the hot waters of the bathtub. The heat soothed his tired limbs and the water washed away the dirt from the journey. He was in his private quarters, located in the Arch Tower.

As a wizard, he had his own lodgings in the tower. There were certainly benefits to being the first wizard in a century. He dipped his head under the water, enjoying the quiet that being submerged brought. In the tub, he could forget about everything. It was also his favourite place to think. He would meet with Grand Master Thanos and ask his permission to head after his mother. The senior mage would probably be able to offer some insight and advice.

He closed his eyes and thought back over the events of the previous few years.

After Eclin, he had tried to seek out his mother, but soon it became apparent that his time in the Void had changed him deeply. He suffered from terrible night terrors and, at times, visions that haunted him in his waking hours. The shakes he sometimes got were a symptom of an illness that Grand Master Thanos had called Void sickness. Nightblades and other spell casters that encountered Fell Beasts and Void tears sometimes suffered from a corruption of their magic. In the Void, magic existed, but like everything else in that foul place it was twisted and wrong. If he wasn't careful, then the sickness could cause him to lose control of his powers. When it struck was unpredictable, but when it did, he often suffered violent fits. Thanos had kept his affliction secret; only he, Thanos and Yepert knew of it.

The hot water let his mind drift to more pleasant memories. His thoughts drifted back to the night two years previously, when he had finally plucked up enough courage to ask Hannah to be with him. For years they had been just friends, but on the eve of the Autumn Festival that friendship had turned to love.

The festival had been in full swing, and Caldaria's central plaza had been alive with jovial celebration. The city's crystal towers had been covered in beautiful decorations such as brightly coloured flags and banners. The mages also did their part by casting fantastically colourful spells that wowed and amazed the enthralled crowds. At the heart of the plaza, a band was playing traditional Delfin tunes. The fiddlers and drummers had the crowd dancing and it was there that Luxon's eyes set upon Hannah. Her blond hair had been tied up into a braid and she wore a flowing white dress. She had been dancing all night long with her friends and her cheeks were flushed red with laughter, and her eyes sparkled with fun and life. He and Yepert had just left a nearby tavern. Perhaps it was the ale that gave him the confidence to move through the crowds and take her hand. The two danced throughout the night, under a night sky filled with fireworks. After the crowds left for their beds, Luxon and Alira had gone to one of the gardens located next to the magic schools. There they had talked until the sun rose in the east, and it was there they had first kissed.

Luxon lifted his head from the water as he heard the door to the bathroom creak open. For a second, he tensed but then soft hands wrapped themselves about his neck and the smell of perfume drifted into his nostrils.

"I cannot believe you did not come to see me as soon as you entered the city," Hannah's voice whispered seductively into his ear. "I would have scrubbed your back for you ... and maybe something else too." Luxon smiled as the soft hands made their way into the water. He groaned loudly when they found their target.

"I couldn't have come to you stinking of the road, Hannah," he sighed.

Hannah giggled and pulled her hands of the water, much to Luxon's dismay. She walked around the tub and sat on the rim. The healer's long blond hair reached down to her shoulders. A large red bow dividing it into a ponytail. Her blue eyes sparkled with mischief as she raised a long tanned leg from under her dress and lowered it into the warm water.

Luxon and Hannah had been in a relationship for two years. Their courtship had been long, and she had been difficult to seduce, but she was his and he was hers. She was five years older than he was, but she was more beautiful because of it.

"I have a lead on the location of my mother," Luxon said.

Hannah's eyes widened in surprise.

"You've searched for clues for years, Lux, and you found no trace of her. What's changed?"

Luxon shrugged his shoulders, making some water spill over the bathtub's rim.

"I know she was a member of the Diasect, and I know she went into hiding after leaving me here to escape Cliria's attention. She knew how to disappear. Perhaps now she wants to be found?"

CHAPTER SIX.

"Or, perhaps she's in danger," Hannah replied, a look of worry on her face. Luxon moved forwards sending water in all directions and wrapped his hands around her leg.

"You've got me wet, you sot!" Hannah laughed.

Luxon smiled and looked up at her with a roguish grin.

"Don't worry. I am going to talk with Thanos about it. This is something I must look into. She is my mother."

Hannah moved out of his grip and took a towel from the nearby rack.

She held it open for him as he climbed out of the tub. She watched him coyly. At nineteen years old, Luxon had grown into a tall, strong man.

His training under Thanos had made him physically fit and muscular. With his sandy blond hair and blue eyes, she was a lucky woman.

"Before you go to see Thanos, perhaps we could say hello properly?" she whispered in his ear. Luxon smirked before wrapping his arms around her and carrying her into the chambers and towards the bed.

"Thanos can wait," he growled.

The grand master of the mages stood with his back to the doorway.

Luxon coughed. He hated it when he had to wait. For five years, he had been Thanos's apprentice, and although the title of wizard outranked that of the Arch Mage, he remained a student.

Thanos turned and fixed his startling blue eyes on his pupil.

"I had hoped you would visit me sooner, Luxon. There is much we need to talk about."

Luxon rubbed his neck awkwardly.

"Yeah, sorry about that ... I got distracted," he replied meekly.

Thanos smirked.

"Young love often causes us to be distracted, my lad. You have nothing to apologise for." The Arch Mage smiled as he offered a cup of wine to his young apprentice.

Luxon took the cup, his face flushing with embarrassment. Thanos smiled knowingly and gestured for him to sit on one of the crystalline chairs tucked behind his desk. Scrolls and tomes lay haphazardly on its surface.

Luxon coughed nervously.

"So, er, back to business Master Thanos," he sputtered.

Thanos chuckled taking his own seat.

"Yes of course," he replied. "I trust your journey to the capital went well? I must admit I was surprised when you told me that Davik had summoned you. Nothing amiss I hope?"

Luxon slouched back in his chair and threw his hands in the air in exasperation.

"Where to start?" he moaned.

Thanos raised an inquisitive eyebrow at his pupil.

"How about the beginning, I always find that's a good place to start."

Luxon took a deep breath and told the arch mage all that had occurred on his journey south. He told him of Davik's theory about his mother, his concerns over the king, the sigil stone, and his run in with the dragon on the King's Road. Thanos sat silently throughout, his eyes not betraying any emotion or concern.

By the time Luxon was done, the sun was starting to go down and the room was getting dark. With a gesture of Thanos's wrist, the candles and lamps affixed to the chamber's walls flared into life.

"This business with the dragons is worrying," Thanos said, pouring himself another drink, "but the thing that concerns me the most is the news of your mother."

"Why?" Luxon asked in curiosity.

"Why? Because she has been in hiding for years, and now, following rumours of Danon's schemes and attacks in the south, she emerges from her hiding place."

Thanos picked up one of the scrolls lying on the desk and unfurled it. He took a small glowing stone from a drawer and placed it onto one of the corners of the parchment to act as a paperweight. Luxon leaned forward. On the scroll was a map of the realm. Several notes had been scribbled in black ink. Thanos pointed to the fortress of the Watchers.

"Your mother passed through the fortress and onto the Great Plains. There is nothing there, save for barbarian tribes and Fell Beasts. Her destination must be the city of Stormglade. I have received reports that the legion fleet has stopped all ships sailing towards the area, and two legions have been sent to reinforce the Watchers. Something is afoot in that city, and I bet you fifty Delfins that it has something to do with Danon."

Luxon's eyes widened.

"The Dark One would not sit back after his defeat at Eclin and cower. No, he has been planning something. He is up to something, and your mother must have an idea as to what that could be. The Diasect had access to lore and tomes that even we mages do not."

Luxon felt a twinge of excitement in his gut. He had been nervous to ask, but it seemed as though Thanos was just as curious over his mother's reappearance as he was.

"Send me after her," Luxon said eagerly. "If Danon is up to something, I will be the only one that can face him."

Thanos frowned.

"Some days you act like a wise old man and yet on others you act like a child," Thanos rebuked; rather harshly, Luxon thought.

Thanos sighed.

"You are right. However, I will not let you make such a journey alone. I fear that grave danger awaits you across the plains. Whatever Danon is planning, it is sure to be terrible."

Luxon could not help but smile. Finally, he would begin his search for his mother.

The door to the chamber burst open with a bang, making Luxon jump.

Thanos glared at the door and at the intruder standing in its frame. Luxon turned. Stood there, his face twisted into an angry snarl, was Ferran of Blackmoor. Without as much as a hello, he stormed into the room and slammed his hands down onto the desk.

"Where did you send her, Thanos?" the Nightblade growled.

Luxon squirmed under his friend's glare. Thanos, however, showed no reaction at all.

"I sent Sophia to Kingsford," he replied coolly. "One of my spies learned of a meeting taking place there between a Sarpi warlord and one of the Baron of Retbit's men."

Luxon gulped at hearing the title of his old enemy.

Accadus of Retbit had been the son of the Baron of Retbit and of the man who had sentenced Luxon's own father to death. The two had hated each other intensely. After the battle of Eclin, Accadus had murdered his own father and taken control of the barony of Retbit, which he then declared a separate kingdom. Since then, the King's Legion had clashed with Retbit on numerous occasions, but no decisive battle had occurred.

"Sarpi? Accadus? What does any of that have to do with my wife?" Ferran shouted angrily.

The Nightblade's hands gripped the desk tightly; the man was shaking with rage.

Thanos raised his hands.

"She volunteered, Ferran. She came to me of her own volition. You were away and time was of the essence."

Ferran stood back from the desk and rubbed his eyes tiredly. He spotted Luxon and nodded his head in greeting.

"Luxon… sorry, I didn't see you there. I get home from that mess in Resden to find my wife missing. I apologise, Thanos, for my rudeness, but where is she? Welsly told me she left Caldaria a month ago. Surely she should have returned by now?"

Thanos smiled.

"She is a very capable woman. I am sure she can handle herself. And I am sure that at this very moment she is on her way back to us."

CHAPTER SEVEN.

City of Kingsford

Sophia looked up at the gibbet swinging gently in the morning breeze. The body of a young mage lay within. His only crime had been to use magic to heal a sick little girl. Sophia had seen horrors in her time as a Witch Hunter, but these past few days had left a mark.

She had hoped to escape Kingsford by sea, but that plan had been dashed after the Legion navy had imposed its curfew. No ships were allowed west past the Crag for fear of pirate attacks. With the western sea lanes closed off, the only other option she had would be to get passage on a ship heading east. But in that direction lay Retbit and more dangers. So, she had tried leaving the city via the roads, but on every attempt, she had spotted more of the Sarpi. They were searching for her; she was sure of it.

Twice she had been pursued through the city's maze of streets. The last time, she had been lucky to escape. She was running out of options.

Eventually they would find her.

She closed her eyes as weariness threatened to overwhelm her; she had not slept properly in days. Her coin had run out and so she was forced to sleep rough. She dared not use an inn again. The Sarpi had tracked her to the inn, and only through sheer luck had she managed to escape their clutches. She had considered going to the city guard but, after seeing what they had done to the poor wretch hanging in his metal tomb above her, she dared not. The guard had set about beating and torturing the lad with sickening glee.

"The poor wretch," a man's voice said from close behind her. "They do this to a boy just because he has magic and they call wielders the monsters."

She swore loudly, her hand instinctively reaching for her dagger. She spun around and thrust the blade tightly against the man's throat.

The man smiled.

"Kaiden?" Sophia asked in disbelief and relief. She lowered the dagger from her friend's throat and stepped back, a look of apology on her face.

"I would not have expected any other type of greeting from you, Sophia," he chuckled. She laughed and hugged Kaiden tightly. She had never been so relieved to see someone she knew.

Stepping back, Sophia took his hand and pulled him off of the cobbled road and down into a side street.

"It isn't safe here, Kaiden. I am being hunted," she explained. She told him of what she had seen and of her ordeal. Kaiden's eyes narrowed when she mentioned the Sarpi.

"I have business with them myself," he growled. "Now that I am here, I will help you. First though, I need to find a weaponsmith and get myself a sword. I had hoped to head straight to Caldaria, but without a weapon I would not last long on the northern roads."

Sophia could sense that there was a deep pain in her friend but refrained from asking its cause. She was sure he would tell her in time.

"Two against three are much better odds," Sophia said with a smile. "Come on, I know just the place to get a sword."

She took his hand and led him through the backstreets.

They crossed through the gardens that lay at the heart of the city to avoid detection. The gardens were more like a miniature forest. They were filled with thousands of colourful flowers, and the treetops bustled with birds.

Autumn was descending upon Delfinnia and the swallows and other migratory birds were preparing for their annual exodus south to the warm jungles at the heart of the continent of Yundol.

It was the height of the day and the gardens were full of folk taking a break from their day's labours. Young lovers ate picnics on the grass and old folk gathered to play chess in the verandas located along the side of the cobbled paths. It was a peaceful place. They hurried through the gardens and came out the other side and onto a busy thoroughfare bustling with merchant traffic.

A cart had been upended and its load of apples lay scattered on the road.

A few people were busy helping clear up the mess, but others swore impatiently at the red-faced cart driver. The tolling of ship's bells could be heard coming from the nearby docklands.

As Delfinnia's largest seaport, Kingsford's docks were capable of anchoring hundreds of merchant vessels at once. With the Legion-imposed curfew, all the ships that would normally sail west around the Crag to Blackmoor in the northwest or turn north to sail up the wide tributaries of the Ridder River, were now all anchored in the port.

Business was booming in the city as the idle sailors spent their coin on food, drink, and whores. The brothel district on the waterfront was seeing record turnover.

Sophia led Kaiden passed the overturned cart towards a walled-off section of the city. Thick black smoke from a hundred chimneys poured high into the air – the reason the district was named Smoke Town. Blacksmiths, shipbuilders, tanners, armourers and chemists all plied their trade in the hectic and stinking streets. Sophia and Kaiden walked deeper into the district until they came to a small building tucked in between a foul-smelling tannery and an alchemist store with windows lined with grime and strangely coloured liquids.

Sophia knocked on the door to the little building three times. Kaiden looked up and noticed a sigil carved into the doorframe. He recognised the pattern as a Nivonian sigil used to ward off unwanted guests. After a while, the door creaked open. A stooped old woman peered at them through the crack. The woman's hair was wild and silver, her ragged face offset by a surprisingly smart pair of glasses which sat on the bridge of her nose.

"What do ya want?" the woman asked rudely.

"Bess. It is I, Sophia. Can we come in?"

The old woman leaned further out of the doorway to get a better look at her visitors.

"Ah, Sophia Cunning, the Witch Hunter. Not seen you round here for years. You got skinny, girly, no weight on your bones at all.' Bess then turned her attention to Kaiden. "And who is this lovely specimen of a man?"

Kaiden smiled at the compliment and Bess cackled.

"Ooh, you are one. I like you already."

"I am Kaiden, my lady," he said with a bow. Sophia rolled her eyes.

Bess clapped her hands together and led them inside. The small building was, in fact, a workshop. A forge dominated the ground floor and weapon racks lined the walls. Scattered about haphazardly were books each adorned with sigils. A larger version of the sigil above the door was on the workshop's ceiling.

"Bess, we are here to get a weapon for Kaiden," Sophia explained. "I know we could have gone to any of the blacksmiths around the city, but I remember that your husband made the best silver swords in the kingdom."

The old woman who was now preparing two mugs of steaming Robintan tea. She stirred a cast iron pot, which sat above a roaring fire pit.

"Ah yes, my Gravik was a fine smith. He made the best swords in the kingdom. He provided silver weapons to the Witch Hunters and Legions he did. Forty years he worked that forge. If you want silver, then you must be going against something magical. What ye hunting? Werewolves? Banshees?"

Kaiden whistled as he looked over some of the weapons in the racks. Each was made of solid silver. One sword caught his eye, its long blade glinting in the light cast by the fire of the cooking stove. Tentatively, he wrapped his hand around the hilt and picked it up. Intricately engraved on the pommel were runes, and as he looked closer, he could see that more were etched into the silver blade itself.

"That is ... was, Gravik's finest work," Bess said sombrely. "He spent a whole year, night and day making that one. He called it Vengeance. He was always so dramatic my husband."

Kaiden stared at the sword. Its name seemed fitting, for vengeance was in his heart. He was about to speak, but Bess held up a bony finger to stop him.

"It is yours. I may be old, but I see the fire in your eyes. Gravik would have wanted his best blade to be used instead of rusting away in this old place."

Kaiden was lost for words.

"Thank you. I swear to you that I will put it to good use," he vowed solemnly.

Bess looked pleased, but Sophia and rolled her eyes.

"Men! Always so dramatic!"

It was getting dark before they left the workshop. Bess told them tales of her time serving in the King's legion as a young woman, and of her time working with the Witch Hunters. Sophia and Kaiden had also eaten well – Bess had wheeled out a huge platter of food. Cheese, bread, and chicken had all been on the menu. Both had eaten greedily. Sophia had not had a proper meal in days, and Kaiden had been famished from his long journey from the Marble Shore.

Cautiously, they returned to the streets and made their way towards the northern gate to where Kaiden had Herald stabled for the day. Finally, they reached the end of an alleyway and peered out into the wide street. The stables were on the opposite side. Sophia swore under her breath as she spotted one of the cloaked figures stood near to the gate, his glowing eyes the only thing giving away his location. Kaiden tapped her on the arm and pointed down the road. Sure enough, the other two Sarpi stalked up the street.

"They always seem to know where I'm heading," Sophia whispered. "It's as though they can track me through my scent or something." She took the bow from off her back and carefully notched an arrow. Kaiden drew Vengeance from its sheath.

"You take the one nearest to the gate. I'll take the other two," Kaiden said. Sophia nodded, drew back the bow's cord and stepped out into the street. As soon as she did so, the Sarpi spotted her. Their piercing glowing eyes narrowed as they picked up her scent. The scraping of blades leaving their scabbards sounded as they advanced. The two from the street hesitated as they spotted Kaiden stood behind her. Sophia loosed the arrow which slammed into the Sarpi at the gate, sending him staggering backwards. Kaiden bellowed a challenge and charged.

Quickly, Sophia notched another arrow and loosed again. This time, the deadly projectile struck the Sarpi square in the head. A pained squeal sounded as the Sarpi staggered backwards.

The clanging of steel sounded as Kaiden's blade clashed with the Sarpi. With skilled footwork, he forced one of his opponents back and ducked under a swing of the other's sword. He rotated his wrists and thrust upwards, slicing deep into his opponent's naval. Another of the Sarpi hit the deck. The last Sarpi was more skilled and more cautious. The two warriors circled each other, each measuring up the other. Sophia and Kaiden had gotten lucky with their surprise attack, but now they faced an opponent who was prepared for them. With stunning speed, the Sarpi charged and ducked Kaiden's sword swing. It took all of Kaiden's skill to regain his balance.

Blow after blow rained upon him as the Sarpi savagely attacked. Sophia tried to get a clear shot with her bow, but her foe was constantly ducking and dodging.

Sweat was pouring into Kaiden's eyes. He had never fought an opponent so skilled and quick. He stepped back, allowing the Sarpi's blade to slide down his own.

Digging his heels in, he pushed forward to bring them crashing together in a knot of straining muscle. He could smell his foe's foul breath and hear its excited breathing.

"What are you? Why did you take my wife and child?" he yelled.

Memories of Alira and Ilene flashed into his mind. Thinking of them scared and alone sent a renewed strength coursing through his tired limbs.

With a roar he pushed with all his might sending the Sarpi staggering backwards.

Sophia let fly.

Her arrow struck home, ripping through the Sarpi's throat, and dropping it like a stone to the ground.

Kaiden placed his hands on his knees and breathed in the cold night air with ragged gasps.

CHAPTER SEVEN.

They had won.

CHAPTER EIGHT.

Caldaria

The training room was a large open space located in the basement of Caldaria's main academy. Straw dummies lined one wall, whilst other equipment took up another. Mages of all abilities were practising their skills. Several dummies were already scorched by a volley of fireballs.

Luxon walked in step with Grand Master Thanos as the leader of the mages regarded the training students with a critical eye. The group that was being put through their paces today was the twenty students studying the mysteries of the Middle Ring.

Each class in the academy was divided depending on their power and skill with the arcane. Those of the Lower Ring were taught the basics of spell crafting. The students of the Middle Ring were of middling ability. Luxon, however, was of the Upper Ring, the class that was home to the most powerful mages in Delfinnia. Even though he had been trained in the Void, and had mastery over the most powerful of magics, he was still learning. Even Thanos took part in the classes to keep his skills honed.

Luxon smiled as Yepert spotted him and waved. His friend was part of the class casting fireballs.

"I have training for you to do, Luxon," Thanos said leading the way to a closed off section of the training hall. "Before I send you out on this mission to find your mother, I want you to learn some skills that I think may prove extremely useful."

The tall mage took a key from the chain at his waist and unlocked a heavy oak door, which he then opened with a push.

They entered the small room. There was no equipment inside, just a mirror which covered the entirety of the back wall. Luxon raised his eyebrows.

"I don't understand. What am I –"

He was cut off by a shrill meow. He looked around and spotted a small black cat sat in the rafters of the room. The cat nimbly made its way down the wooden beams and leapt to the floor. Thanos walked over to it and stroked its back before picking up a grey robe which was hanging from a peg behind the door. He chucked the robe onto the cat. Luxon stared at his mentor as though he had lost his marbles.

"Master ... what are you doing?"

Thanos smiled.

The robe moved and then, to Luxon's amazement, rose from the ground. The outline of a man appeared. The figure struggled for a few moments before turning around.

A skinny man with wild white hair faced him and smiled.

"Master Kvar?" Luxon asked dumbly.

"Yes, yes, that's me," Kvar said bowing. "Grand Master Thanos told me that it was time I taught you the ways of Transmutation."

Luxon had been trained in all of the other schools of magic – Alteration, Illusion, Healing and Combat – but so far he had not been taught the ways of possibly the most dangerous school of them all. It was said that Transmutation had a strong effect upon the caster's mind; its users had a reputation for being more than a little crazy. It was because of that reputation that few mages were willing to train in it.

"I will leave you two to it," Thanos said. He placed a strong hand on Luxon's shoulder and looked him in the eye. "Listen to Kvar in all things. Transmutation can destroy your mind if you are not careful. Kvar is the most skilled in the art in the whole of Caldaria, so heed his words."

Luxon nodded.

The door closed and Kvar clapped his hands loudly, making Luxon jump.

"A wizard! I have never had the honour of training a wizard. Did you know that Zahnia the Great was a master of Transmutation? In one of his many battles he transmuted himself into a wildcat. In another, he leapt from a falling tower and turned into an eagle and just flew to safety." As Kvar rambled on, his eyes darted in all directions.

Luxon gulped. He was a madman.

"Stand in the centre of the room," Kvar fussed. "Go, go, go!"

Luxon did as he was told.

"Before you can turn yourself into something else, it is easier to first master the ability to turn things, into other things." The master reached into his robe and took out an apple. He tossed it to Luxon, who caught it easily.

"Transmutation requires focus. A spell caster must put their very being into the thought, and then they must channel their power into it. Concentration is vital; that is why you should not attempt such magic whilst under pressure. Only the most powerful, the most focused, can do that. Now, turn that apple into a lemon," Kvar said seriously.

"Okay, I'll give it a go," Luxon answered, doubt evident in his tone.

Kvar stomped his feet like a child and waved his arms about wildly.

"No, no, no!" the master cried. "You must not have any doubt in your mind at all. You must believe it can be done. That is why Transmutation appeals to the strange, the dreamers. They believe anything is possible ... and it is!"

He pulled another apple from his robe and held it close to his chest. Kvar closed his eyes and muttered to himself. A light flashed in his hands.

With a knowing smile, he opened his palm. Sure enough, the apple was no longer there. In its place was a juicy looking pear, which he then proceeded to take a bite out of.

Luxon gawped in amazement. He narrowed his eyes in determination and concentrated. He pictured the apple in his mind's eye and imagined it turning into a lemon. He opened his mind and focused the magic within him. He could feel his forehead dripping with sweat, and pain coursed through his body. He focused harder. He could feel the texture of the apple begin to change, and the smell of lemons filled his nostrils.

With one last effort, he squeezed his hands tighter until he felt juice covering them.

Slowly, he opened his eyes and laughed in surprise. In his hands was a crushed lemon. He held his hand up to his mouth and tasted the sour juice.

Kvar smiled happily.

"You see – anything is possible. We must work on your control. We will train until you can transmute a rock into a diamond!" the master cackled manically.

Luxon was exhausted. Master Kvar had made him practise non-stop for five hours. His eyes were red, and his head ached. He wasn't annoyed, however; after his initial success, he had quickly progressed. He had managed to turn a stone into a piece of coal and then into a gemstone, before passing Kvar's test of turning it into a diamond. He had asked the master why he didn't spend all day turning rocks into diamonds; he could easily become the wealthiest man alive.

Kvar had laughed hysterically before replying. "It may look like a diamond. It may feel like a diamond, but it is not a diamond. In time, the magic fades and it will turn back into a rock."

Luxon was outside and making his way back to his quarters when he saw a group of mages gathered in a group. They were all chatting excitedly. Curious, Luxon walked over to see what had caused all of the interest.

The mages were huddled around a poster that had been nailed to a wall.

The sound of marching feet prompted the crowd to part and scurry away in all directions. Luxon took the chance to step closer to the poster. Written in black ink were the words:

Accadus, Baron of Retbit, offers all magic users' sanctuary in his lands. The persecution of magic wielders must end. Join Accadus and live free of hatred and revulsion.

Luxon stared at the words, his heart sinking. Angrily, he ripped the poster off the wall. He scrunched it up and tossed it onto the ground.

The sound of marching feet grew closer. Welsly and two other Nightblades rounded the corner. Welsly stopped as he spotted Luxon. He picked up the paper, unfurled it and read the words.

"Another one of those blasted posters," he grumbled. "By the gods, who keeps putting these things up?"

"How many have you seen?" Luxon asked. More and more mages were returning to Caldaria telling tales of abuse and persecution.

"Too many. Things outside Caldaria are getting so bad that I've even heard rumours that some mages are considering taking up Accadus's offer. If they join him then, he will have a force of magic users at his command."

"How can anyone trust Accadus?" Luxon said angrily. "He is a murderer. Hells, if the rumours are true he is in league with Danon himself."

Tiredness almost overwhelmed him. He said goodbye to Welsly and continued tiredly back to his room.

CHAPTER EIGHT.

---◆O◆---

The nightmares came to him, as they often did. Luxon tossed and turned in his bed. His cries woke Yepert, whose bedroom adjoined that of his friend's.

In their training, they had been told that dreams were important to mages, but to a wizard like Luxon they could prove to be vital, even prophetic. Yepert lay awake and stared at the ceiling of his small room. The shouts and cries of his friend grew in volume. He resisted the urge to wake him.

A scream made him flinch. Whatever Luxon was dreaming of must be awful.

Slowly he got out of bed, put on his robe, and made his way silently into his friend's room. From the doorway he could see Luxon thrashing around. The sheets were strewn across the floor and soaked with sweat.

---◆O◆---

Fire consumed the land. Dead things moved and consumed the living. Luxon stood on a high wall of a mighty fortress overlooking a vast flat plain; at his side were his friends and warriors that he did not recognise. Soldiers of the King's Legion manned the walls, their bows and catapults trained on the approaching foe. All were grim-faced, their weapons held tightly in their hands. In the distance was the shape of a city, its towers crumbling like dominoes. Winged creatures filled the sky and the earth was covered by shambling undead. Behind the zombies marched a black-armoured army.

It numbered in its tens of thousands; glowing eyes glinted through the visors of helmets and from the shadows cast by hoods. He looked to his left. On the sea were hundreds of ships in battle and countless bodies drifting amongst the turbulent waves. Cries of the dying and the crashing of wood carried on the cold night air.

Fire consumed the sea. He felt panic and fear. They would all be consumed by the horde. He could feel himself scream as the army parted and a man walked to the fore. He looked familiar, his hair was black, his face pale and twisted, his eyes red with hatred. The figure raised a hand and pointed straight at him. "Danon comes for you all," a voice boomed. "Your doom is at hand"

Luxon's eyes snapped open, his breaths coming fast and panicked. His body was clammy with sweat and his hands ached from where they had gripped the sheets too tightly. He looked around and sighed in relief as he realised he was safe. His bleary eyes focused on Yepert who was standing nearby. His friend's face was covered in black soot.

"Are you alright?" Yepert asked, taking a mug from a nearby shelf and filling it with water from a jug.

Luxon accepted the drink gratefully and gulped down the cool liquid.

"I'm fine. It was just a nightmare ... are you alright?" he replied hesitantly, pointing to his friend's blackened face.

"I'm okay ... you sort of set the curtains on fire. I managed to put it out with a spell."

Yepert gestured to the still smoldering curtains. "That was the worst one I've ever heard you have, Lux, and you've had a fair few over the years. What was it about?"

Luxon ran a hand through his sweat-soaked hair and sighed in exasperation.

"It was nothing ..." he muttered.

CHAPTER NINE.

"Let me tell you of the Sarpi," Thanos began solemnly.

Luxon, Yepert, Ferran and the newly arrived Sophia and Kaiden were sat in the Arch Mage's study. In the week that had passed, Luxon had improved his skills in transmutation to such an extent that he could transform objects nearly at will. Turning himself into another creature, however, still eluded him.

Sophia and Kaiden had arrived in Caldaria the previous night, and the news that they had brought with them had spurred Thanos into accelerating his plans.

Preparations were underway to equip Luxon and the others for the long journey south to the Watchers, and beyond to the Great Plains and the city of Stormglade.

"Once, long ago, there were four great empires of man. The Tulin, Yundol, Nivonian and Sarpi. Each of these empires ruled their respective continents, with the Nivonian ruling what we today call Delfinnia. These empires came under threat in the Second Age when a disciple of Danon created the N'gist cult – a group of mages perverted by dark magic and necromancy. The leader, as we know from the tales of Estran, was called

Necron. Within a few years, the N'gist's influence corrupted the empires of the Tulin, Sarpi and Yundols. Their emperors submitted to the will of Necron and his army of N'gist followers. The war that followed saw the Nivonian Empire battle the others, but they too were bested. Danon returned and his first Dark Age began."

Ferran yawned loudly, eliciting an annoyed look from Thanos. Sophia leant over and slapped her husband playfully on the arm.

"Sorry, Thanos, but we've heard this tale a thousand times," Ferran said sarcastically.

Thanos crossed his arms, unimpressed. The arch mage stared at the Nightblade until Ferran looked away and mumbled an apology.

"As I was saying," Thanos continued, "the Dark Age was ended by Zahnia the Great. In his struggle to liberate the peoples of Esperia from Danon and the N'gist, he travelled to the four empires. The Tulin and Yundol joined him in his war against evil, but the Sarpi refused, for they had embraced the ways of the N'gist fully. Danon was their god, and the N'gist their new, foul religion. Zahnia left the Sarpi, but after his victory and the banishment of Danon to the Void, he returned with a fleet to Sarpia's shores. As punishment for their wicked ways and devotion to evil, Zahnia cursed the Sarpi Empire.

"'If they loved darkness so much then they can live in it forever,' Zahnia proclaimed. Using his powers, he made it so that the sun would never again cast its warmth and light upon Sarpia. He moved a rock drifting in the blackness of space and made it so that it would always blot out the sun over the landmass of Sarpia."

Luxon whistled in awe. To be able to do such a thing would require more power than he could imagine.

"We do not know what happened after that, as the Golden Empire avoided Sarpia and after the Magic Wars, contact with the outside world was mostly lost. I surmise that Sarpi mages must have come up with a way to allow the Sarpi people to survive in the perpetual darkness. Perhaps that is why their eyes glow," Thanos finished.

A silence fell over the room as its occupants reflected on the story.

Kaiden broke the quiet.

"I do not care what they are," he said, his voice cracking with emotion. "They took my wife and daughter. I will do whatever it takes to get them back." He rose from his seat and stood before his friends. "We went through hell and back at Eclin. Now I beg you to no doubt do the same in the south. If we can best Danon once, we can do it again, Sarpi army or not."

Ferran leaned back in his chair and drummed his chin with his fingertips.

"I suppose I'm in."

Sophia nodded.

"You don't even have to ask. I will help you," she said.

A look of determination was on Yepert's face.

"Last time, I was just a terrified boy. Now I am a man and I am still petrified, but I cannot let my friends walk into danger without being by their side. Count me in."

They all turned to look at Luxon, who was looking at his hands.

"Our paths lie in the same place. Kaiden. I will go with you beyond the Watchers and the plains, but my quest differs from yours. I go to find my mother, but if it means saving Alira and your daughter in the process, than I shall."

Kaiden bowed to his wizard friend.

"There are no better friends a man can find than you."

The following day passed in a blur as final preparations for the journey south were made. Horses were shod, supplies packed, weapons sharpened and Luxon was put through his paces by Master Kvar and Thanos.

Thanos had set up an obstacle course that filled the whole training level of the college. Climbing ropes, gymnastic horses and other equipment were laid out. A crowd of students sat to one side, all eager to watch Luxon's challenge.

"A magic user's biggest weakness is their reliance on their powers," Thanos preached to the students. "What do you do if you are incapacitated, if your powers are drained, or your concentration is lacking? To survive, you must also hone your body as well as your mind. Skills with mundane things such as swords and bows could save your life in such situations."

Yepert stood to one side next to his friend.

"You ready for this?" he asked Luxon, who was taking off his shirt and limbering up his arms and legs. He punched the air in rapid succession.

"Yeah, I think so. I've been working on my fitness, remember? I just wish Thanos hadn't invited the whole college to watch me make a tit of myself."

Thanos finished his speech and waved to Luxon. Taking a deep breath, Luxon rolled his shoulders and stepped up to the starting line.

"Watch this wizard tackle the course," Thanos said. "He will soon depart on a dangerous mission and all of his skills will be put to the test, both magical and physical. Learn from him, for one day each of you must pass the same course if you wish to be anointed full mages."

Luxon went into a sprinter's position and waited for the arch mage's signal. Thanos raised his arm; Luxon's heart was pounding in his ears.

The arm dropped and Luxon shot forward at a sprint. The first obstacle was a set of monkey bars which he attacked with vigour. His strong arms bore him across with ease and he leapt to the ground and rolled. Instantly he rose to his feet and ran forward. The next obstacle was a narrow beam placed over a pit built into the hall's floor. Using magic, Thanos had set sacks filled with sand swinging across the beam. Luxon slowed and crouched, his eyes watching the bags. He tensed as he waited for his chance to advance. The pace of the bags swings increased in speed. Luxon sat back on his heels and tossed Thanos a look of annoyance. The arch mage smirked playfully.

Taking a deep breath, Luxon closed his eyes and channelled the magic within him. He felt power flood into his body. When he reopened his eyes, the room around him looked different. Everything now moved in slow motion. The enhancement spell had worked a treat. The bags swung out of the way slowly and Luxon made his move. Spreading his arms out to his sides to keep his balance, he moved as fast he could across the beam. He dispelled the enhancement and the room returned to normal. Behind him, the bags continued to swing at their rapid pace.

A chorus of gasps came from the on looking students as they spotted Luxon on the other side of the beam. Yepert clapped his friend eagerly.

Luxon flashed Thanos an arrogant smile and saluted sarcastically, eliciting a laugh from his mentor. He ran forward and leapt over a trap door that snapped open beneath him.

The next obstacle was a high pillar with no visible way of reaching the top. He narrowed his eyes and spotted the tiny holes etched into the pillars surface.

Slowly, he placed his hands into the lower holes and hauled himself upwards. The climb was tough, and sweat poured from him as his muscles strained. He was glad he had joined the Nightblades in their training after Eclin; the tough physical training they did had aided him well.

His sweaty hands slipped, almost causing him to fall, and creating more gasps from the watching students. Swearing under his breath, he stretched for the hole he had missed. With a grunt, his fingertips made contact and he pulled himself higher. His arms shook with tiredness and his legs felt like lead as he reached the top of the pole. There was no time to relax, however, as the next task was to get back down. He could jump or he could use magic. He thought over what Thanos had said to the pupils, and heeded his words; he had to learn to do things without always relying on his powers. Slowly and painfully he opted to climb back down rather than leap and use levitation to ease him gently to the ground. At the back of his mind, he knew that in real life and if he was in danger he would take the magical option.

Eventually, his feet touched the cold floor of the training room. His breathing was ragged and every sinew of his body ached. He continued forward to the final obstacle and stopped in bemusement. A large block of wood barred his path. It was too high to climb, and its only noticeable feature was a tiny hole at its base. Master Kvar was stood nearby, a smile on his face.

Luxon moaned as he realised that this was Kvar's final test of his transmutation skills. He walked over the hole and knelt down in front of it. Only a tiny creature would be able to squeeze through such a space. Closing his eyes, he focused. He imagined a tiny field mouse scurrying about his feet, and channelled his power into the thought. Weariness flooded his body and his head ached as pain spiked within it. A strange sensation filled him as he felt himself get smaller and smaller. A wave of excitement passed over him as the spell took effect. He felt his trousers fall to the floor in a heap.

He opened his eyes and saw darkness. He felt panic as he realised that something was pressing down on his body. He moved forward and headed towards a sliver of light. His limbs felt different, but apart from that he felt fine. He crawled under the object and into the bright light. He cried out as the wooden block towered over him like a mountain. He jumped as the cry came out as a squeak. The tiny gap now looked a chasm and he scurried into it. The tunnel felt miles long, but eventually he emerged out of the other side to be met with a chorus of cheers and applause. A massive hand reached down and scooped him up off of the floor.

Master Kvar chuckled as he stroked the squeaking mouse in his palm.

"Well done Luxon, well done indeed," he praised.

Carefully, he placed the mouse onto the ground and gently placed a robe on top of it. A light began to shine from underneath the material, and the robe began to rise from the ground as Luxon reverted back to his original form.

Panting, Luxon covered himself and gratefully took the trousers offered to him by Yepert, who had snatched up his clothes after his transformation.

"That was the weirdest sensation I think I have ever felt," Luxon said happily. He wiggled his fingers and toes after putting on the robe to cover his modesty.

"I do believe that you are ready for what is to come," Thanos declared.

Luxon crossed his arms in annoyance. Upon returning to his chambers, he had found Hannah waiting for him. He was surprised to see that she was dressed for travel, a brown bag hung over her shoulder. In her left hand was a silver staff which was plain along its shaft, save for the healer's emblem etched into the weighted head.

"Thanos said that it is okay for me to go with you," she explained hotly. "I let you go last time and you vanished for months. Hells, you ended up in the Void!"

The two had been arguing for a good while.

"I can look after myself,' Hannah added as she continued ticking off points with her fingers. "Master Erin says that I am one of the best pole staff users in his class. I am a skilled healer, which, from what you told me of your last adventure, would have come in handy and … well … you need all the help you can get. The Great Plain is full of dangers; having me along will make things easier."

When she had finished, she planted her hands on her hips, her blue eyes staring at Luxon defiantly.

CHAPTER NINE.

All of her points were valid. She was smart enough to know the perils of the journey, and having a healer in the group would come in handy.

"I'm not a bad healer myself…" Luxon grumbled lamely. He knew when he was beaten.

Hannah's expression softened. She walked over to him and hugged him tightly.

"You do not have to worry," she whispered into his ear before nibbling it gently. Luxon groaned as the hairs on his neck stood up. He started to laugh and pushed her gently away.

"Damn it, woman, you always know how to wear me down," he laughed. "C'mon, we'd better finish packing; we have to meet the others at the stables by noon."

CHAPTER TEN.

Barony of Retbit

The legion soldiers were kneeled in a line, their armour stripped off their bodies. The rain was pouring, turning the battlefield into a mass of foul-smelling mud. All around came the screams of dying men and horses. In the distance, catapults thundered as they unleashed a volley of deadly missiles at the legion fort on the opposing shore of the Zulus River.

Pacing in front of the captured legionaries was Accadus, the rebel baron of Retbit. He had murdered his father and brother five years previously to claim the mantle of baron. He had refused to pledge allegiance to King Alderlade, and so a long bloody war had raged on Retbit's borders. Neither side had been able to overpower the other, but now things had changed. Accadus's master, Danon, had sent him reinforcements from Sarpia, and with those extra troops he had been able to drive the legion back across the Zulus River.

"How many men are in the fort, Commander? I do not want to have to ask again," Accadus said softly to one of the legionaries.

Dressed in his black plate armour and long black cloak, Accadus was an imposing presence. He had grown taller and muscular as he had trained with sword and spell at the feet of his master. His long black hair framed a strong, narrow face, and dark brown eyes that could intimidate any man. The legionary shivered in the cold, but kept his mouth shut. His green eyes stared at the baron defiantly. Blood dripped from a wound on his shaven head to run into his greying beard, the rain doing its best to wash the crimson liquid into the soaked earth.

Accadus tutted and gave the signal.

A burly man dressed in mail armour, bearing the sigil of Retbit, stepped behind one of the kneeling soldiers. He raised his axe high and brought the sharpened head down onto the legionary's skull.

Bone and blood sprayed onto the mud. A sickening crunch prompted another of the prisoners to vomit. Accadus smirked cruelly. Casually, he gestured to another of the prisoners and the axe fell again. Panicked shouts came from the stripped legionaries.

"Two hundred!" the commander yelled, as the axe man stood behind him.

Accadus smiled and crouched in front to the terrified man.

"So, you let your men die, but when it comes to saving your own miserable life you sing like a canary," he mocked. With a smile he nodded to his man again. The commander screamed for mercy but the axe silenced him. Accadus looked at the other prisoners.

"I am a merciful man. All I want is what is rightfully mine. I want the Sundered Crown and the realm. My father had a lawful claim to the crown and yet this upstart child, Alderlade, is king. How do we know that he is truly the son of the previous king? He could just be a fake, put on the throne by the council to act as their puppet."

He walked down the line of kneeling men. None could match his gaze. Men would do almost anything to save themselves, even if it meant breaking their oaths. Very few were willing to die for their leaders.

A cloaked Sarpi approached, his blade dripping with blood. The survivors of the battle were being rounded up and loaded into wagons. With the powers taught to him by Danon, Accadus would turn his enemies into obedient slaves.

"Ah, Sintinius," he greeted. "I was just about to seek you out. Your forces performed admirably. The Sarpi are deadly indeed."

The Sarpi looked at the bodies of the legionaries and chuckled.

"Lord Danon was correct," the Sarpi hissed. "I did enjoy putting Delfinnians to the sword. My forces are ready to attempt a crossing of the river. All you need do is give the word."

Accadus smiled and looked over the scene of carnage. The battle had been brutal; both sides had lost many men. The difference was that Accadus could still use the dead. He watched as his men dragged the bodies of both legionaries and his own forces into a pile in the centre of the boggy battlefield.

"Danon told me to wait. He wants to be sure of victory, if we move too quickly then we could be outnumbered. No, we will wait for his signal. We will attack from the east and he will strike from the west. The legion is weak and the barons are too busy squabbling amongst themselves. Our victory is assured."

Sintinius hissed in annoyance.

"What about the wizard?"

Accadus scowled and his hands knotted into fists at the mention of his old enemy. Luxon had humiliated him at Caldaria, a shame that still made his cheeks flush in anger.

"He will not stop us," he snarled as he stalked over to the growing pile of bodies. "He will try, but our plans are too far advanced for him to interfere. If he does appear, then I will deal with him. Master Danon has trained me well."

"He has taught me the ways of the N'gist. Life through death!"

"Life through death," Sintinius repeated reverently.

Accadus planted his sword into the muddy earth before standing next to the pile of bodies. He closed his eyes and summoned the magic within. Darkness filled him as he tapped into the foulest of powers. The air grew bitterly cold and ice began to form on his armour and upon Sintinius's hood. Soldiers stopped to watch, and those that had been moving the corpses stared. Accadus stepped forward and placed his hands upon one of the dead; he channelled the dark powers through him and into the pile. To those watching, he was engulfed in shadow and the faint light being cast by the sun dimmed.

The Sarpi gathered closer and fell to their knees in prayer. The men of Retbit however backed away; they feared their lord's power.

"Life through death," they chanted.

The field fell into shadow as the light from the sun faded into nothingness and a whirling vortex of wind began to blow and surround the dead. The wind grew louder and louder until it stopped abruptly and an eerie silence fell. The darkness retreated, and the light returned. The Sarpi stopped their chanting.

CHAPTER TEN.

Accadus stepped back and waited.

The corpse he had touched twitched. The fingers on the slain warrior's hand began to move slowly. A moan came from the body as the dead man awkwardly picked itself up from the pile. Around him, the other dead began to writhe, their own horrific moans joining the first. Soon, all the bodies were moving and the moans turned into a near deafening howling. Men who had been slain just hours before began to stagger and walk. Some had gaping wounds on their torsos, others had limbs missing, but all moved like macabre puppets.

"Life through death," Accadus whispered darkly.

It was dark when the moans grew in volume. The nervous legionaries manning the wall of Fort Zulus peered out into the blackness, their hands gripping their swords tightly. They had been waiting for an attack all day and their nerves were shot. The bulk of the Retbit forces had withdrawn, but the horrors they had left behind wandered the boggy ground across the river.

"The undead will come soon," bellowed the fort's commander. "The night will drive them towards prey and so we must be ready for them."

The man was called Stalvos, a grizzled veteran who had battled the realm's enemies for over twenty years. He had killed Fell Beasts, undead and all the other dark things that the old enemy sent his way. He had been the commander of the Ridderford garrison until the War of Claimants had begun. He had fought and bled at the Golden Hills, and now he found himself commanding a fort on the front lines in a war with Retbit.

"Light the braziers," Stalvos shouted. Men rushed to and fro to carry out his orders. Soon, the torches lining the fort's stone battlements were ablaze. Some of the younger men cried out when they saw the shambling host coming towards them.

The flowing waters of the Zulus River knocked some of the zombies off of their feet and carried them downstream. They would no doubt cause problems for some poor village.

The moaning grew louder as the zombies fixed their gaze on the lit torches. The crowd of undead staggered like drunks coming home from a night on the town.

"Ballistae!" Stalvos shouted.

The fort was small, but was still outfitted with two ballistae. The devastating weapons could shoot a six-foot-long bolt hundreds of meters and with lethal accuracy.

The ballistae operators quickly loaded the weapons and aimed. Stalvos held his arm high in the air and waited. More of the zombies began to enter the water; some fell, but most pressed on, their desire for flesh driving them onward. Stalvos dropped his arm and the ballistae fired with deafening twangs. The bolts flew, striking the hoard and carving a large furrow through the crowd, destroying a dozen undead in one strike.

"Archers, nock arrows," Stalvos yelled. "Remember, fire destroys the dead."

The men on the walls hefted their bow and lit their pitch-tipped arrows at the braziers. As one, they pulled back their bow strings and loosed. The flaming projectiles fell like rain, striking dozens of the shambling corpses. Some fell to the ground aflame, but many strode deeper into the river's waters, dousing the flames.

Stalvos felt sweat break out under his helmet. The zombies continued to shamble towards the fort, and the fire which normally destroyed the undead so easily was having little affect. A panicked cry came from further down the wall. He turned his head, his eyes straining in the darkness to see what was going on.

"Undead at the walls sir," came a panicked shout.

Stalvos swore loudly and drew his silver-tipped sword. He marched down the line, shouting at his men to keep shooting. Sure enough, six zombies had managed to reach the base of the fort's wall and were clambering up the stonework. He could see the snarling faces of creatures that had once been people.

A legionary impaled one of the climbers with a spear, but the weight of the zombie threatened to pull the spearman over the wall. Other soldiers rushed forward to hold their friend in place as the other zombies grabbed at the spear.

"Let the bloody thing go," Stalvos ordered. The soldier did as he was told. The impaled zombie fell into the river with a loud splash, its arms feebly trying to remove the spear lodged in its guts.

The bulk of the horde had reached the base of the fort, their hands reaching skyward in an attempt to get to the legionaries above. The soldiers kept shooting, but the waters of the Zulus prevented the flaming projectiles from destroying the undead.

Stalvos peered over the side of the wall. He frowned as an idea formed in his head.

"Cease fire," he commanded wearily. "Save your arrows."

"Sir, they will surround us if we don't stop them," said one of his men in a panicky tone.

"I know, son. Better they stay focused on us than head deeper into the kingdom. Also, by keeping them here and fixed on us, the Retbit forces are going to have to deal with them before they can get to us. Those monstrosities might do us a favour when Retbit attacks in force."

The soldiers glanced at each other uncertainly.

"Will help come, sir?"

Stalvos looked at his men. Most were just out of boyhood and training. They would never be able to hold the fort if Accadus unleashed his full strength. Despite that, he forced a confident smile onto his hard face.

"Aye. Help will come," he said with more confidence than he felt. "The legion will not abandon us. When Retbit tries to take this place, we will stand strong and kill them all,"

He turned and walked back down the wall towards his quarters. He looked to the stars and muttered a prayer to whoever would listen.

They would surely need divine favour.

CHAPTER ELEVEN.

Luxon was glad to be on the road again. As much as he enjoyed Caldaria, the sense of excitement that travel always created couldn't be beaten. They had left the mage city under cover of darkness, in the hope that any spies sent by Accadus or Danon would miss their departure. Thanos would do his best to maintain the ruse that they were still in the city, but the enemy would no doubt learn the truth before long.

Their journey would be in two stages. Firstly they were to head to Sunguard, and there meet with Davik. A messenger had arrived in Caldaria the previous day requesting that Luxon returned to the capital. No reason was given but the message was stamped with the King's seal.

The second part would be the long trip south-westward to the Watchers and the Great Plains.

The two moons were high in the cloudless sky; the air was cool and the smell of winter was on the breeze. Each of the travellers wore thick woollen cloaks over their usual attire to keep out the chill. They were on the King's Road heading south towards the capital. Ferran led the way. The Nightblade's knowledge of the kingdom's terrain was unmatched, save for the rangers that wondered and defended the wilder places of the realm. The road was paved and in good repair thanks to the work of the King's Legion. Trees and hedgerows were cut back and drainage ditches ran along both sides.

They had been travelling for a good while before they reached one of the sigil stones. The mysterious monoliths, that were dotted around the country and found within the realm's towns and cities, had been created eons ago by the ancient mages of the Nivonian Empire to protect the land's roadways and settlements from Fell Beasts. The stones resonated with a lost magic that kept the beasts of the Void away. Travellers often camped close to the stones, and tonight proved no exception. Ferran whistled in warning, and Luxon and the others slowed their mounts to a stop. The Nightblade urged his horse forward, his hand resting close to the hilt of his tourmaline sword. Sophia dismounted, readied her bow and moved quickly into the darkness to outflank whoever was here.

Two red tents were erected next to the stone, a slowly dying cooking fire giving off the only illumination at the camp. Ferran stepped closer and paused. The sound of people waking up with a start made him to drop into a combat stance.

A cacophony of swearing sounded, before the tent flaps opened and three tired looking people staggered outside. The tallest of the bunch held a spear whilst the only woman of the group carried a small knife. They shivered in the cold night.

"We mean you no harm, friends," Ferran said soothingly. "We just want to share the safety of the sigil stone until the dawn."

The tall man hesitated as he looked Ferran and the others over. His eyes widened as he spotted the weapons attached to their belts. Slowly, he placed his spear onto the ground and gestured for the woman to do the same.

"Aye, you lot look capable and don't look like bandits, so I guess you can share the stone with us," the man said, offering his hand. "My name is Tuilin, this is my wife Una, and this is my son Rendil."

Ferran stepped forward and shook hands, explaining that they were a simple group of merchants heading towards the capital. Tuilin glanced at the others in suspicion.

Ferran waved Luxon and the others forward and they quickly went about setting up a small camp of their own. Within a few minutes, Kaiden had started a small fire and Sophia remerged from the trees lining the roadside, a dead rabbit hanging from her belt. Yepert, Luxon and Hannah took care of the horses, then sat down next to the fire.

Sophia cooked the rabbit as they all made small talk amongst themselves and the travelling family. The chill of the night was replaced with warmth and it wasn't long before sleep came to them.

Luxon however didn't feel tired, so offered to take the first watch. He sat next to the fire, his mind distracted by the journey ahead and thoughts of his mother. He hadn't seen her for eight years. Would she be different? Would she even recognise him? His thoughts were interrupted by Tuilin's voice.

"Not long until dawn, judging by the stars," the man said.

Tuilin had a thin face topped off with a head of brown wispy hair. He now wore a thick travel coat as he settled next to the fire.

Luxon nodded. The clear sky revealed all the constellations he had read about in the books from Caldaria's Great Library. The Swordsman stood proud and the Beggar sat low on the horizon. Luxon had learned that when the bottom most star of the beggar constellation dipped below the horizon, the sun would begin its daily rise.

"So, where are you heading, if you do not mind me asking?" said Tuilin, throwing a fresh log onto the fire. The wood burned brightly for a moment as the wood caught flame.

Luxon hesitated for a moment.

"We're travelling to Plock," he lied.

The stranger nodded, his eyes not leaving Luxon who shifted uncomfortably.

"You're a bad liar, lad," Tuilin said quietly. "Your dark-eyed friend said the same, but I have a talent for spotting liars. You're a bunch of mages going somewhere – not to Plock, but somewhere."

Luxon felt the hairs on his neck stand up. Something was wrong. The man sat opposite him was no ordinary traveller.

"Who are you?" he demanded. He channelled the magic within, ready to fight.

Before Tuilin replied, the woman Una and the young man Rendil quietly stepped out of the darkness. Una carried a long silver-tipped spear whilst Rendil held two short stabbing daggers. Around their necks hung amulets of a design Luxon had never seen before.

"I would drop your weapons. Otherwise you might get hurt," Luxon warned.

Tuilin chuckled menacingly.

"Is that right? We know who and what you are, lad. You're the wizard, the one worth a small fortune. You can try and resist. It won't do you any good."

Luxon stood. He raised his arm and focused his power. To his amazement, nothing happened. He tried again to use the telekinetic spell to disarm the strange folk, but again nothing happened. Panic filled him as weakness flooded into his body. The group advanced menacingly.

"Help!" Luxon cried as a wave of tiredness washed over him. Desperately, he lunged towards the fire and with a yell hurled the cooking pot at the attackers. Boiling hot water splashed out, striking Rendil in the face. He collapsed to the floor in an agonised scream. Tuilin swore as the camp burst to life. Kaiden scrambled out of his tent his sword held at the ready. Ferran and Sophia, too, rushed to Luxon's aid. They were all bleary eyed, but the sight of danger quickly brought them to their senses.

"Get behind me," Ferran shouted as he pushed Luxon back. In his hand was his ignited tourmaline blade. Kaiden stood shoulder to shoulder with the Nightblade. Yepert and Hannah were also armed, Yepert with his short sword and Hannah with her pole staff.

Tuilin sneered at the group before grabbing his wounded "son" by the arm and dragging him backwards. Una keep her spear aimed at them.

"This isn't over, wizard," Tuilin snarled. "Know that you and your friends are hunted. We will meet again."

"Shall we pursue?" Kaiden growled as the sound of the fleeing footsteps faded.

Ferran shook his head.

"No. It's too dangerous to venture far from the rune stone whilst the darkness lasts. Hopefully a Fell Beast will do them in, whoever they were."

Luxon sat heavily onto the ground, weariness threatening to overwhelm him. Whatever the amulets had been enchanted with, they had a power the likes of which he had never felt before.

"Slavers most likely," Kaiden growled. "I've heard rumours that someone has put a high price on live mages. The real mystery is how they got their hands on those amulets."

"Those amulets made it feel like my powers were being drained from me. It felt like the N'gist amulets used by the Baron of Retbit when he attacked Caldaria, but these effects were far more potent."

Hannah rushed over to him and placed a hand to his forehead. She reached into a small pouch attached to her belt and pulled out some herbs.

"Here, chew these," she said her voice full of worry. "They should restore some of your energy."

"We need to get moving, Ferran," Kaiden said. "Fell Beasts or no, they could come back and in greater numbers. We're not far from Sunguard; another few hours and we will reach the capital. Perhaps Davik can shed some light on things."

A few moments passed before the Nightblade nodded in agreement.

"You're right. Pack your gear and saddle up. If we are to reach the capital in one piece we are going to have to ride hard and fast."

CHAPTER ELEVEN.

The first of the sun's light was met with welcome relief as it began to appear in the eastern sky. They had ridden throughout the remainder of the night. Luckily, they had not encountered the strange attackers again, but they had heard various creatures moving through the undergrowth. With the sunrise, the threat of an attack by Fell Beasts was reduced, but they would not be truly safe until they reached the sigil stone of Sunguard.

Ferran called for the group to slow down in order to give the horses a break. The loyal beasts had run for hours without complaint, but now they panted heavily. The companions reached a small clearing which contained a well.

Over the centuries the King's Legion had built dozens of the watering holes along the kingdom's main roadways to keep the soldiers and mounts watered. Kaiden dismounted. With a grunt, he lifted the heavy grate which covered the well and began to lower a bucket into its depths. Yepert, too, dismounted and helped out with the time-consuming task.

Luxon sat back in his saddle, his eyes heavy from exhaustion. The sound of the early morning birdsong began as the creatures of the Great Wood stirred from their slumber. The spot was peaceful and he couldn't help but smile. His face dropped however when he heard Kaiden swear loudly. He opened his eyes to see the former knight gagging as he tipped the contents of the bucket onto the ground. Instead of sweet clear water, a vicious black fluid oozed from it.

"What in Niveren?"

Ferran dismounted and walked over to the well. He dipped his head into it and sniffed.

"Goblin tar," he muttered. "A lair must be close. They're probably under our feet right now."

"Goblins this close to the capital?" Sophia said in surprise.

"Surely the Legion should keep these wells and roads clear," Hannah said.

Ferran gestured for Kaiden and Yepert to get back onto their horses.

"It's just another sign that the kingdom is falling apart," Ferran sighed. "A Nightblade would normally take care of such things, but Thanos has ordered them to stay in Caldaria because of the attacks. C'mon, let's keep moving."

The day had turned grey and cold as they reached the bluff which overlooked the plains of Sunguard. In the distance, the towers of the capital stood strong, and distant banners could be seen fluttering in the breeze. As they got closer to the city, the road widened became increasingly busy as merchants and soldiers moved to and fro from the capital. A line of small stone legion forts ran alongside it, and several taverns and inns were filled with patrons despite the early hour. The group dismounted at one of the taverns, and Ferran, Luxon and Sophia continued to the city on foot. The others paid a stable boy to feed and water the horses before going inside to the warmth of a fire and a hot meal.

CHAPTER ELEVEN.

Luxon, Ferran and Sophia walked through the city's main gate without issue. Each pulled their hoods closer around their faces just in case anyone was watching out for their arrival.

They quickly made their way through the wide streets to the base of the hill on which the King's Spire stood. The legionary guarding the heavy iron gates gave them a dubious look as Luxon identified himself. He noticed that the soldier's hand drifted subconsciously to the hilt of his sword. After a few moments, the gates opened and the trio was escorted up the hill and into the Spire. As they walked upward, the city below sprawled out in all directions. Easily visible was the Great Church of Niveren and the plaza where the king had been crowned. Unlike that day, the huge open space was packed with people.

After passing through several guarded gates, they arrived at the King's Spire. The palace was built into the side of the tall pillar of stone which stood tall over the city below. No one knew how the great pillar had been formed, but legend said that it had been placed in its current spot by a god. The first men had settled at its base, and over the millennia many different cities had been built, each bearing the name of the first: Sunguard. It had been the capital of Niveren's people, the Nivonian Empire and the Golden Empire. Now, it was the beating heart of Delfinnia.

A steward ushered them inside and led them through the maze of marble-walled corridors. Many of the walls were covered in paintings depicting key scenes from the realm's history. Ornate tapestries covered other walls, and works of art were strategically placed to emphasise the wealth and power of the realm.

Eventually, the steward gestured for them to wait in a small side room. Compared to the rest of the palace, the room was bland. A table decorated with gold leaf and two rather uncomfortable looking couches were the only furniture.

Luxon sat on one of the chairs and closed his eyes. If things were going to go the same way as his last visit to the palace then there was a good chance they would have to wait a long-time before being seen.

The sound of the heavy oak door opening made him raise his eyebrows in surprise. The steward poked his head around the door and waved them to follow him. They were led once again through the warren of corridors. The deeper they got into the palace, the more opulent the decoration. Gold leaf covered most of the walls, and the white marble floor was polished to a bright shine. Portraits of old kings and barons lined many of the walls, and ornate swords hung from golden pegs. Luxon tried to get his bearings but quickly gave up; the palace was like a maze. His curiosity grew the longer they walked. He had never been in this part of the palace before. Finally, the steward stopped outside a large wooden door. He took a large iron key from his belt and put it into the keyhole. With a loud click, the door unlocked and, with a grunt, the steward pushed it open. He waved them inside before bowing and retreating back down the corridor.

They were in a large chamber lit by a dozen wall-mounted lanterns. The walls were painted white, and tapestries depicting the royal family's coat of arms dominated them. On the floor, the king's coat of arms was inlaid in serpentine, and on the ceiling was a painting of what looked like Zahnia the Great's victory over Danon. The wizard was depicted as muscular, despite his age, and his long grey beard and hair flowed behind him. In his right hand, the wizard held a golden sword infused with light and in his left he wielded his staff, Erdasol. Danon was depicted as a black shadow retreating from the light. Luxon marvelled at the painting; the detail was exquisite, suggesting that it had been created by one of the realm's master painters.

CHAPTER ELEVEN.

"Danon's Second Fall," a quiet voice spoke from the far end of the chamber. "A marvellous painting is it not? Painted by Rusious, the master painter of Balnor."

Luxon, Ferran and Sophia knelt as they recognised the small boy walking towards them. King Alderlade was now eight years of age, but from the stern look on his young features he appeared older. His black curly hair reached his shoulders and his blue eyes shone with intelligence. The boy king wore an outfit of purple velvet, with a small red cape over his shoulders. A gold chain hung around his neck, and at its centre was a glistening jewel: the King's Jewel.

"Sire," Luxon greeted.

"I thought we were here to meet Davik?" Ferran muttered under his breath.

Alderlade gestured impatiently for them to stand.

"How can we serve you, Your Majesty?" Ferran asked respectfully.

The boy king paced the room, his small hands clasped tightly behind his back.

"Somebody stole it! Somebody stole my stone!" the king whined, his voice quivering with emotion.

Ferran and Sophia glanced at each other in confusion.

"Forgive me, Sire but what are you talking about?" the Nightblade asked.

The king stopped his pacing and glared at Ferran. The boy's face was flushed red and tears threatened to flow from his eyes.

Luxon placed a hand on Ferran's shoulder and leaned in close.

"Could you two wait outside? I know what the king is talking about. I think he will be calmer just speaking with me."

Ferran hesitated for a moment before taking Sophia's hand in his. They both bowed before slipping out of the room.

"You are talking about the sigil stone, aren't you?" Luxon asked his king softly. "The one that you held in Eclin, the magic stone." He knelt before the small boy and looked him straight in the eye.

Alderlade nodded, wiping his eyes clear. "My uncle says that no one should ever see me cry … that as king, I have to be strong," the boy said, puffing out his small chest.

Luxon smiled. "I have met your uncle Ricard. I wouldn't listen to him too closely if I were you, Sire. Now, tell me what has happened to the stone."

Alderlade explained that a man had broken into the king's vault and stole the sigil stone. The thief had been highly skilled as no guard noticed his presence.

"The scoundrel was a Fleetfoot! I got Davik to send men to look for the stone, and they found a man's body hidden in a ditch not far from the city limits. He had been murdered!"

Luxon looked away. This news was troubling indeed. As well as all the other issues he faced, the theft of the sigil stone might prove to be the most important. A dark thought entered his mind. Why would someone kill just for a magical stone? Was Danon behind the theft? That was a sobering thought. When he had touched the stone in Eclin, visions had flashed into mind, visions that still haunted him. The stone was more important than he first thought.

"Sire, were there any clues as to who killed the thief?"

The king looked at his hands his brow furrowed in thought.

"Perhaps. My men arrested all the known Fleetfoots in Sunguard. Maybe they know something?"

Luxon smiled and squeezed the boy's shoulder.

"With your permission, Sire, I would like to see those prisoners. Keep this between us, though, as I think we should keep the importance of the stone under wraps for now. It will be our little secret."

The king nodded in agreement.

"Forgive me, Sire, but where is Davik?" Luxon asked. "We assumed that we would be meeting with him, also."

The King frowned.

"Davik is in the east overseeing the redeployment of troops … I think."

The boy pouted. "No one tells me anything."

Luxon left the room and waved for Ferran and Sophia to follow him. The steward that had led them to the king's chamber was patiently waiting further down the corridor.

"You," Luxon said. "Take us to the jail, please."

Ferran, Sophia and the steward all looked surprised at the request.

"What the hell is going on?" Ferran mumbled.

"I'll explain later, but we had better send word to the others that we will be delayed."

The steward guided them back through the maze of corridors until they reached the top of a spiral staircase which was guarded by two grim-faced legionaries. As they approached, the soldiers barred the stairs with their spears.

"No entry. Baron Ricard's orders," the taller of the two guards said.

Luxon sighed in annoyance. He reached into his cloak and pulled out a small piece of paper.

"We have the king's permission. Last time I checked, the word of King Alderlade superseded that of his uncle, or am I mistaken?"

The guard read the note. He coughed nervously, his face flushing red in annoyance.

"Well ... that does look like the king's seal. Fine, you can go on down, but we will be watching you closely, wizard," The guards parted their spears and waved Luxon and the others through. Sophia glared at the men as she passed them.

"Disrespectful sods," she muttered under her breath.

Ferran led the way down the spiralling stone staircase, the others close behind. The way was lit with flaming braziers lining the stone walls. When they reached the bottom of the stairs, they found themselves in a narrow corridor. The air was heavy with damp and the place stank of sweat.

One of the guards pushed himself past Ferran.

"C'mon then, I haven't got all bloody day. The scum you want is in the cell at the end. Don't take too long," the guard grumbled, before turning on his heel and ascending back up the staircase.

Ferran took one of the torches from the wall and led the way deeper into the dungeon. They passed half a dozen cells which contained a large number of miserable looking men and woman. As they passed, some of the prisoners reached out through the iron bars to feebly plead for their release. As they reached the cell mentioned by the guard, Ferran chuckled.

"I should have known."

Sat on a wooden stall and picking dirt from under his fingernails was a heavyset bald man. A scar ran from the top of his skull to his chin, but his eyes suggested a keen intelligence. Upon seeing Ferran, the man stood up and smiled.

"Thrift, you old dog," Ferran greeted warmly. "I really should have guessed that you would be caught up in this." He reached a gloved hand through the bars, which Thrift shook.

"I can't believe it, Ferran of Blackmoor, Sophia Cunning and the wizard. You've gotten tall, lad. How long's it been?"

"Five years, Thrift. It's good to see you," Sophia answered. The thief reached through the bars and took her hand, before kissing it smoothly.

"What brings such distinguished guests to my humble jail cell?" Thrift asked with a wink.

The last time Luxon had met the thief was during the battle of Eclin, when Thrift had led a force of Fleetfoots in the fighting. The thieves guilds were renowned for their skills with bow and blade, and their support had been vital in liberating the city. After the fighting had ended, Thrift and the other Fleetfoots had been pardoned for all past crimes, but true to their nature many of them were soon back on the rob or back in jail.

"What do you know about the break in at the Hall of Treasures?" Luxon asked, leaning closer to the bars.

The colour from Thrift's face paled and his roguish smile slipped, to be replaced by a look of fear. The thief stepped back from the bars and shook his head.

"Nope. I am not getting involved in that nonsense, not again. I've had it up to here with magic and monsters! Leave me out of it, wizard."

Luxon arched an eyebrow at the reaction.

"So you do know something about it. Tell us what you know, and I promise to get you released and leave you alone."

Thrift looked at him a pleading look in his eyes. Conflict played behind them before he relented with a deep sigh.

"I've heard rumours ..." he began warily. "Apparently, a master thief called Untir was hired to break into the Hall of Treasures. The Fleetfoot chapter house in Sunguard refused to back him up, but apparently the gold on offer was so great that Untir got greedy and went in solo."

"Do you know who the contractor was?"

"Again, this is just rumour, but my contact in Sunguard told me that the contract was signed by the Merchant King of Stormglade. The guild refused the contract because it doesn't like to get involved in politics, but as I said – the promise of a lot of gold sometimes supersedes the rules."

Luxon looked at Ferran and Sophia; all roads were leading to the city of Stormglade.

CHAPTER TWELVE.

After they left the palace Luxon and the others reunited with Yepert, Kaiden and Hannah at the Weary Traveller Inn. After a quick bite to eat, they saddled their horses and got back on the road.

"It cannot be a coincidence that everything is pointing to Stormglade," Yepert moaned to his friend. "The Sarpi, your mother and the theft of the sigil stone ... why do I get the feeling we are heading towards some terrible danger?"

Despite his worry, Luxon couldn't help but smile. He glanced to his right; Hannah was riding at his side, her beautiful face deep in concentration. In her hand she held a wilted rainbell flower. Her mouth moved as she quietly uttered an incantation. A white light began to shine from between her fingers when she closed her hand into a fist. A few seconds passed and she opened her palm. To Luxon's surprise, the wilted flower now looked healthy and vibrant. Hannah whooped in happiness.

"Finally! I've been working on that spell for weeks," she laughed.

"See, Yepert, we'll be fine. We have a great healer at our side," Luxon said with a wink.

The group followed the King's Road south until they reached the Sundial Inn. Ferran decided that as the sun was still high in the sky, they should press ahead to the sigil stone located on the border of the barony of Balnor.

As the days passed, they travelled through a number of small farming settlements, and on their left hand side was the shimmering waters of the Lakelands. Smoke rose lazily on the autumn air from the hundreds of houses in the town of Midlake which lay at the heart of the Lakelands. A small fleet of fishing boats drifted on the lake's surface, and children splashed and played on the banks.

As the day wore on, they left the Lakelands behind them and the road began to dip. The soft rolling hills and pine forests gave way to large open fields which were filled to the brim with crops almost ready to be harvested. Wheat and corn were the most common, but spread between them were orchards filled with apple trees. In the western sky the sun began to dip lower on the horizon, and long shadows began to stretch out. Ferran raised a hand to signal them to stop. Luxon trotted his horse to the front of the group to see what prompted the halt. He gasped at what he saw. The setting sun lit up the sky and made it look as though it were on fire. In the far distance was the outline of a city, its tall towers standing strong and its banners flapping proudly in the soft breeze.

"Behold. The city of Bison," Ferran said softly.

The city was built on a raised patch of ground which allowed it to dominate the Bison plains that stretched for hundreds of miles in all directions. Luxon narrowed his eyes and smiled as he spotted a huge plume of dust. Hundreds of black dots were moving quickly on the plain. As his eyes adjusted, the dots turned into horses.

"We are lucky," Ferran said with a smile. "It's very rare to see one of the famous Bison herds this close to the border, and at this time of year.

Normally they stick to the northern plains which border the Blackmoor." The Nightblade raised a hand to shield his eyes and pointed at a small settlement which lay to the west of the city.

"We will camp there, at the sigil stone of Akadems. It will be the last civilised place we will see until we reach the Watchers."

"How long until we reach the Watchers?" Kaiden asked. Unlike the others he had no smile on his face; instead, he wore a look of determination.

Ferran's smile faded. The cause for their journey was not a pleasant one, and grave danger surely awaited them.

"Three days if we're lucky and the weather stays calm. We shouldn't have to worry about Fell Beasts on the plain, though, as the Baron of Bison's cavalry patrol the roads."

"Good," Kaiden said softly, before spurring his horse onward towards Akadems.

The small town of Akadems was a relic from the ancient days. Crumbling stone buildings dating back from the days of the Nivion Empire stood alongside wooden structures built by the settlement's current inhabitants. The town's largest building belonged to the mayor who, upon Luxon and the others' arrival, had scurried out to greet them. The place was a mish mash of architecture, as one half was comprised of the swirling stone pattern of some much older building, and the other was built from wood and rock.

The mayor himself was a chubby man who obviously loved his drink. His bald head was offset by a thick black beard and small eyes which shined with intelligence. For such a big man, he was surprisingly energetic as he ordered a small band of villagers to bring out food and drink to their honoured guests. Luxon learned that the man's name was Hori, a relative of the current Baron of Bison.

"Any news from the watchers?" Luxon asked after their horses had been taken away to be fed and watered. Hori had then invited them into his house, and now they sat at a long oak table which was covered in plates full of food.

It seemed as though half of the town was at the feast, and the noise of chatter and a bard's lute filled the stuffy warm air.

The mayor was greedily stiffing his face with cheese, and ale dripped from his beard.

"Nay, not heard much from the garrison there in a good while," Hori replied through mouthfuls of food. "S'pose that must be a good thing, rather no news than ill news."

Hannah was sat next to Luxon, and she squeezed his hand gently; next to her was Yepert, who was a smaller mirror image of the mayor. He was never happier than when filling his mouth with grub. At the other end of the table were Kaiden, Ferran and Sophia. They were huddled close and in deep conversation.

"What do you suppose they're gassing about?" Hori asked, reaching for another piece of mutton. "Anyway, what brings a group such as yourselves to this little backwater town of mine?"

Luxon glanced at Hannah who gave him a look of warning. Upon their arrival, Ferran had introduced themselves as a band of merchants hoping to set up a trade route to the Watchers; he had been careful not to give away their true identities. As a result, Luxon had made sure to conceal his staff by hiding it in his horse's saddle bags …

"I hope you're not here to cause mischief like that woman did. Ended up having to chase her out of town we did. Flipping magic wielder," Hori moaned.

Luxon's eyes widened. Hannah shook her head in warning but he couldn't help himself, he had to ask.

"Er, this woman, what did she look like?" he asked nonchalantly. "Just in case we run into her on the road …"

Hori picked up a tankard of ale and downed it in one. Hannah had a look of disgust on her face. The mayor slammed the tankard back down onto the table and let out a loud burp, which was promptly followed by a fart.

"She was a witch! Her hair was as black as her wretched soul and her eyes were an icy blue, cold enough to freeze an honest man's heart. She came to town with men in hot pursuit, she sought shelter, I told her to keep travelling, no wielders are welcome in my town I said!"

Luxon felt himself getting angry; only the calming touch of Hannah stopped him from leaning over and punching the man's fat, pig-like face. Ferran was glaring at him from the other end of the table and shook his head slowly in warning.

Luxon closed his eyes and took a deep breath to calm himself.

"These men who were chasing her … who were they?" he asked through gritted teeth.

Hori filled his tankard up again before pausing in thought. After a while he snapped his fingers as he remembered.

"They said they were Witch Hunters. Sent by the Baron of Champia to rid the world of magic's evil. They said that they had been chasing her for many miles. If they caught her or not, I do not know. I hope they did."

Luxon clenched his fists under the table. The Baron of Champia knew of his mother, but how? Was it he who had sent those so-called Witch Hunters after them on the King's Road? He stood from the table and stormed out of the hall. Ferran gestured for Hannah and Yepert to stay put as he, too, stood and followed his friend outside.

"What's angered your friend so?" Hori called out through a mouthful of mutton.

"Apologies, Mayor," Ferran replied. "My young companion does not handle his drink too well. Go back to enjoying your meal."

Ferran found Luxon sat outside the hall with his back pressed against the structure's wooden wall, his head in his hands. The sun had set a few hours earlier and only the sounds of the revelry inside the hall carried on the cold air. The twin moons were shining brightly and casting their lunar light over the vast empty plains that stretched off into the distance.

"Feels like the first frost of the year may fall tonight," Ferran said as he sat down next to Luxon. He picked a blade of grass and twirled it between his fingers.

"That bastard Ricard …" Luxon muttered quietly. "He is up to something. He sent those Witch Hunters after us on the road; he sent them after my mother. How can we travel so far into the wilderness when that snake sits so close to the king?"

Ferran nodded, understanding his young friend's frustration.

"Ricard is a very powerful man, Luxon. I share your doubts about him. During the civil war he fought to take the crown for himself – not once did he believe that his nephew lived. Even when rumours to the contrary were spread, he did nothing to find him. With no evidence, however, we cannot take our concerns to the king. We must stick to the mission at hand and trust that Davik will protect his majesty. Whatever is happening in Stormglade, it links everything, I am sure of it."

Luxon sighed heavily before standing up.

"If that idiot mayor insults magic users again, I am going to set his beard on fire, I swear," he grumbled.

Ferran laughed.

The rest of the night passed without incident, and Luxon even ended up enjoying himself. He and Hannah had danced along with the mostly drunk villagers, and for a time the troubles of the world fell away. As the feast had wound down, the two of them snuck off to the stables where they made love in the hay. It was there that Ferran found them. Luxon's thick robe lay across them, protecting their modesty.

"C'mon you two, times a wasting." The Nightblade held a bucket of water in his hand which he placed nearby. "Here, wash yourselves with this and meet us in the town square when you're ready."

Luxon moaned, his head aching from the amount of ale he had consumed. Hannah leant over him and kissed him softly on the lips.

"Here, let me fix that hangover," she said playfully. She placed her palm on his forehead and closed her eyes. She muttered a spell and Luxon gasped. Warmth flooded his head, and the pain immediately subsided. He blinked and shook his head. Even the taste of stale ale had left his mouth.

"You could make a fortune charging drunks for such a service," he joked. He pulled on his trousers before walking over to the bucket and dunking his head into the cold water.

Hannah likewise pulled on her travel tunic and robe before scooping up a handful of water and washing her face. She then reached into a pouch on her waste and pulled out two small leaves.

"Here chew this," she said, handing Luxon one of the small strong-smelling green leaves. "It is Robintan mint; it will make your mouth feel nice and your breath fresh, and they're also very good for your teeth."

Luxon popped the leaf in his mouth and chewed as instructed. Instantly, his mouth was flooded with freshness. They quickly gathered up the rest of their affects and hurried outside. Upon seeing the couple, Yepert let out a wolf whistle. Hannah flushed red in embarrassment, and the others laughed.

"Mount up you two!" Ferran ordered. "We still have a long way to go until we reach the Watchers. From here the road will be more like a dirt track and the wilderness will be more unforgiving. Keep your eyes open for Fell Beasts, and pray to Niveren that we don't encounter any dragons!"

CHAPTER THIRTEEN.

Despite Ferran's dire warnings, the rest of the journey passed without incident. True to his word, however, the road did narrow until its stone surface stopped and was replaced by a dirt track. Thanks to the cold nights and rain showers that dogged them, once they left Akadems parts of the road had turned into a muddy quagmire. The horses found it hard going, and more than once the travellers had ended up in the dirt. Kaiden had suggested that they leave the road to avoid the mud, but Ferran did not agree.

At night they heard the sounds of Fell Beasts, the wail of a banshee bringing bad memories to Yepert especially. It took them three days and nights to reach the fortress of the Watchers. Its mighty towers dominated the horizon and its long thick walls stretched for two miles from north to south. The citadel defended the narrow stretch of land which divided the Great Plains from the rest of the kingdom.

As they got closer they could see the banner of the King's Legion flapping in the breeze and armoured legionaries patrolling the battlements. Kaiden frowned as he spotted another flag flying. Upon its field was a white background, and in the centre was a seven pointed gold star.

"Impossible ..." he muttered. The flag was that of his old order, the Knights of Niveren.

"I thought the order disbanded after Eclin," Luxon said as he recognised the banner. Like the others, he was covered in mud, and the dark rings under his eyes betraying his tiredness. Sleeping out in the wilderness without the protection of a sigil stone had been a nerve-wracking experience, and one that had not allowed them much rest.

A haunted looked crossed Kaiden's features. "A Knight Vigilant perhaps?" He had lost so many friends at Eclin, and out of the thousands of knights that fought in that terrible battle, less than a handful remained.

"What's a Knight Vigilant?" asked Hannah, who was riding next to Luxon.

"They are legends, really," Kaiden began. "There are only three at a time, and they are the greatest warriors in the order. They are tasked with roaming the world and keeping a vigilant lookout for dangers that pose a threat. If they do find such a threat they are sworn with trying to destroy it before it emerges ..."

"If the rumours about Stormglade are true, then its little surprise such a Knight would have passed through the Watchers," Luxon said.

"There's only one way to find out, and that's by going inside," Ferran added from behind them. He spurred on his mount and led the way to the Watchers.

CHAPTER THIRTEEN.

As they approached, a legionary on the battlements ordered them to halt. He then turned and called down from the wall to his comrades.

Luxon patted his horse's neck as it stamped its feet nervously, and flashed a reassuring smile to Hannah and a very nervous looking Yepert. The younger mage had little love for legionaries. He turned back to the fortress as the sound of grinding metal emanated from the gatehouse. The huge iron portcullis slowly rose into the air and a dozen heavily armed soldiers on horseback galloped out toward them. Each of the riders had a cloak of the darkest red draped over their armour, and red plumes atop their helmets.

"The Bloodriders!" Yepert exclaimed in awe.

The mounted warriors now circling them were members of the Legion's legendary cavalry unit. They had earned their fearsome reputation during the Yundol invasions. At the battle of the Ridder, the Bloodriders had smashed the enemy forces in a single charge, an action that had turned the tide in that savage conflict.

Ferran raised his hands high and gestured for the others to do likewise as the Bloodriders formed a circle and surrounded them, their lances lowered and aimed.

"Who are you?" demanded one of the riders. The horseman's plume was larger than the others, indicating that he was the squad's captain.

"We are here by order of the king," Ferran replied. "If I may?" he asked. The captain nodded and the Nightblade slowly reached into his tunic and pulled out a wax-sealed scroll. Davik had sent it to Caldaria shortly after

Luxon's first trip to the capital. Without it they would not be able to enter the Watchers and enter the Great Plains.

The captain trotted his horse forward and took the scroll from Ferran's hands. He broke the seal and unfurled the parchment. A few uneasy moments passed, and Luxon noticed Yepert shift uncomfortably in his saddle. The captain grunted and handed the scroll back.

"Well, that seems to be in order," the captain said, his voice changing from one of gruff irritation to one of less gruff irritation. "Welcome to the Watchers." He barked an order to one of his men, who then sped off back towards the citadel before raising a hand above his head. He then waved to the legionaries gathered on the walls. Luxon gulped as he realised that many of them had bows aimed in their direction. The tense atmosphere faded. The Bloodriders lowered their lances and escorted them through the gate.

Yepert whistled in surprise once they were inside the safety of the walls. The fortress was huge. Once through the gate they found themselves in a vast courtyard lined with dozens of stone buildings. Many of the structures were store houses and barracks, but others were more like what you would find inside a town or city. There were taverns, shops and armouries, as well as a walled-off residential district that housed the garrisoned soldiers' wives and children. The placed brimmed with activity. Soldiers marched along the cobbled avenues or were shoring up the defences. The sounds of barked orders came from all directions, and the air smelt of smoke from the blacksmiths' forges. The Bloodriders led them deeper into the fortress until they passed through a second thick stone wall.

Something gnawed at Luxon's consciousness, and he stopped. Hannah looked over her shoulder.

"Are you okay?"

A heavy feeling spread into his limbs as though some invincible force was staying his feet. He looked around and his eyes settled on a man. The feeling grew heavier. The man was chained to a wooden stake, his torso bare, exposing his scarred skin. His hair was long, lank and brown. The man looked at him, his grey eyes piercing deeply into Luxon's own. As they watched each other, a feeling of foreboding filled him. Luxon shook his head and looked away. He smiled weakly at Hannah.

"Just a slight headache. I'll be fine," he lied.

He glanced at the man in chains again before hurrying after Hannah and the others.

Now they were in the heart of the citadel and its command centre. A tall stone tower dominated the space; anyone stood at the top would be able to see for miles in all directions.

A man dressed in a simple brown tunic and trousers greeted them. He was tall and well-built, and his hair was cropped short in the legionary style, the only clue that he was indeed a member of the King's Legion. He smiled warmly at them.

"Greetings and welcome to the Watchers. My name is Fritin, the commander of this mighty citadel. I hear that you seek to cross the Great Plains. You have come at a very unfortunate time, I am afraid."

"Unfortunate? How so?" Ferran asked.

Fritin dismissed the Bloodriders and gestured for Ferran and the others to follow him inside the tall stone tower.

"The tribes are restless," the commander said. "My scouts have fallen under attack every time they venture onto the plains. What information we have gathered suggests that they are warring with one another. The Plains are dangerous at the best of times, but with the tribes in conflict I cannot allow you to cross. It would mean certain capture or death."

Hr led them into a large room. A stone hearth dominated the room; the only furniture was a long wooden bench.

The feeling he had felt outside crept back into Luxon's mind. Before he could think, he spoke.

"Who is that man chained up outside?" he asked, with more force than he had expected.

The commander blinked in surprise at the sudden interruption. He rubbed his neck awkwardly, refusing to meet Luxon's hard stare. Ferran frowned at his young friend; he could sense the magic coursing through his veins.

"He ... he is a criminal, a cattle smuggler, nothing more ..." Fritin answered nervously. Luxon's blue eyes bore into the commander's.

"You're lying. Tell me who he is," Luxon demanded. The wizard's voice grew deeper rose in volume. Yepert threw a surprised look at his friend and the others stepped back. The atmosphere of the room became heavy.

The commander shrank under the wizard's hard stare, the colour draining from his face.

"Luxon. Stop this," Ferran said calmly. A breeze began to blow in the room, causing the flames in the fireplace to flicker, and the lit braziers hanging on the walls to extinguish.

Luxon ignored the Nightblade.

Ferran reached into his cloak for the hilt of his tourmaline sword, and Kaiden's hand drifted for his own blade. Sophia and Hannah retreated to the other side of the room. Yepert however stepped forward, planting himself between the now petrified commander and his friend. Luxon's eyes were no longer blue, but black and terrible.

"Luxon. Calm yourself," Yepert pleaded. "Please, you must listen to me. Take control; remember what Master Thanos taught you." The soft breeze was now a whirlwind and Kaiden and Ferran found it difficult to stand upright.

"What is happening?" yelled Kaiden over the howling winds. Outside the chamber came frantic banging on the door and the shouts of concerned soldiers.

"He has lost control," Ferran shouted back. "Something has triggered his power. I have seen this once before, long ago. Something is working through him."

In Luxon's mind, the horrors of Eclin screamed into his consciousness, and the nightmares he had suffered roared into life. Through the haze, however, he could see Yepert pleading with him.

"Luxon!"

He gasped and staggered backwards. The wind dropped and Hannah rushed forward, catching him before he collapsed entirely. Tears poured from Luxon's eyes and the colour in his face was gone. He was a deathly white.

Fritin clambered back onto his feet, his back pressed against the wall. The shouts of the soldiers carried through the door.

"I'm fine. Stand down," he shouted to his men. "Get a medic in here now!"

He stared at the young man who was now unconscious on the floor.

"Release that cur in the chains and bring him to me," he ordered. "I want some answers."

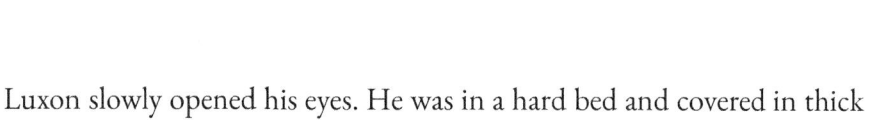

Luxon slowly opened his eyes. He was in a hard bed and covered in thick woollen blankets. Hannah's head rested on his chest, the gentle rise and fall of her body showing that she was asleep. Sat in a chair on the other side of the bed was Yepert, who was reading a book.

"An interesting read?" Luxon said. His voice sounded croaky, as though he had not drunk for a long time.

Yepert looked up, a soft smile on his face. The mage's eyes were dark from tiredness. He put down the book and reached for the pitcher of water and cup that was on the floor at his feet.

"Not really," he replied offering Luxon the cup after filling it with the cool liquid. "I found it in here. It's just a book on military tactics."

"How long was I out?"

"Two days. We were afraid you were never going to wake up." Yepert paused, his brow furrowing into a look of genuine concern. "It was the Void again, wasn't it?"

Luxon looked away. He had done his best to keep it a secret, but Yepert had found him in a similar state more than once since Eclin. Memories of the long years he had spent in the Void struck without warning. Once, he had collapsed on a walk in the woods outside of Caldaria. He had lost control of his power there, too, and almost set the trees ablaze. Other instances had occurred in the years since, but nothing as serious as now.

"It comes without warning," he stammered. "Visions burn into my mind until I feel as though I am back there. I see such horror ...Fell Beasts ... monsters ... Danon."

He downed the contents of the cup and sighed as the water soothed his throat.

"I dread to ask why my throat is so sore," he muttered.

"It was because of the screaming," Yepert replied quietly. "Ferran says you have something called Void sickness. He said that long ago, the mages who created the sigil stones and the Nightblades that fought the Fell Beasts often succumbed to it. The Void corrupts the magic in any mage or magic user that comes into sustained contact with it. You went into the very Void itself..."

Luxon stared at the stone ceiling, his mind racing at the revelation. His thoughts drifted back to the man in chains. Why had the attack come when seeing the man? He had to know.

"What time is it?" he asked.

"Not long till dawn," Yepert replied after yawning loudly.

Yepert and Hannah helped Luxon get washed and dressed before leading him to the courtyard where the man in chains had been. The man was gone, but a strange sense emanated from the spot where he had been tied up. The hairs on Luxon's arms stood on end as he approached the spot. He crouched down and touched the ground. Closing his eyes, he focused his magic. He felt a familiar presence ... his mother! His eyes snapped open. She had been here, and she had met the chained man. He turned and ran inside the tower, Yepert and Hannah close behind.

Luxon called out for Ferran and the others.

Sophia peered out of a side room and smiled upon seeing him up and about.

"Thank Niveren you're alright. C'mon," she said waving for them to follow her. "Ferran is with commander Fritin and the prisoner." After leading them deeper into the citadel tower, they came to a set of heavy oak doors. Kaiden was stood outside, a grim look on his face. As he spotted their arrival he stepped forward.

"I advised against it, but there was no stopping them," he said sombrely.

Luxon raised an eyebrow at his tone, but ordered the legionary posted outside to push open the doors.

Luxon strode into the room determinedly, but stopped short as he saw the prisoner on his knees in the centre of the circular room.

Standing over him, rubbing his bloodied knuckles was Ferran. Blood dripped from the prisoner's lips, and his face was a mass of bruises. Commander Fritin stood by, watching.

"He's out cold again," the commander said.

"What is the meaning of this?" Sophia cried from behind him. Ferran stared at his wife.

"He could be a spy for the enemy," the Nightblade replied weakly. "We had to get answers out of him."

"By torturing the man?" Sophia snapped, before storming out of the room. Ferran looked at Luxon.

The wizard shook his head disapprovingly, before pushing past Ferran to stand before the beaten man lying on the floor. Hannah hurried over to him and began to tend to his wounds.

"There was no need to torture him. What happened was not his fault," Luxon said quietly. He knelt down next to Hannah. "Will he be alright?"

Hannah brushed a lock of blond hair behind her ear and closed her eyes. She ran a hand over the wounded man, a faint glow emerging from her palm.

"Yes. I do not sense any permanent damage. I can revive him if you want."

Luxon nodded and Hannah channelled her magic with an incantation. The light from her hand spread over the prisoner until, with a gasp, he awoke.

"Easy, you're safe," Luxon said in a calm voice.

The man looked around in confusion, his eyes wild. Then they settled on Luxon.

"You ... you are the one ..." he muttered. "The woman told me that you would come. She told me to help you, but I failed!"

Luxon placed a calming hand on the man's shoulder.

"Who are you?" he asked.

The man stared at him and gulped before replying.

"My name is Faramond, prince of the Keenlance clan. You are the wizard Luxon Edioz, son of Drusilla Edioz, mistress and keeper of the Diasect."

Luxon stepped back his heart racing.

"You're mother came to my tribe for aid," Faramond said. "She told me to watch out for your coming and to warn you to turn back," he added, a hint of pleading in his voice.

"Turn back? I have been looking for her for years. Why would I turn back now? She came out of hiding for a reason, and I need to know why."

The prince looked away, a haunted look on his face.

"I am sorry, but that is all she said to me," Faramond looked at the wizard pleadingly. "I came to the Watchers to beg for safe passage for my people. The Great Plain is no longer safe. Evil prowls the grasslands and preys on the tribes," He glared at the now sheepish-looking commander Fritin. "For my trouble, I was attacked and taken prisoner. The legion will pay; they are blind to what is coming."

Luxon stroked his chin in thought.

"If you promise to take me and my companions to my mother, I will get you released and try to help your people if I can."

Faramond stared at him for a moment as he considered the offer. A few moments passed before he dropped his head.

"You have a deal, wizard," he said softly.

CHAPTER THIRTEEN.

Kaiden stood on the Watchers' high wall, his gaze focused on the distant horizon. Grey clouds were sweeping across the plain, promising to bring rain. He glanced up at the banner that was flapping gently in the breeze. The seven-pointed golden star of Niveren on the white field, the sigil of his order. He frowned. How could the knights be here? After Eclin, there had been so few of them left alive that it was decided to disband. It had been a terrible decision to make; not once in a thousand years had the order been so decimated. Now as he stood on the walls at the end of the world, the banner of Niveren flew proudly once again.

"Kaiden?"

He turned at the sound of his name.

Sophia was stood at the top of the stone steps which led to the top of the wall. Her cheeks were red from the climb. She pulled her cloak tighter around her body to keep out the chill that was beginning to make its presence known in the autumnal air.

"I asked Fritin about the Niveren flag," she said as she leaned on the wall next to Kaiden. "He told me that a knight left it here about six months ago, before heading out onto the plains. Apparently, all the knight said was that his was a mission of vital importance. The commander said that he looked as though he had been in the wilderness for a long time, and that his tunic was filthy and his hair wild. Whoever it was hadn't been near to civilisation in years."

"Thank you for asking, Sophia," he said softly. His gaze once again looking to the horizon. Somewhere out there was his wife and daughter.

First he would save them, before worrying about the mysterious knight.

"How are you? You seemed upset with Ferran," he asked.

Sophia sighed heavily.

"I shouldn't be mad at him. He was worried about Luxon. Sometimes I forget what he is, and the things he has done in the service of the realm. I forgave him for what he did to my father, but sometimes, like today, the pain and the anger comes flooding back."

Kaiden nodded.

"It's hard to escape our pasts," he said. "No matter how hard we try to put them behind us, they seem to have the nasty habit of coming back to haunt us."

CHAPTER FOURTEEN.

It had been surprisingly easy to convince commander Fritin to set Faramond free. The smug legion officer had even provided them with an extra horse for him to ride on.

Luxon paced the courtyard nervously. Had he made the right choice? Had his need to find his mother blinded him to danger? Those thoughts tormented him as he walked. The others were nearby checking over their supplies and weapons, and loading them onto their mounts. He looked up when the sound of heavy footfalls sounded on stone. Faramond stood before him. His long hair was now tied into a loose pony tail, and the blood and dirt on his face had been scrubbed clean.

He wore a shirt and greaves made of chainmail and a pair of leather boots with iron soles. His bare arms were muscular, no doubt from the years of shooting a bow that the tribal folk of the plains was famous for. Now that he was back in his armour, Faramond held his head high and confidently. When they had first met, Luxon would never have imagined that the man before him was of noble blood. Now, however, it was apparent.

"They will not return my weapons," Faramond grumbled as he walked over to Luxon. The man was a good foot taller than the wizard.

Luxon shrugged his shoulders.

"They wouldn't agree to free you if you were armed. I am sorry."

"Simpering cowards ... they will regret this." Faramond bellowed out loud: You will regret this! I want my weapons; I will fight any man here for them!"

The others stopped what they were doing, and stared at their new companion. Luxon winced; he could see the patrolling legionaries stop and glare.

"He has a temper ..." Yepert muttered.

Luxon hoped that no one would take the tribesman up on his challenge.

A few tense moments passed, before a voice replied.

"I will fight you, you tribal piece of scum," said a massive legionary, who was pushing his way through a group of his comrades.

Luxon gasped; the legionary was the biggest man he had ever seen. The soldier was as big as a bear. The brute took off his helmet to reveal a shaven head and a face that only a mother could love. A livid red scar ran down the side of his cheek, and his smile revealed a set of broken, yellowish teeth.

"Bolgar! Bolgar! Bolgar!" cheered the legionaries.

Faramond smiled and rubbed his hands together.

"So, you Delfinnians aren't all cowards," he mocked. His words caused the growing crowd to boo and jeer. Bolgar laughed heartily.

"I will enjoy pulling your arms and legs off, little man," the big man chuckled. He turned to his companions and took the two short swords given to him. He threw one to Faramond who caught the blade easily. With impressive skill, Faramond twirled the blade through an intricate pattern in the air until it moved so fast that it was just a blur. Bolgar crossed his massive arms and joked with his friends.

Luxon and the others, meanwhile, had stepped out of the way.

Faramond stopped his display and rolled his shoulders. He then raised the sword point high. With his free hand, he gestured for his foe to attack, a smile on his face.

Bolgar stalked forward, his own sword in an en guard position. The crowd began to cheer as they sensed a good fight was in the offing. The legionaries took bets on the combatants, and gold flowed freely between them.

"I cannot let Faramond be harmed," Luxon muttered to Yepert. His friend was enthralled at the display; he had long dreamed of being able to wield a sword like the heroes of old. But if Faramond got himself killed, then the one lead Luxon had on his mother's whereabouts would be lost. He narrowed his eyes and watched the fight closely; if he had to, he would use his power to intervene.

"What is this racket?" bellowed commander Fritin, who had stormed outside, a squad of soldiers at his side. He took one look at Bolgar and Faramond and smiled. Luxon hurried over to him.

"Faramond just wanted his weapons returned, that is all. I tried to explain your decision, but, well … he wasn't very happy about it. If you would just let us be on our way, I'm sure I can convince him to forget ab–"

Fritin held a hand up dismissively and laughed. He walked forward so that he stood in between the two big men.

"We haven't had much chance for entertainment in this fortress lately," he said loudly so that he could be heard by the quickly growing crowd of onlookers. "I will not deny my lads the chance to witness a spectacle such as this"

"I must protest, Commander," Luxon snapped. He didn't have time for this foolishness. Fritin glared at him, all humour gone from his features. Slowly, he stalked toward the wizard, his guards close behind. Luxon tensed as he sensed Ferran and the others move closer. The Nightblade stood at his left, his hand gripping the hilt of his tourmaline blade; to Luxon's right, Kaiden's hand rested on the pommel of his own sword.

Fritin stopped short at the sight of their grim expressions. For a moment the tension built to painful levels. The watching legionaries bristled at the standoff. The commander smirked and reached into his tunic pocket. He pulled a piece of paper marked with the seal of the Baron of Champia.

"A rider arrived in the night. He brought a very interesting message from the capital. The king has decreed that all magic wielders are to be outlawed from stepping foot outside of Caldaria. These orders were given by Ricard of Champia, the king's uncle." He shrugged his shoulders. "I am in a very difficult position, for you see, here you stand – a wizard, a Nightblade and mages, all far from home." Fritin turned to face the crowd of soldiers and raised his voice so that all could hear him.

"Do I do as our king commands and arrest these people, or do I follow the request of wielders?"

Luxon and the others slowly stepped backwards towards the horses. Sophia now had her bow drawn and aimed at the commander. Yepert held his short sword at the ready and Hannah gripped her staff tightly, a determined look on her face.

"The king was the one that sent us here in the first place!" Ferran argued. "Lord Davik signed the papers himself, and last time I checked it was he, not Ricard of Champia, that is regent." His words caused some of the soldiers to call out in agreement. It was well known that there was no love lost between the two most powerful men in the kingdom.

Luxon's group continued to slowly move back towards the horses. Fritin and his guards drew their swords, eliciting protests from some of the watching legionaries.

"Not all of your men seem to agree with you, Fritin," Ferran said. "Let us leave, there is no need for violence."

Luxon stepped forward. He gestured for his friends to lower their weapons. They were outnumbered.

"How about a wager, Commander," he asked.

Fritin raised an eyebrow, his curiosity peaked.

"Go on."

"If Faramond wins the fight with your man, you must let us go."

"And if my man wins?"

Luxon threw a look at his companions.

"If your man wins, then we will surrender ourselves into your custody without a struggle."

Ferran shouted out in protest, but Sophia placed a calming hand on her husband's shoulder.

"Trust in Luxon. He knows what he's doing ... I hope," she said with more confidence than she felt.

Fritin thought for a moment, before nodding in his head. He faced his men.

"You heard the wizard. If Bolgar wins, the magic yielders will surrender. Their fate is now in the hands of Niveren."

The crowd cheered, the earlier tension now eased. The prospect of a good fight outweighed their concerns over the politics of the capital. The cheers faded and a new tension filled the air as the two warriors circled each other. Faramond had a wry grin on his face and his eyes were fierce. Suddenly, Bolgar dashed forward and brought his sword down in a slice. Faramond spun on his heel like a dancer, and the blade whistled as it swept through empty air.

The prince chuckled. To Luxon's amazement, the man was actually enjoying himself, as if he had no fear. Bolgar grunted as he swung again; this time the blade was deflected aside easily. The crowd roared back into life as the sound of clashing steel broke the spell of silence that had fallen over them. The large legionary shuffled forward, hacking and slashing as he advanced. Faramond danced backwards, only using his own weapon to parry any blows that got too close. Bolgar roared in frustration at the prince. Already, sweat was pouring into the soldier's eyes. Despite the autumn chill that filled the air, the man was hot and flustered as his foe kept dancing out of range.

"Fight me, you coward!" Bolgar roared as he launched a combo of cuts and slices.

Faramond ducked and dodged. Bolgar sneered as mid-swing he rotated his wrists and aimed the sword point at his enemy's feet. The crowd gasped as Faramond acrobatically cartwheeled out of the way. He laughed at the stunned expression on Bolgar's face.

CHAPTER FOURTEEN.

With a grace that would put a trained dancer to shame, the prince ran at Bolgar, dodging a swing by skidding onto his knees mid-run. The sword's deadly blade passing narrowly over his head. Still in motion, he rose from his knees and launched himself into the air. Bolgar staggered backwards as Faramond's knee connected solidly with his chest. Now it was Faramond who went onto the offensive. As at the start of the fight, he whirled his sword around so that it whistled through the air. At such a speed, Bolgar had no chance of seeing the blade. With sheer luck, he shifted his weight onto his heel and brought his own weapon up. The sound of clashing steel rang out again. The two men fought hard, their faces mere inches from one another; they could smell each other's breaths. Both men grunted as they fought to gain the upper hand over the other. Bolgar growled; his sheer size and bulk was giving him the advantage. To his surprise, however, Faramond winked mischievously. With a speed that caused the crowd gasp, the prince disengaged his blade and launched himself into a back flip. With no resistance, Bolgar staggered forward and fell onto his knees. It was then that Faramond made his move by delivering a savage kick to the side of the legionary's skull. Teeth and spittle flew from the big man's mouth, his eyes rolled into the back of his skull and he crashed to the stone-flagged ground with a thud, unconscious.

The crowd gawped in stunned amazement at what they had seen. Faramond sheathed his sword into his belt and knelt over his beaten adversary.

"The bigger you are, the harder you fall to the earth like a sack of shit," he chuckled.

Luxon sighed in relief. He walked over to the prince and shook his hand. Next he turned his attention to Fritin. The commander's face was red with rage.

"Looks like we win, Commander."

The commander was about to reply when a horn sounded in the distance.

A bell began to ring out on the western wall.

"To your battle stations!" bellowed a centurion.

The stillness that had settled over the crowd ended as the soldiers scrambled to their positions, the standoff between their commander and the magic wielders forgotten. More bells began to toll as the alarm spread through the mighty fortress. Legionaries hurried to the armouries or to positions on the wall. It was chaos.

Ferran gripped Luxon by the shoulder and pushed him towards the horses.

"This is our chance, mount up!" he called to the others. Kaiden leapt into Herald's saddle and the others quickly followed suit. Luxon mounted his brown horse, pleased to see Faramond do likewise.

A large contingent of legionaries marched past, their heavy armour clinking noisily. Many of the soldiers looked terrified, giving away the fact that they were rookies.

"I recognise that horn," Faramond whooped. "My people have come for me!" He kicked his boots into his horse's flanks and shot off towards the western gate.

With an exasperated sigh, Luxon and the others followed. Very soon, they began to struggle to keep pace with the prince. His equestrian skills were something to see. He commanded his steed with authority and grace. Skilfully, he steered his mount around the now running legionaries.

The tolling of the bells grew more frantic as they approached the western gatehouse.

CHAPTER FOURTEEN.

As with the eastern gate, it was an impressive barrier of stone and iron. A massive portcullis had been locked into place and archers had taken up positions along the battlements. Commander Fritin was bellowing orders to his men. Clumsily, the soldiers formed up into ranks: spearmen in front, swordsman behind.

Faramond reached the gate and trotted his horse in front of the petrified ranks of soldiers. He smiled happily and raised his head high.

"Release me, Fritin, and allow my new friends here to leave, or my people will attack this fortress!" he shouted so that all of the legion could hear.

Commander Fritin glared at his former prisoner, his eye twitching in rage. Luxon and the others trotted their mounts over to Faramond. The sound of thousands of galloping horses carried clearly on the cold air.

Luxon dismounted and bounded up a set of stone steps which led to the battlements. He pushed his way past the archers gathered on the walls and looked out.

An army numbering in the thousands was amassed just out of bowshot.

Every warrior was on horseback, a bow in their hands. The earth shook as the Keenlance tribe kicked their heels into their mounts' flanks. As one, the horses stamped their iron shod hooves onto the frost bitten grass of the plain. A single rider emerged from the massed ranks, a horn held high in the air.

"Seems they want to talk, sir," one of the archers called down to Fritin.

The commander snorted derisively.

"Of course they do," he replied loudly. "It would take a million of those dirt eating tribesmen to breach the walls of this fortress."

Some of the legionaries chuckled.

Sheathing his sword, Friton climbed the steps that led to the battlements. Arrogantly, he pushed his way past Luxon and leaned on the parapet.

The rider holding the horn trotted forward. He wore an iron helm decorated with a tall red plume. The face piece was simply decorated, and only revealed the man's mouth and chin. Like the other riders, he wore a suit of armour made of many individual small armour scales of various shapes, which were attached to each other and to a backing of cloth or leather in overlapping rows. Their arms were bare, and leather bracers were attached to the wrists, attesting to the importance they placed on the bow.

"Release our prince, fiend, and we will retreat from your walls," the rider shouted. "If you do not, we shall attack." Enforcing his threat, the warrior turned in his saddle and pointed.

Moving through the massed ranks of horsemen trundled six trebuchets, pulled by horses. Upon seeing the deadly siege weapons, some of the colour drained from Fritin's face. He swallowed visibly as he imagined the damage such contraptions could inflict upon the fortress's walls.

He rubbed a hand over his face as he contemplated his options. He had too few men to make repairs. With most of the legions fighting in the east against Retbit and Fell Beasts, he just didn't have the manpower. If the tribes knew just how weak the garrison at the Watchers was, they would surely attack en masse.

Without men to adequately defend the mile-wide walls, they would eventually be overrun.

"I guess you had better let us leave, Commander," Luxon said softly. Fritin's shoulders tensed, and for a moment Luxon thought that the man would strike him. He channelled the magic in him, ready to defend himself. But with a reluctant sigh, Fritin's shoulders sagged and he called down to the legionaries bracing the gates.

"Open the gates and let them leave." he said defeated. "We can't afford to risk the fortress, not with all the weirdness occurring on the plains."

With a loud screeching the massive portcullis began to slowly rise. Dust fell as the huge iron doors creaked open. As they did so, the legionaries lowered their spears in preparation for an attack by the tribesmen. Luxon hurried down from the walls and climbed into his horse's saddle.

"Will you take us to my mother?" he asked Faramond, whose horse stood next to his own.

The man nodded.

"I shall, and I will show you why my people have risked everything to escape the plains."

CHAPTER FIFTEEN.

It had once been a city of hope, a place where the disparate folk of the plains could gather in safety. Now, it was a city of nightmares. Stormglade had fallen into darkness.

Black clouds roiled in the skies above the city; beasts of the Void stalked the lands outside its walls; and men with glowing eyes patrolled its high walls. In the streets, the dead prowled, and dark mages of the N'gist performed their foul incantations. It was a city of evil, a city of death … the city of Danon.

In the city's harbour, a black-sailed ship slid into port. Aboard were hundreds of prisoners captured during the Sarpi's raids along the Marble Shore. Men, women and children were chained and huddled together in fright as the ship slowly pulled alongside a stone quayside. Among them were Alira and her little girl, Ilene. As the ship juddered to a halt, one of the Sarpi captors banged his spear on the deck.

"Get them up and get them processed," the Sarpi hissed. Rough hands gripped Alira and pulled her up onto her feet. She held tightly onto her daughter, pressing her close to her breast.

"Fear not, my sweet. Papa will come and save us, I promise," she whispered into her daughter's ear. The little girl buried her head into her mother's hair. The two of them were chained together by the wrist, and Alira was attached the other prisoners by a chain attached to her ankle.

Miserably, the prisoners slowly marched off the ship and down a wooden ramp that had been attached to the starboard side. Standing at either side of the ramp's base were two more cloaked Sarpi warriors, their eyes glinting menacingly in the darkness. Each held a long spear tipped with a jagged steel point. Between them was a man; not a Sarpi, but a normal man. He was short, with weasel-like features, and wore a black cloak with sleeves trimmed with scarlet red material. In his left hand was a large book, and in his right a quill with which he used to scribble notes on the tome's pages. The prisoners were forced to file passed him, and as they did so he would write something in the book. Alira reached him. Immediately, she felt dizzy and weak. She cried out as she staggered. Ilene clung onto her tighter.

"Wait," the robed man said.

He scurried over to Alira and grabbed her by the hair, and she cried out in pain. He leaned in close, his foul breath almost making her gag. A bony hand brushed her cheek and pinched her cheeks. The man sneered.

"This one has magic in her veins," he chuckled wickedly. He turned and gestured for one of the Sarpi to grab her.

"Take this one and her brat and put them with the other gifted ones," he ordered. He smiled, revealing a mouth of broken and yellowed teeth.

"You should be happy, my beauty," he cackled as he gestured for the line to keep moving. "You will be spared the digging. You will serve the master."

Alira and Ilene were pushed towards a small group of prisoners huddled miserably to the side. There were four of them altogether. An old man with a kind face stood close to a young man who looked petrified. Two young girls – twins it seemed – held on to each other tightly.

A woman dressed in the same robes as the wicked-looking man emerged from the shadows. As she did so, Alira and the other prisoners moaned as the strange weakness overwhelmed them. It was then that Alira noticed the strange amulet hanging from the woman's neck. They were pushed forward by a Sarpi whose spear butt jabbed them in the back whenever they faltered. All the while, the robed woman stayed close, and the sense weakness came with her.

They were led from the docks into a wide open plaza which was lined by ruined buildings. The sound of metal striking rock filled the air, peaking Alira's curiosity. They moved through the plaza, which was now filling up with the other prisoners and up a flight of stone steps which led to the city's inner defensive wall. Despite the weariness she felt, she did her best to take in all that she could. Now that they were higher up, they could see down into what must have been the city's centre. The prisoners stumbled, as they gawped at the sight before them. Huge stone temples were in ruins and a massive man-made crater filled the space which once would have been a wide open forum. Thousands of people with pickaxes and shovels were hard at work digging deeper into the earth. Overseeing the workers were more Sarpi and more hooded figures. The prisoners gasped as they spotted a digger fall to his knees in exhaustion. One of the hooded figures stepped forward, raised a hand and blasted him with magical fire. The man's shrill, agonised screams filled the air, and the stench of cooked meat wafted on the breeze. The woman in the cloak ordered for them to stop, a wicked smile on her lips.

"Watch. Witness the power of my master. Watch what will happen to all who oppose his will."

The hooded figure that had set the prisoner ablaze signalled to another who was stood outside a small stone hut located at the edge of the dig site. A frail-looking old woman came out of the structure, pulling a black cloak tightly about herself as she did so. Slowly, she shuffled over to the burned corpse of the prisoner. Then she leaned over it and began to loudly make an incantation.

From their vantage point, Alira could not make out the words clearly. As the woman's voice rose in volume, the air grew icy cold, and what sources of light there were seemed to dim. A white mist appeared as if from nowhere to envelope the dig site. Alira's breath now came out as steam as the temperature dropped even further. Frost began to form on their clothes, prompting her to hug her daughter tightly to keep her warm. As quickly as it had formed, the mist began to dissipate and the temperature rose. After a few moments, the old woman stepped back from the body. To the prisoners' horror, the corpse began to twitch and a terrible moan filled the air.

"Undead!" Alira whispered in horror "By Niveren!"

"N'gist ..." the old man in front of her muttered in disbelief. Alira's eyes widened at the name, it was the name of the cult of Danon, a cult long thought extinct.

The now reanimated zombie picked up a pickaxe before going back to work.

"You see," their captor chuckled. "Even if you die, we can still make use of you."

The Sarpi grunted and shoved the group forward with the end of his spear. All the while, Ilene buried her head into her mother's shoulder. Alira did her best to calm the petrified child. What were they digging for?

They followed the inner wall until they reached a tall stone tower. The N'gist cultist opened a heavy wooden door and gestured for the prisoners to go through it. They did so to find themselves in square-shaped chamber, a single lit brazier offering the only light source. Other people were inside huddled in groups.

"This door is magically sealed, and this chamber is enchanted," the woman said cruelly. "So don't even bother using your powers to try and flee."

A last shove from the Sarpi and the door slammed shut with a loud bang.

Alira's eyes quickly adjusted to the gloom. She counted twenty other people in the chamber. Some wore the robes of Caldarian mages; another group wore the armour of Nightblades. Some just looked like ordinary people, wealthy and poor mixed together. She flinched as the old man who had spoken earlier touched her hand. He peered at her as though he knew her.

"Forgive me, child, I mean you no harm. My name is Grig and that –" he said pointing to his younger companion, "is Huin. Have we met?"

Tentatively, she shook the old man's hand, and he broke out into a kind smile.

"I don't believe so. If we did then I cannot remember, I am sorry. My name is Alira, and this is my daughter Ilene." Her daughter poked her head up, looked at the man, and then buried her face back into her mother's blond hair.

"You said something on the wall … you said those people are N'gist?"

Grig nodded, his smile fading.

"Aye. I did. For a long time there have been rumours that mages and magic users outside the safety of Caldaria had been disappearing. When the civil war ended, we left Caldaria and set up shop in Kingsford. As healers we made a pretty good living for ourselves. Then men claiming to serve the Baron of Champia came to our shop. They arrested us, saying that magic was forbidden. Poor Renly was taken prisoner. We tried to resist, but they wore strange amulets that prevented us from using our powers. They beat us, and then piled us into the back of a wagon which took us to the coast."

"And here we are!" Huin chimed in miserably.

"What do they want with us?" Alira asked as she pressed her back to the chamber's wall and slid to the ground. Ilene shifted to get more comfortable before starting to snore softly her small hands holding tightly onto her mother's hair. The child was exhausted.

"They want to turn us," came a voice from deeper in the room. They looked up to see a blond-haired man walking over to them. He wore the black leather armour of a Nightblade. "They want to turn us into one of them, and make us join the N'gist."

Alira looked at Huin, whose eyes widened at the words. She shuddered as memories of the witch Cliria surfaced in her mind. The bride of Danon had possessed Alira when she was just a teenager. For years, she had been the unwilling vessel of the witch. After Eclin, she had been freed from Cliria's possession, but in the years that followed, vague memories of the foul deeds she had been made to commit haunted her in nightmares.

"I would rather die than become one of them," she said quietly.

"How do you know this?" Huin asked the Nightblade, who introduced himself as Torbin.

"There were six of us. Now there are just two. The others were turned." He gestured to the door. "The woman who led you here, she was one of us," he said, his hands knotting into fists.

"How is that possible?" Grig gasped.

Torbin looked away before taking a deep breath to get his emotions under control.

"Magic. Dark and ancient. Of a sort I have never seen before. All I know is that the others were dragged away and returned as one of them." He paused as a deafening roar sounded from outside their prison. Alira gasped and Ilene began to cry.

"Then there is that. Whatever that is," Torbin added quietly.

Memories of the battle of Eclin flashed into Alira's head. She would recognise that sound anywhere, for it still haunted her dreams. The roar came again; it shook the chamber's walls, and dust fell from the rafters in the ceiling. The roar contained something within it. It wasn't the terrifying feral sounds that she remembered; if she had to guess, it was a roar of pain.

"A dragon ... they have a dragon?" she whispered.

The Nightblade nodded.

"Every night we hear it."

"It sounds like it's in pain," Huin said, his head tilted to the side to listen.

At the sound of footsteps outside the chamber, they all moved away from the door, which opened to reveal a red-cloaked figure. Silently, it stalked into the room, two Sarpi guards close behind. It sniffed the air before moving quickly across the chamber. A bony hand reached out and grabbed Torbin by the arm.

"This one ..." the figure hissed.

The Nightblade struggled but the cloaked figure was remarkably strong. With a violent twist, Torbin's arm snapped loudly and he screamed in agony.

"No! I will never join you ... I will never join you!" he screamed as the Sarpi dragged him out of the chamber.

The cloaked figure cackled.

"That is what they all say."

CHAPTER SIXTEEN.

Sunguard

The royal palace was a hive of activity as the Grand Council prepared to meet. The barons of Delfinnia had been summoned, and all had arrived at the capital. The only problem was that Davik had not called such a council. Being the king's regent, only he had the authority to issue such a summons. He didn't have to think hard to know who had gone behind his back. Ricard was making his move.

Davik had returned from his visit at the eastern front as quickly as he could upon hearing the news that the council had been summoned. He had wasted no time in ordering the Sunguard legion to accompany him back to the capital. If Ricard's aim was to oust him from the regency, then he would surely hesitate when he saw an army at his opponent's back.

The soldiers marched through the gates before taking up positions throughout the palace. A handpicked squad of six legionaries was sent to the king's quarters. Whatever game Ricard was playing, Davik was sure that it involved the king. He watched the troops filing past from the saddle of his white horse. The fighting in the east was not going well for the kingdom. Eclin was lost, the ruined city now the home of swarms of pucks and other foul creatures which had emerged from the dark places of the mountains. With no Eclin rangers or Knights of Niveren to guard the region, the Fell Beasts had multiplied in numbers. All he could hope to do was prevent the creatures from spreading across the kingdom. The legion had retreated to Plock and the valley of Summil. Hundreds of miles of territory had been lost. To the south east, Accadus of Retbit continued to harass the forces based along the Zulus River. Tales of dark magic being used, and rumours that Sarpi were fighting in the rogue baron's army only confirmed his fears that Danon, too, was ready to reveal himself to the world once more. Davik sighed heavily and rubbed a gloved hand over his face. He was exhausted. Ricard had outmanoeuvred him at every turn. The wretch had spread dissention among the populace. His anti-magic rhetoric had struck a chord with the people, so much so that magic wielders were fleeing to Caldaria in their hundreds. With the mages fleeing, the rest of the realm would be vulnerable to the magical forces arrayed against it.

"Davik. I must speak with you."

He looked up to see the king's nanny striding towards him from the palace. She pushed her way through the leering soldiers until she was stood next to him.

"Elena," he greeted tiredly. "What is it?"

The young woman bit her lip nervously.

"It's the king. I fear for his safety," she replied.

Davik snapped his fingers to summon a stable hand. A young boy rushed forward and took the horse's reins. Gingerly, Davik dismounted, wincing in pain as his old injuries made their presence felt. Elena offered him her shoulder to lean on, and he grunted in thanks.

"Come. Let's talk inside."

CHAPTER SIXTEEN.

Davik poured himself a glass of Robintan wine and sighed contentedly as the delicious fruity liquid slid down his throat. He and Elena were in his private quarters, safe from the prying eyes and ears of any potential spies working for Ricard. They sat at the room's small table. Upon his arrival, servants had brought him a plate of venison and boiled vegetables. It sat untouched; he had little in the way of an appetite.

"The bastard has bested me again. I should never have left the capital," he chuckled humourlessly.

Elena looked away, tears in her eyes.

"I have been denied access to the king," she fumed. "Ricard has replaced me with his own servants. He said that a girl from peasant stock has no place mentoring a king." The news took Davik by surprise. Anger surged through him. He slammed his glass onto the table.

"What gives him the right? First he turns the realm against those with magic, and then he goes behind my back and summons a Grand Council, and now this! I will have him arrested for treason."

Elena looked at her old friend in sympathy. Davik had never wanted to be regent; in the years since he had been bestowed the title, the stress had caused his hair to turn white, and deep lines had taken root on his face.

"There's something else ... I think I know why Ricard wants me out of the way," Elena added softly. "Whilst you were away, Luxon Edioz and some of his companions met with the king. He commanded them to find that strange stone, the one found in the Eclin Mountains. After they had left the city, I overheard Ricard talking with the king. He said that the stone was being used by magic wielders to corrupt his mind – and that magic was not to be trusted. I fear the king believed every word."

Davik slumped in his seat. He had little understanding of magic, but he did know that Luxon Edioz was someone who could be trusted.

"What is he up to?" he muttered. "Why has the wretch waited until now to sow such discord? Could it be he is a traitor?"

The thought was too awful to contemplate, but it was one that made sense. With the Grand Council divided and their attention focused on power politics, the realm's enemies would be able to press their advantage. He closed his eyes and sighed. He was a fool. He had again played into Ricard's hands by bringing the Sunguard legion with him.

The borders were already overstretched.

"It would make sense that he is a traitor," Elena said quietly. "He has resented you for years for being made the regent. Before Alderlade was crowned, Ricard was one of the main contenders for the throne. It would not surprise me that he seeks the Sundered Crown for himself."

Davik rubbed his eyes tiredly. He hated politics. He stared into his now empty glass, his thoughts racing.

"Think about it, Davik," Elena continued, her tone growing angrier. "Who would be the best defence against Danon and Accadus?"

"The mages!" she added, answering her own question. "By turning the people against them, Ricard has removed the best defence against the enemy's magic. Instead of fighting at the legions' side, the mages and

Nightblades have been forced to flee and hide in Caldaria, as far from the battle as possible."

She stopped talking as someone knocked on the room's door.

"My lord regent," came the voice of a steward. "The Grand council has gathered in the King's Hall,"

"I'll be right there," Davik replied gruffly. He stood up and walked over to the full length mirror in the corner of the room. He checked his clothes over, pulled his tunic straighter and adjusted his sword belt before spitting on his palm and slicking his hair back.

"Wish me luck. I think I'm most definitely going to need it," he sighed before leaving the chamber.

Davik walked down the long brightly lit corridor leading to the King's Hall. He nodded in greeting to the legionaries standing to attention. As ceremonial guards, their armour was polished so that reflected the light cast by the chandeliers hanging from the ceiling. Davik stopped outside the large double doors that led into the hall proper and sighed. Facing the barons was the last thing he wanted to do. He nodded to the smartly dressed steward who was waiting patiently to open the doors.

With a loud creak, the doors opened.

Silence greeted him as he strode into the hall. He held his head high and thrust out his chest. He may not be a skilled politician, but he was a warrior. As was custom, he took his seat on the plain-looking throne located in the centre in the hall. Arrayed in a semicircle in front of the throne were the barons in high-backed chairs of their own. To the side sat the clerks and stewards who would transcribe all that would transpire in the coming meeting. Davik caught the gaze of the realm's most powerful men. The only seat that was empty was the one reserved for the barony of Retbit. The young Baron of Balnor smiled, but the rest masked their intentions. Sat in the centre chair was Ricard, a slight smirk on his handsome face.

The door to the hall opened again and the barons stood as Archbishop Trentian shuffled inside. The old man was in his eighties and was the leading religious leader in the kingdom. With no gods to speak of, the peoples of Delfinnia worshipped Niveren, the hero who had delivered the world from evil and led mankind to glory. Trentian was the head of the Niveren cult and was tasked with overseeing the Privy and Grand councils. The old bishop took his place at a lectern, which was carried into the room by two servants.

"I, Trentian, archbishop and loyal servant of Niveren and the realm hereby announce this meeting as begun."

Immediately, Ricard rose from his seat. He smiled cruelly at Davik.

"Lords of the realm, I summoned this Grand Council," he announced. The barons grumbled at the revelation. The Baron of Balnor stood.

"Lord Ricard, what gives you the right to summon such a council?" the thirteen year old boy baron snapped, his high-pitched voice a stark comparison to those of the other lords. "By law, only the king – or in this case the regent – can do so."

Davik leant back in his seat and touched his fingertips together.

You have overreached yourself Ricard, he thought as the other barons nodded in agreement with Balnor's words.

To his credit, Ricard covered his annoyance at the young baron well. He kept a thin smile on his lips.

"Forgive me, my lords, archbishop. That is indeed correct, but I felt as though such a gathering was necessary."

Ricard moved from his chair to stand in the centre of the hall. "This past month has seen the situation across the kingdom deteriorate to such an extent that I know some of you believe we need new leadership."

The barons shouted in protest.

"What gives you the right?" demanded the baron of Kingsford.

Wyatt Foralis was a man in his forties with a reputation for guile. His skills on the battlefield, however, were questionable as he was one of the only barons to not get embroiled in the civil war for the crown that had raged five years previously.

"I have the right of a concerned member of this council!" Ricard snapped. "Sarpi raiders harass your shores, Foralis. Dragons torment yours, Blackmoor, and Fell Beasts plague everywhere east of the Greatwood. We should all be concerned." he faced the Baron of Balnor and glared at him. "And the rogue Baron of Retbit threatens your lands."

Ricard then jabbed a finger at Davik. "This man is no leader. He is just a warrior; violence is all he knows. He has failed spectacularly to bring peace and order to the realm. He allows magic wielders to roam the land freely and corrupt the minds of the people. He is in league with the wizard Luxon Edioz who, according to my agents, even now is heading west across the Great Plains, for what nefarious purpose I know not."

Trentian banged his fist on the lectern. Ricard bowed to the archbishop.

"The accusations of negligence and the regent's love of magic wielders is indeed a cause for grave concern," the archbishop said. "I have heard from my priests that the common folk are turning from the light offered by Niveren to the mages of Caldaria for their salvation. This heresy must not be allowed to continue."

Davik slumped in his seat. So that was Ricard's plan. He and Trentian had made a deal. The cult had no love for mages; they saw magic as heretical and impure.

"Perhaps they turn to the mages because it is they who are our best hope of defeating our enemies," Davik growled.

"Blasphemy!" Trentian shouted angrily.

The other barons began to argue amongst themselves. Some were in favour of replacing Davik, but others like Balnor were opposed. The shouting grew louder. Ricard smirked in silence. Trentian banged the lectern again to restore order

"My lords! We are divided on this matter, that is clear to see, but I urge you all to think long and hard about what is good for the souls of the people. The mages plunged this world into war before and the wizard Luxon Edioz proved that magic remains the path to ruin. All the ill that has befallen our realm has come as a result of Luxon and the mages' actions at Eclin." Trentian's face was flustered. His hatred for magic was well known.

"Does the king not have a say in this matter?" said Rusay Broadmane, the Baron of Robinta.

He was in his thirties, tanned by Robinta's mild climate, and strongly built. He was the best swordsman in the realm, having won numerous tournaments over the years. The barony under his control was the bread basket of the kingdom, more famous for its wines and tea than for its strength at arms. Nonetheless, Rusay held considerable clout with the council for without the food Robinta provided the realm, the people would soon go short. It was for that reason that Rusay had remained mostly neutral in the fighting during the civil war.

Ricard clapped his hands and the stewards opened the doors. The barons all stood and bowed deeply as King Alderlade was led into the hall by two legionaries. The eight-year-old monarch smiled and waved at Davik, who smiled warmly back. Davik stood from the throne and stepped aside. Ricard took the boy king's hand and lifted him up onto the now vacant throne.

Sat in the high-backed chair, the king's diminutive size was apparent. His little legs couldn't even reach the ground. Trentian gestured for the barons to sit again. Davik, however, remained standing.

"Your Majesty,' Ricard began, 'as your uncle, everything I do is for your benefit and the benefit of the kingdom. We are gathered here today to discuss whether it is time for a new regent to be appointed. The realm is in peril, nephew; it is time for a change in strategy."

The king looked to his uncle and then at Davik, confusion evident on his face.

He is just a child, Davik thought. He felt himself getting angry.

Trentian moved from the lectern and shuffled over to stand at the king's side.

"You must do what is best for the people, my king. Faith in divine Niveren keeps the souls of your subjects pure. Magic is like a disease – it poisons the mind and corrupts men's morals. Davik has served the realm admirably, but his love of wielders blinds him. I believe that your uncle would prove to be a better candidate to guide you. Niveren wills it, Sire."

Davik glanced at the barons. They were whispering amongst themselves. In his heart, he knew they would vote in favour of replacing him. What bribes or deals Ricard had made with them, he did not know, but he knew that he had been bested. The barons of Bison, Kingsford, Blackmoor and Zahnia would vote in favour of Ricard. None of those men had love for magic wielders, and all of their lands had suffered from attacks by dragons, Fell Beasts and raiders. Perhaps if he had been more ruthless, perhaps if he had ignored the plights of the commoners and focused on waging war, then the realm would not be in such a dire mess. He shook his head angrily; ever since becoming regent he had doubted himself.

"This is madness!" shouted the Baron of Balnor. The anger in the teenager's voice caused the others to stare at him. With the gaze of his peers upon him, he flushed red in embarrassment.

"Davik is a good man and not all wielders are wicked folk, Archbishop," he continued angrily.

"Watch your tone, boy," Ricard growled in warning. "Trentian is the holiest of men, show him some respect."

"Holy? Just because he holds such a title does not make it true," the baron shouted, his body trembling with rage. "If you continue down this road and replace Davik as regent, you kiss Balnor's support goodbye."

Davik winced at the words. The chamber erupted in a cacophony of shouting, and accusations flew. Most of the barons had battled each other for the crown in the civil war, and no love was lost between them. The shouting grew louder as the men squabbled. Davik looked at Ricard. The bastard was doing his best to hide a smile. It was the king who put a stop to the arguing. He stood on his chair and screamed. It was a childish act, but it worked at silencing the barons.

"I, too, am a boy, uncle. Would you dare dismiss my views as easily?" Alderlade scolded. The smile on Ricard's face dropped and Davik felt his chest almost burst with pride at the king's words.

"I will not allow my barons to be divided. I may just be a child but I am also a king. To settle this matter I will strike a balance. Davik will remain as my regent."

Davik sighed in relief, he stepped forward to thank the king, but was halted as Alderlade held up a hand.

"And my uncle shall be co-regent," the king added. "You will either work together or fail. I need you both."

"That could have gone better, but it could also have gone a whole lot worse, too," Rusay Broadmane said as he poured himself a mug on wine. After the council meeting, Davik had retreated to his quarters. The barons of Balnor and Robinta had joined him, they were the only allies he could rely on in the council.

"Does the fool want another civil war?" Balnor muttered. The young man was staring out of the window. Outside, in the palace gardens, the sound of birds singing and the gurgling fountains carried on the breeze.

"Balnor is right, Davik," Rusay added. "The decision by the king has calmed things for now, but it will only be a matter of time before Ricard tries again to remove you. I fear the king himself is in grave danger. Ricard has always lusted for power, always sought ways to gain advantage over his rivals. With enemies pressing upon the kingdom's borders, I fear he will lead us to ruin,"

Davik ran a hand through his hair. He was getting too old for this. He downed his own glass of wine.

"I do not trust the man. My spies have reported that dark things are afoot in Retbit and Stormglade. If he divides us now, our true enemies will destroy us. He has Trentian on his side, and now as co-regent he can press on with his campaign against magic wielders with a vengeance."

Balnor slapped his hand against the wall in frustration. He had seen first-hand what dark magic could do to people. His own mother, father and sister had all been slain by the witch, Cliria. Despite all that, he had no ill feeling towards the mages; some were even his friends, and he included Luxon in that list.

"We must expose him, then," Rusay said thoughtfully. "If your fears turn out to be true then Ricard must be stopped by any means necessary."

There was a knock on the door, and the men glanced at each other nervously.

Slowly Davik rose from his chair and opened the door.

A young woman in a red dress curtsied. In her hands she held a bottle of wine.

"A peace offering from my master Ricard, sirs," the girl said politely.

Davik took the offered bottle and dismissed the girl. The label on the bottle said Robintan wine 265. Rusay whistled as he read the words.

"A 265! Even I do not have a bottle of that in my cellar. 265 is a legendary vintage, Davik. Perhaps Champia is truly sorry. It would have cost him a fortune to get his hands on a bottle."

Rusay took the bottle out of Davik's hands, he then popped the cork and poured himself and the others a glass each.

"A toast, my friends. The world may be in dire straits but at least Davik here has survived his enemies plot to have him removed from power!"

"I'll drink to that," Davik chuckled. He drank a large gulp and gasped at the taste. A whirlwind of flavour assaulted his tongue

And then the pain hit him.

"Argh!" he cried.

His throat felt like it was on fire. The sweet tastes of the wine were quickly replaced by the foulness of poison. Rusay and Balnor were just about to drink their own glasses, but threw their glasses aside as they rushed forward to help their friend.

"Davik, Davik what is wrong?" Rusay asked desperately.

The colour drained from Davik's face as the poison took effect. He screamed in pain as the liquid burnt its way down his throat and into his guts.

He collapsed to the ground with a thud and writhed in agony.

"Guards!" screamed Balnor.

The veins on Davik's face bulged until they looked as though they would burst. His pained scream spluttered as blood spat from between his lips.

With one last violent spasm, his back arched and snapped like a twig.

He lay unmoving …

Dead.

CHAPTER SEVENTEEN.

Luxon had read in one of the dusty tomes in Caldaria's Great Library that the Plains were vast. Now that he was riding on them, he understood why the tribes called it the Ocean of Grass.

The terrain was flat for hundreds of miles in all directions. They had been riding for an entire day, and they had yet to encounter any other people. The Keenlance army rode behind their prince, who was in deep discussion with one of his commanders. Luxon was nervous. He wasn't sure whether Faramond would keep his word and take him to his mother, or kill them all.

He glanced over his shoulder to see Hannah. She smiled at him sweetly. Yepert rode next to her, his face looking green. The lad always suffered from motion sickness. Ferran, Sophia and Kaiden were further back, chatting. What about, he couldn't quite hear, but whatever it was, he bet it involved the next stage of their mission.

The sun was slowly sinking under the horizon, and the first of Esperia's two moons was beginning to make an appearance to the west. Night would soon fall, and with it, the dangers posed by Fell Beasts would rise. With no sigil stones anywhere in sight, he wondered how they would find safety. They were highly exposed. There was nowhere for them to hide if it came to it.

"Luxon," called Faramond. "Come up here. We have much to discuss."

Luxon nodded.

With his heels, he spurred his horse into a trot and took his place at the prince's side.

A smile was on Faramond's face. He took a deep breath and sighed contentedly.

"You smell that, lad? That is the smell of freedom, the smell of the plains, and the smell of home."

Luxon sniffed.

"Smells like dust and horseshit to me," he chuckled. "My home smells like wood smoke and chemicals. The alchemists of Caldaria always come up with weird new odours for us to sample."

Faramond laughed heartily.

"Home is important to all folk, master wizard," he said seriously, a dark expression crossing his face. "I fear that mine may soon be lost. Evil stalks the plains, and not just Fell Beasts. We have always had to endure those horrors, but now something else threatens us and all the tribes."

Luxon looked away, unable to meet Faramond's fierce gaze.

"Undead stalk the lands near the city of Stormglade, armies of ghouls and werewolves assault our encampments. Worst of all, though, are the men in cloaks. At night they come and take away our people, for what foul purpose we do not know. Entire tribes have been taken. Only ourselves and the other warrior tribes resist, but we do not have the strength to keep fighting. I fear whatever is in Stormglade will soon be ready to spread across the Ocean of Grass and beyond."

"The cloaked men. Do their eyes glow?" Luxon asked, looking over his shoulder. The army was kicking up a massive dust cloud that could no doubt be seen for miles around. He was worried; if there were any of the enemies nearby, they would have to be blind to not see their location.

He narrowed his eyes and, with a slight gesture, used his magic to create a light breeze that made the dust cloud scatter. Now, to any observer, they would be a lot harder to spot.

"The Sarpi we know," Faramond continued. "The men I speak of look more like mages to me. The only thing they have in common are the amulets they wear and their use of magic."

"Mages?" Luxon said in surprise. He thought back to the posters he had seen in Caldaria. Had mages truly joined the enemy? He shook his head. He could not believe that any of the mages he had grown up with would willingly choose to serve the dark powers.

They rode on for another hour. The dying light of the sun lit up the horizon, casting an orange glow and long shadows over the plain. As the light faded, the column of riders grew quiet. The warriors pressed closer together and drew their weapons. Most had bows, but the riders at the edges held lances. Luxon and his companions were ushered into the centre of the line, the safest place to be.

"It's too quiet …" whispered Kaiden. He had drawn in his own sword and held it in a tight grip on his lap.

"The plains are known for night stalkers, Fell Beasts that run as fast as a horse and have fangs like a snake," said Ferran, who was riding at his side. "The worst however are the gargantuans, massive beasts that can tear a man apart limb from limb."

The Nightblade had never been on the plains before, but he had met others from his order that had, and the tales they told made even his hairs stand on end.

Both men were shushed to silence by one of the Keenblade warriors.

Only the sounds of the horses and the clinking of weapons and armour could be heard.

Finally the last of the sun's light vanished and night fell. The sky was cloudless and revealed the stars which were hidden in the daytime. The column continued its march. With no landmarks or sights to break up the boredom, it felt like the journey had latest forever to Luxon and the others. The safety of the Watchers' walls was miles behind them; only danger lay ahead.

A roar sounded from somewhere in the distance. The column tightened further. The roar came again, this time closer. The warriors strung their bows and lowered their lances. Kaiden raised his sword and Ferran ignited his tourmaline blade. The two men ushered the others to get behind them. Luxon pulled Dragasdol from the sheath attached to his saddle. Whatever was out there didn't sound friendly.

At the head of the column, Faramond made a motion with his arms. Immediately, a dozen riders broke off from the main army and galloped off into the darkness. The rest of the riders drew torches from their saddles and lit them with firestones. The sight of the magical stones surprised Luxon. They were made in Caldaria and were widely used across Delfinnia. All a user had to do was hold the stone up to a flammable object and rub it against it three times. The riders did so and the torches burst into life. The light they provided offered some comfort and enabled the army to see any incoming dangers.

A scream sounded from the rear of the column. A trumpet blared.

"Form a circle!" Faramond commanded.

With amazing skill, the Keenlance warriors wheeled their horses around until they formed a fast-moving circle. Luxon and the others were in the centre, along with the prince and a handful of warriors. They now dismounted and hammered long spears into the ground, the deadly points facing outwards.

Another scream sounded, and this time Luxon saw what had happened. A large creature darted in from the darkness and plucked one of the riders off their terrified horse.

"Nightstalkers!" Ferran shouted.

The riders loosed a volley of arrows outwards. Some of the projectiles struck home, eliciting a pained screech.

"My Lord!" yelled one of the warriors to Faramond. "It's a pack, and more are on the way."

The prince shut his eyes before looking at Luxon.

"We were fools to allow ourselves to be caught out in the open like this. We will lose many men this night. Break circle! Attack!" he roared.

The warriors broke the circle and shot off in small groups. Now that the wall of horsemen was gone, Luxon could see the Nightstalkers. There were too many to count. The plain was filled with the fast-moving creatures. With the protection of the circle now gone, Luxon and the others were now open to attack.

One of the snarling beasts charged towards them, but was downed by one of Sophia's silver-tipped arrows. More of the beasts came at them. The scene was one of carnage as the Keenlance forces battled the Fell Beasts. Horses and men were being slain by the dozen, their pained screams echoing in the night. Despite the losses, the warriors fought on. One of the Nightstalkers was impaled by a rider wielding a lance, whilst another was brought down after being riddled with arrows. They were brave, but Luxon could see that bravery would not be enough to survive. He looked at Yepert and Hannah.

"We have to help them. Use your magic!" he cried as he spurred his horse forward, Yepert and Hannah close behind. He raised Dragasdol and aimed the staff at a Nightstalker who was about to devour a wounded tribesman. He focused his power and vaporised the beast with lightning. Yepert and Hannah, meanwhile, used their magic to launch fireballs.

To his right, he spotted Ferran hacking and slashing at the Fell Beasts, his Tourmaline blade flashing brightly in the darkness. Kaiden, meanwhile, cut one of the monsters down before reaching from his saddle to pluck a wounded warrior to safety. Sophia had joined the Keenblade horse archers and was shooting arrow after arrow, and most were hitting their targets.

Luxon turned his horse; he aimed for the heart of the Nightstalker pack. Narrowing his eyes, he summoned the magic within. Sweat broke out on his forehead as he channelled his powers. Raising his right hand, he called the winds. A howling gale began to blow across the plain, and dark storm clouds appeared as if from nowhere as he focused. He aimed the wind at the Fell Beasts. It grew in intensity until it turned into a whirlwind. The power of the swirling vortex ploughed into the pack, taking the beasts high into the air. The monsters' pitiful cries were silenced as they were sent flying in all directions in a tangle of broken limbs.

Luxon wasn't finished. Raising Dragasdol to the sky, he summoned more power to himself. His eyes shone bright blue as the magical energy surged through him. With a roar of rage, he thrust his staff at the vortex. With a deafening boom, lightning split the sky and struck the staff. Dancing fingers of electricity surged through it to strike the Nightstalker pack. Some burst into flames; others exploded.

Ferran yelled a warning as he rode hard towards his friend. Luxon was too focused on the spell he was casting to notice the Nightstalker charging towards him. With a vicious snarl, the beast leapt, its jaws sinking into the flesh of Luxon's horse.

The mortally wounded animal bucked in agony and threw the wizard from the saddle. Luxon cried out as he crashed to the ground. The force of the impact sent his staff flying from his grasp. Weariness filled him; he had exerted too much magic and now he was helpless against the Nightstalker, which advanced menacingly towards him. He scrambled back on his hands but the beast leapt. He cried out as the weight of the creature pinned him to the ground. All he felt was fear. He was a wizard, but what good is that if he could not use his magic?

Desperately, he tried to conjure a spell, but his fear and tiredness kept breaking his concentration. With a roar, the Nightstalker opened its fang-filled mouth. Luxon could smell its foul breath.

Just as he thought his end had come, Ferran's sword sent the Nightstalker's head flying off.

Luxon fainted.

Luxon was stirred by the aroma of cooking meat. Slowly, he opened his eyes. He was lying on a bed of animal pelts, in what appeared to be a large tent made of cloth. From the faint light trying to penetrate the material, he surmised that it was daytime. He winced. Every part of him ached, and his head swam as he tried to sit up. In the centre of the tent was a large fire with a spit placed above it. A pig was cooking nicely. Cushions of many different colours and designs were scattered around the grass-covered floor. The only furniture that he could see was a wooden desk and stool. At his bedside was a large clay jug filled with water and a simple cup. If he had to take a guess, he would say that he was at the camp of the Keenlance tribe.

Tilting his head he could make out the sounds of a busy camp. Somewhere nearby, a blacksmith was hard at work, their hammer clanking against metal.

He sat up again, this time fighting the dizziness that tried to keep him down. He was still wearing his clothes, although they were now covered in dirt and what looked like soot. Staggering to his feet, he could see that he was alone inside the tent.

Where is everybody? he thought.

Concern for his friends filled him.

Was Hannah safe? Was Yepert? What about the others?

Looking around he saw his staff lying at the end of the makeshift bed. He picked it up; its weight reassuring.

He tensed as the tent's flap opened. A tall, elegant woman with long black haired stood in the entrance. Her large green eyes widened when she noticed him. Around the woman's neck hung an amulet with an unmistakable pattern upon it.

It was the sigil of the Diasect.

Luxon stepped back and lowered his staff.

"Could it be?" he whispered.

The woman smiled softly.

"Hello ... my son."

CHAPTER EIGHTEEN.

Luxon shook at the sight of her. So many years had passed, so many years where he had believed that she was dead. He could feel his eyes fill with tears.

He dropped Dragasdol to the ground and ran to her. Opening his arms wide, he grabbed her in a tight embrace, and laughed. His heart swelled with happiness, Drusilla's own joy mixed with her son's. She held him close and stroked his hair, while he breathed in her scent. It was comforting, and reminded him of the days when his family had been all together and happy.

After a while, she eased out of the embrace and held him at arm's length. Her eyes were wet with joyful tears.

"You've gotten tall, Luxon," she laughed. "And strong, like your father was."

Luxon rubbed his eyes with the sleeve of his tunic.

"I've missed you, mother. I never stopped searching for you. I never stopped believing that you were still alive."

Drusilla brushed her son's cheek affectionately, her expression soft.

"I missed you too, son," she whispered. She took his hand in hers and led him over to the fire. "You must be famished. You slept for a whole day and night. Your friends were very worried about you."

Luxon blushed.

"I overdid it with my magic ... I lost control. Mother. But what are you doing here? Why are you on the Great Plains?"

Drusilla held up a hand to stop him talking.

"Not now, my son. I will tell you what I can later. For now, we will eat and enjoy this moment. Tell your friends that the food is ready."

Luxon smiled. His questions could wait. His mother was right: he was starving.

The tent was full of laughter. Luxon and his companions laughed and joked with members of the Keenlance tribe. To Luxon's surprise, the Keenlance people were friendly and very generous hosts. The warriors that Luxon had saved hailed him as a hero. Ferran and the others had been relieved to see that he was well. They were all sat around the fire telling each other stories and cracking jokes, some of which went right over the heads of the tribal folk. Different cultures often take time understanding one another, after all. Faramond was standing in front of the fire, a horn full of mead in one hand and his sword in the other. The prince had just finished telling them a story which had resulted in the tribes folk rolling about the floor in laughter. He then turned to a group of musicians, who had been waiting patiently to one side, and told them to play.

A rattling tune started up, and tribesfolk burst out into song.

Luxon smiled as the prince hauled a laughing Sophia to her feet and began to dance with her around the tent.

"I can't remember the last time we had a night off as fun as this!" Yepert slurred.

"I do," Luxon said. "It was the Feast of the Brave Knight last year. If I recall, you got so smashed that you ended up trying to kiss Marisha Dinlow. But before you could do the deed, you puked up all over the poor girl."

"Oh yeah ... she still hates me," Yepert chuckled.

Luxon stood and patted his friend on the head.

"Go get some sleep, Yepert. We can't have you hungover tomorrow."

Yepert took another swig of his mead before slumping onto the ground. Within seconds, he was snoring loudly. Luxon laughed.

In the centre of the tent, Faramond bowed deeply to Sophia and kissed her hand. She returned the bow before sitting with Ferran at the fireside.

The band now changed its tune to a more sombre melody. The tribal folk stopped laughing and bowed their heads.

"They sing for the dead," Faramond said to his guests. He bowed his head and began to sing:

"The sons and daughters of Keenblade return to the gods that made them.

"Dying with lance in hand and arrow in flight, they died with honour. They died defending their lord, and ridding the world of the most ancient of mankind's foes.

"They will live on forever in the memories of their descendants."

As the song came to an end, the tribesfolk raised their horns of mead in the air before downing the contents. Luxon did likewise and lowered his head. So many people had died battling the Fell Beasts and the dark powers that continued to torment the world. He knew that many more would perish over the coming days. In his gut, he knew that Danon was plotting and preparing. Soon, he would be ready to unleash his full power upon Delfinnia. At Eclin, Danon had been weak; he had relied on the strength of his dark bride, the witch Cliria. Thousands had perished just so that he could be freed from the Void. After Eclin, some even believed that he had been destroyed – the lich that he had used for a body had been found, after all. Luxon knew better. Thanos and the other masters had known better. Danon was not so easy to kill.

"Son?"

He was brought out of his thoughts by his mother. She stood next to him, a hand on his shoulder.

"Sorry. I was thinking."

"What troubles you?" Drusilla smiled. "I spoke with Hannah – a lovely girl. I am very happy that you have met someone to share your life with. I think I intimidate her though."

Luxon chuckled. "Of course you do. I've spoken of my quest to find you for years. I guess I must have built you up quite a lot." He looked at the woman who had abandoned him years previously at the gates of Caldaria.

"I think it's time you answered my questions," he said seriously.

Drusilla nodded.

"So do I," she replied quietly. She took his hand and led him outside of the tent.

Hundreds of tents and campfires were spread across the plains. The people of the Keenblade tribe were all around them. Beyond the edge of the city of cloth was a tall wall, built from long wooden stakes that had been hammered into the ground. The wall was vital, due to the lack of rune stones. The tribe's survival depended on the palisades keeping at bay the Fell Beasts that stalked the nights. As the tribes were nomadic, the stakes were easy to remove and pack onto the long wagons that were lined along the walls perimeter. Armed warriors patrolled the edge of the camp on horseback constantly.

Drusilla led her son away from the centre of the camp. The two moons were high in the sky and casting their glow upon the world below. There was not a cloud in the sky, and the chill of the approaching winter made its presence felt. Away from the fires the temperature dropped, and Luxon wrapped his cloak tighter about his body. His mother appeared to not notice the cold; she wore a loose-fitting dress that exposed her tanned arms, and a purple cloak. She led the way through the maze of tents to the walls, then looked around to see if the coast was clear.

"Follow me, Luxon. Use your gifts," she said mysteriously.

She crouched and closed her eyes. Her hand touched the amulet around her neck. Luxon stepped back as the amulet began to glow brightly. The light grew in intensity until he was forced to look away. When the light faded, his mother was gone.

"Follow me."

To his surprise the voice came from the other side of the wall. He pressed his face to the wood and looked out through a small hole at the plain beyond. His mother was stood a hundred paces away on the other side.

Closing his eyes, he channelled the magic within. He bent his legs and pushed off of the ground, leaping high into the air and easily clearing the tall wooden stakes that comprised the camp's wall. He landed nimbly on his feet and jogged over to his mother.

"Nicely done," Drusilla praised. "I see you've been trained well by Thanos and the mages of Caldaria."

"How did you do that? Did you teleport?" Luxon asked. He had only heard rumours that teleportation spells were real. The grand masters claimed that they could perform such magic, but Luxon had never seen it being used in real life before.

"Yes. Teleportation comes in very handy when you are in hiding like I was. Numerous times, Cliria's agents almost found or cornered me. Teleportation was my way of escaping their clutches." She tilted her head as though listening. "We cannot linger here for too long. Fell Beasts have already caught our scent."

She took Luxon's hand, and together they ran further into the night.

"Where are we going?" Luxon asked.

"Somewhere safe; somewhere we can talk in safety."

They ran for what felt like miles. Finally, they reached a small lake with a smaller island in its centre. The body of water appeared out of place in the sea of grass. As they drew nearer, Luxon could sense the magic radiating from it. Drusilla stepped into the shallow water and pulled her son after her. They waded through and clambered out onto the small island. The magic was stronger here. A single tall tree stood on the patch of the ground. The bark of the tree had markings carved into it – magical carvings.

"What is this place?" Luxon asked in wonder. He placed a hand on the tree's trunk and the carved words lit up with magical power.

"A very long time ago the whole world was in danger of being destroyed by the Fell Beasts," Drusilla said. "Men with magic hunted them, and to protect themselves and others, they created places of safety in the wilderness. The same magic that gives the rune stones their power resides in this single tree. I learned of it whilst reading the ancient texts in the Diasect library. We will be safe here."

Drusilla reached into her cloak and pulled out a firestone. She gathered some sticks that had fallen from the tree and created a small fire. The two of them sat close to the flame.

Luxon looked at his mother. For so long he had assumed that she had been just an ordinary woman, the wife of a noble in Sunguard … his mother.

A sadness filled him as he realised that in reality he knew nothing about her. The many trips away she had taken, that his father had said were to visit family, were lies. She possessed magic, and she had known that he too had it. She knew that the blood of the first wizard Aljeron flowed through their veins.

"Why didn't you tell me?" he asked sadly.

"It was for your own protection, son. I … was made a member of the Diasect long before I met your father. My own father had been a member himself, and with the title being hereditary it fell to me to take his place. Our task was to watch for signs of Danon and his minions. I soon realised that the other members of the Diasect had long forgotten that purpose. They had grown fat and lazy – complacent. Perhaps it was because I was young and new to it, but I tried to do what I was supposed to. You remember all those times when I wasn't around?"

Luxon nodded.

"During those times, I was travelling the realm, meeting contacts and making enquiries. I remained vigilant, even if the others did not. The night the king was assassinated- I tried to warn them." Drusilla's voice cracked at the revelation. "I learnt of Cliria and of her plan, but I was ambushed and delayed by her followers. The Diasect's fortress at Tentiv was attacked and destroyed. I had no choice but to flee."

"So, that's why you weren't there that night," Luxon muttered, a hint of bitterness in his voice.

The Night of Tears had seen Sunguard ripped apart by riots, and the legion tore the city apart as they sought the king's murderers. Luxon had been protected by his father, Garrick, but he still remembered the worry he'd had for his absent mother. His mother had returned three days later. He remembered her staggering into the family home, her clothes soaked in blood. Garrick had told him that everything was fine, and as a ten year old boy he had believed his father.

A few days after that, the Privy Council had gathered to decide on who would succeed the slain king. Garrick had been a noble in the Sunguard court, and he had testified that the king's youngest child still lived. His words had caused strife among the barons and set the stage for the war that had followed.

"Garrick was the bravest man I ever met," Drusilla said softly, her eyes focused on the crackling flames of the fire. "What happened to him was unjust."

"I understand why we had to flee the city," Luxon said. "What I don't understand is why you left me at Caldaria. I was just a kid, I knew no one, and you left me there without a reason why. For a long time I thought I had done something to make you abandon me, for a long time ... I hated you."

"I am sorry. As soon as we left Sunguard, Cliria and her agents were after us," his mother said. "She knew of our bloodline; she knew that if she caught us she would be able to free Danon from the Void. I left you with the mages because Caldaria was the one place she could not get into. I thought it best that I disappear. For years, I took odd jobs in Blackmoor and worked in Robinta. All the while, I kept my identity safe and secret. The world was at war, but at least it was safe from Danon."

Drusilla stood and began to pace, her hands fidgeting. After a while she stopped and sighed deeply.

"I know it was not your fault. I know that Cliria tricked you ... but, my son, Danon walks upon Esperia once more. After Eclin, I watched and waited. As the realm did nothing to prevent it, Danon set his plans into motion."

Luxon wiped the tears in his eyes. It was his fault Danon had broken free from the Void.

"What made you come out of hiding and come here?" Luxon sniffed.

"The sigil stone," Drusilla replied, her voice barely louder than a whisper.

Luxon stared at her in confusion.

"The stone? What is so important about it?" he asked, his stomach knotting in dread.

Drusilla stopped her pacing.

"As a member of the Diasect, I was a guardian of the realm's most vital secrets. We knew where the stone was hidden, as did one other: the former Baron of Balnor. The Balnor family dates back to the days of the first king and were tasked with protecting the secret of the stone, in case the realm had need of it. The stone was supposed to remain hidden from evil. But at Eclin, Alderlade used it to fend off Danon. After that, Danon knew of it and hired a thief to steal it from Sunguard."

Luxon slumped onto his back and stared at the night sky. His suspicions had been correct after all. The sigil stone was important, and he had the horrible feeling that he was about to find out why.

"The stone is one of three, created to protect the sword of the gods, Asphodel. They were made by mages under the command of King Riis the First at the ending of the Magic Wars." Drusilla hesitated before continuing. "They were made to react to only those with the blood of kings in their veins. That is why it reacted to Alderlade. Only those people were trusted to wield it."

Luxon sat up, his eyes wide.

"It ... It reacted to me!"

Drusilla looked away, unable to look her son in the eye.

"Danon's magic is old and very powerful. Perhaps he broke the spell set upon the stone. What I do know is that he saw where the second stone is hidden."

"Stormglade? The second stone is there?" Luxon asked.

His mother nodded.

"It is. Riis most trusted champion, Alectae, hid the stones. The first he hid in the frigid mountains of Eclin; the second, in his homeland of the Great

Plains; the third and final stone- well, that we have to discover. Danon has brought his N'gist followers to him, and has enslaved the city to his will. Even now, evil is being drawn to him. I saw it with my own eyes. I came out of hiding, made it through the Watchers and across the Great Plain. I even made it inside the city walls. The poor inhabitants of the city are now his slaves or worse. The Merchant Kings now hang from the walls of their palaces. It is a place of darkness."

Luxon poked at the fire with a stick. His eyes narrowed as he took in all that his mother told him. His mind drifted back to the time he had touched the sigil stone.

A golden sword cast back a cloud of darkness. A ruined tower nestled in the heart of a dark forest ... except, no, it wasn't a forest.

He doubled his concentration. The vision he had seen had been distorted, uncertain. The forest wasn't a forest ... at least not any longer.

"There was a forest on the plains ... when Stormglade was first built ..."

"Yes. The forest was cut down. The lumber was one of the city's main exports until the merchants got too greedy and cut all the trees down. How did you know that?" Drusilla asked hesitantly.

"The vision I saw when I touched the stone after Eclin," Luxon said. "It makes sense that the vision imprinted upon it would show the place at the time it was created. You said you got inside the city?"

Drusilla nodded. "I did. I was discovered and barely escaped with my life. I was wounded as I fled across the plains. A Keenblade scout found me, brought me back to their camp and nursed me back to health. Listen to me, son: the stone that Danon posesses has led him to Stormglade, and in turn, the stone he seeks will lead him to the final and most important stone. For that final stone will lead to the final resting place of Asphodel.

In my reading, I learned that the first two stones act as way markers, like a trail, but the third is the key to obtaining the sword.

"Here," she said pulling a small book from her cloak pocket. "This book will tell you all you need to know. I managed to salvage it from Tentiv."

On the horizon, the sky was turning orange to hail the arrival of a new day. To Luxon's surprise, they had been talking all night. The woman sitting across from him was his mother, and yet he felt as though she were a stranger. He realised that he had not known what to expect when he found her, because he had been so fixated on finding her in the first place.

"We should head back to the camp before our absence is noticed," he said. "We need to plan our next move. We must get the stone from Danon, and discover what he's up to."

The next morning, Luxon and the others were treated to a huge breakfast comprised of wild fruit and freshly baked bread. The generosity of their hosts made Luxon question the books he had read about the tribes in Caldaria's Great Library. The authors had made them out to be mindless savages who had no interest in the finer things in life. So far, Luxon's experience had been very different. He smiled as thoughts of returning home and writing a book on the tribes entered his head. He looked up as a shadow was cast over him. Faramond was standing over him, a big smile on his face. In his hands he held two swords. He dropped the one from his left hand onto the ground in front of Luxon.

"Pick it up," the prince said, still smiling.

Luxon glanced nervously at the others, who all looked surprised. Ferran smirked and gestured to the weapon. Hesitantly, Luxon stood and picked up the blade.

Faramond laughed.

"Don't look so scared, master wizard. Come with me," he chuckled, before walking off. Luxon followed, leaving the others to joke amongst themselves.

"The way you saved my men the other night was very impressive," Faramond said. "My grandfather used to tell me stories of mages; he always made magic out to be this terrifying power. After seeing what you're capable of, I see that his tales were true."

Faramond led Luxon deeper into the camp. They passed several large pens which contained the tribe's livestock and horses. As they walked, the people they passed all bowed down low.

"They honour you, Prince," Luxon muttered in an attempt to make small talk. He wanted to go back to the tent and finish off the fruit that he could still taste on his tongue.

"My people respect strength more than anything, master wizard," Faramond replied as they walked. "They are bowing to you. Word of your power has spread throughout the camp like wildfire, and rightly so. They see you as a beacon of hope, something that we have not had in a long time."

Luxon looked at the prince in surprise, before looking up at the sky. Now he knew what the saying having the weight of the world on your shoulders meant.

They passed a coral housing a dozen saddled horses, and reached a patch of bare ground. The grass covering the plains had been removed and replaced with sand that had been shaped into an oval.

"The power you have obviously has limits," Faramond continued. "What happens when your use of magic wears you out? How can you defend yourself without it? There are tales from the past which tell of magic wielders amongst the tribes. As well as spell casters, they were also great warriors. They were known as War Wizards."

Faramond gestured for Luxon to stand in the oval of sand. He raised his sword.

"Defend yourself, wizard."

Luxon cried out in surprise as the prince dashed forward and brought his blade down. Instinctively, Luxon raised his own sword and deflected the blow. The impact of the heavy iron blades clashing together reverberated painfully up his arm.

"Good. Use your instincts," Faramond said as he took a step back and lowered his sword once again. "I am going to teach you how to fight with a sword. Do not think of it as a replacement of your magic but rather a skill that complements it. Let's try again."

It was dusk by the time Luxon and Faramond made their way back to the others. The prince had put the wizard through his paces and had worked him to near exhaustion. At first, Luxon had been hesitant, but as the hours passed he grew more confident in his skills with a sword. He hadn't been a total novice after all – after Eclin he had spent time with the Nightblades and had learned the basics of swordplay. But Faramond had shown him techniques he had never seen before, and his hunger for knowledge had allowed him to absorb the skills quickly. By the end of the day, Luxon had managed to hold Faramond to a draw in a duel. It had felt good to get sweaty and tired, to use his body as a tool rather than relying on his magic.

"What happened to the War Wizards?" Luxon asked as they walked back to the tent. He carried his cloak in one hand and his training sword in the other. His linen shirt was tied about his waist. The cool evening air felt good on his bare skin.

A dark look crossed Faramond's face.

"According to the stories, they were all killed during the great purge of magic users that followed the Magic Wars. Inquisitors from the Knights of Niveren swept the plains and slaughtered anyone who possessed magic. Those who could flee did; they ran to the coast and from there are said to have sailed westward across the Boundless Sea. Some say they returned to the lands of our ancestors; others say that they all perished."

"It seems we magic users and your people have a lot in common," Luxon muttered. "Both have suffered persecution and both are regarded with mistrust."

"My people are seen as lesser than those who live in their cities and cower behind stone walls," Faramond agreed. "We were once like them, before the Cataclysm that forced us to flee across the sea."

Luxon remembered reading of the Cataclysm, an event that had occurred over a thousand years ago. Scholars in Caldaria were constantly arguing over what exactly the Cataclysm of Vucrar was. Some argued that it had been a cataclysm that had come from the stars; others thought that it had been the result of a volcanic eruption. Even the tribes themselves no longer knew. It was common practise among the mages to vigorously debate the matter during their studies.

"My father, the king, is old and ill," Faramond said quietly his eyes hazy. "I pray to Niveren that he will pass so that he does not have to watch the death of his people."

Since their arrival in the Keenblade camp, Luxon had only seen the king briefly. The man was ancient and feeble.

"Then it is up to you to lead them," he said. "I know we've not known each other long, but I think you will be up to the task."

Faramond smiled and ruffled Luxon's hair.

"It seems we both carry the hopes of many upon our shoulders."

Chapter Nineteen.

Sunguard

The city was in chaos. Thick black smoke filled the sky, and swirling vortexes of flame leapt from house to house in the merchant's district. Men, women and children fled through the streets or tried to hide as the soldiers of the Sunguard Legion rampaged. Davik, their commander and their regent, had been slain. Those responsible would pay the ultimate price for his murder, even if it meant ripping the city apart piece by piece.

Ricard stared out at the carnage occurring far below. He was on the balcony of his quarters in the King's Spire. In his shaking hand, he held a glass of wine. What had happened? He hadn't wanted any of this. He leant heavily against the stone railing and stared at the billowing smoke rising in the cool autumn air. He'd had no love for Davik, but to murder him? The very thought made him feel sick to his stomach.

Word of Davik's poisoning had spread like wildfire, the young Baron of Balnor had practically yelled it from the rooftops, and he, Ricard of Champia had been accused as the culprit. Balnor had stormed out of the city, Robinta close behind. Both men had vowed to take vengeance for Davik's death.

Civil war would come to Delfinnia once more.

He bit his lip as he thought. Who would gain from such a crime? The people and the barons blamed him of course, but he knew that he had not ordered the deed. Someone was setting him up and deliberately steering the realm towards war. The kingdom was already at breaking point, and now with the barons at each other's throats once more, its ruin was at hand. He finished his drink and angrily threw the glass over the side of the balcony. He watched as it fell, and shuddered. The door to his chamber shook as someone pounded upon it.

"Ricard. I know you're in there," came the petrified voice of Archbishop Trentian.

Ricard rolled his eyes. The people rioting in the city below knew of the role the old man had played at the Grand Council. In their minds, the bishop was just as guilty as he was. Reluctantly, he walked back inside and opened the door.

"Niveren save us!" Trentian cried as he pushed his way into the chamber. "The mob has reached the merchant quarter; soon they'll reach the Plaza of Kings. Niveren's cathedral will be burnt to the ground!" The old man was flustered, and his normally pristine robes were crumpled.

Ricard glared at the archbishop.

"Perhaps you should pray to Niveren to spare his cathedral. And whilst you're at, it ask him to save our hides as well," he growled sarcastically. "Fear not, Archbishop. I have two hundred of my own men guarding the plaza, and the Ridder Legion has been recalled to the capital."

He noticed the scepticism on the archbishop's face.

"The Ridder Legion is loyal to me," Ricard asserted. "As of now, I will need all of the men I can find."

Trentian rounded on him, a bony finger jabbing into his chest.

"If it was not for your foolish pride and ambition, we would not be in this situation. If you had been content with Davik being regent, we could have avoided all of this. Our plans against the wielders would have been completed regardless."

Ricard scoffed at the cowardice of the man. They had been framed by who knew who, and yet the so-called man of religion's hatred for wielders still came to the fore. He slapped himself as a thought struck him.

"Wielders! Who but they would benefit from me being framed for Davik's murder? They hope to end the persecution against their ways by discrediting me, by disgracing me. It all makes sense now."

Trentian gawped at the baron, belief in his eyes. He paced the room before snapping his fingers.

"Yes, yes it must be them. We were framed by the wielders – that must be it! We must tell the people that this is what has happened. They will forgive us and turn their ire against wielders. We must spread the word through the city at once!"

Trentian turned to leave, hope on his wrinkly old face.

"I will order the scribes and priests to begin spreading the word at once. I fear, however, that harsher action will be needed to get the Sunguard Legion back under control. They were loyal to Davik; they will not back down unless they are stopped by force!"

The archbishop scurried out. Ricard shut the door and poured himself another glass of wine. The archbishop's words may ease the anger of the populace, but in his gut he knew that Balnor and Robinta would be much harder to convince that he was innocent. Blaming the wielders was their only option.

The girl ran through the smoky streets. With agile grace, she skipped over the body of a dead city guard. The man's head was hanging at a funny angle, the iron scythe that had almost took it off still lodged in the neck. His was not the first body she had seen as she made her way from the King's Spire to the southern gate. A fire had been started in the merchant quarter and the blazing inferno was quickly consuming the western side of the city. The soldiers who were not desperately trying to contain the rioting were all rushing to join the effort to halt the fire's spread. She sniffed the air; smoke filled her nostrils. It was the smell of victory.

Panicked screams sounded from a nearby alleyway; many people had perished in the rioting. Hurrying through the backstreets, the girl encountered a group of laughing legionaries dragging a girl of a similar age to herself down a side street. For a heartbeat, she contemplated helping the poor wretch, but soon thought better of it.

None of the people in this wretched city deserve to live, the girl thought a wicked smile playing on her lips. They think they know fear; wait until my master comes here with my brethren.

She had played her role to perfection. It had been surprisingly easy for her to infiltrate the royal household as a serving girl. All she'd had to do was bide her time. She reached into the pocket sewn into the inside of her dress and giggled as her fingers played with the bottle of poison she had hidden within.

She rounded another corner and skidded to a halt.

A large bald man covered in tattoos blocked the narrow path. She tilted her head. The man wore the clothes common to the city's poor; his tunic was filthy and streaked with blood. The body of a small child was at the man's feet. Whatever foul act that had occurred had happened very recently. It wouldn't surprise her if the thug had come from the city prison. The rioters had made a beeline for the structure and freed the scum inside.

Upon seeing the girl, the man smiled cruelly. The girl laughed.

"You think that you are scary? How funny," she mocked.

The man moved towards her menacingly.

"I am scary, you little whore," he growled. "I'm gonna show ya just how scary I am. I'm gonna make you beg for death before I'm done with ya."

Again, the girl laughed. "You don't know what true scary is," she said softly. "I would like to show you, but I am terribly late."

The man continued to advance. The girl raised a hand and wagged a finger at him, like a mother scolding a naughty child. With a flick of her wrist, the man was sent flying backwards and crashed into a heap against the wall. He scrambled to his feet, his eyes wide in surprise. The girl giggled again, and rotated her wrist. A sickening snap reverberated up the narrow street as the man's spine was violently twisted to an unnatural angle. The man screamed as he collapsed onto the ground, his spinal cord severed. The girl admired her handiwork for a few seconds before continuing on her way.

The now paralysed man sobbed in agony.

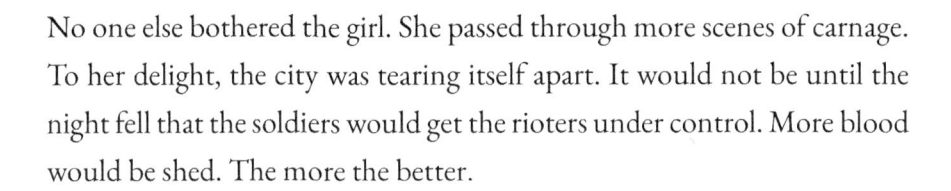

No one else bothered the girl. She passed through more scenes of carnage. To her delight, the city was tearing itself apart. It would not be until the night fell that the soldiers would get the rioters under control. More blood would be shed. The more the better.

Finally, she reached the southern gate. This part of the city was quiet in comparison to the other districts. Very few people were out on the streets, and those that were made it clear that they were armed. A woman and her small daughter hurried inside a house. An old man stood outside his property, a rusty old legion blade in his hands.

The girl smiled.

If a riot could instil such fear in these people, then they were going to lose their minds when her master came.

Her smile widened as she spotted the tall cloaked figure stood next to the gate. The cloak was the colour of crimson. At the figure's feet lay the cooling corpses of the guards tasked with defending the gate.

"Did you encounter any trouble, Yinnice?" the figure hissed.

The girl shook her head. "Nothing that I couldn't handle. The plan has gone perfectly. Civil war will come. We have sown enough discord that they will all soon be turning on one another."

"And the mages?"

The girl laughed and clapped her hands in happiness.

"Oh, don't worry, the mages will be blamed. I made sure to leave a trail that will point the finger at them. Our enemies will be powerless to stop us."

CHAPTER TWENTY.

Five figures moved silently through the long grass. The night was pitch-black save for the dim light cast by the waning twin moons. Luxon, Sophia, Ferran, Kaiden and Drusilla were on their hands and knees, crawling ever closer to the high walls of Stormglade. They had approached the city from the north east, using the marshy lands created by the sea for cover. Drusilla had devised the plan; she had successfully infiltrated the city once before. According to her, there was a small drainage ditch built low in the walls that would provide them with their way in.

Cautiously, Luxon raised his head above the tall grass. He could make out small dots of light moving along the crenulations. Men were on patrol. The enemy was being vigilant.

Aside from the sound of the marsh's wildlife, he could hear what sounded like hundreds of iron hammers striking stone. He ducked back down as Ferran gave out a low whistle in warning. Ahead, and moving through the long grass, was an animal. The lack of light made it impossible to see, but whatever it was, it was big. As the creature lumbered closer, the damp earth shook slightly. Luxon looked to his right to see Ferran crawling over to him. The Nightblade was covered in mud and his face was painted black just like Luxon's own.

"It's a Gargantuan," Ferran whispered "There's no way we can take it out without being spotted. We're going to have to go around. Follow me."

Luxon nodded and crawled after his friend.

Close behind him was his mother, now dressed in an outfit of black trousers and tunic, and Sophia. Kaiden was just off to Luxon's side. His limbs were growing tired from the crawling. He narrowed his eyes and focused his magic, channelling the power into his tired limbs, and sighing as the tiredness evaporated. Enhancing physical attributes was a skill often used by Nightblades when they were in remote and often physically tiring situations. He had no doubts that Ferran was using similar magic. He glanced behind and saw that his mother had cast the spell, too. She smiled at him. Kaiden, meanwhile had no talent for magic; he was just using his determination to find his wife to keep him going. They skirted round the Fell Beast without being detected.

It took them another hour before they finally reached the bottom of Stormglade's walls, but they had done it without being spotted. Cautiously, they followed the wall south until they reached the culvert that Drusilla had described. Dirty water was pouring out of a barred grate and flowing into the marsh. Luxon dreaded to think what horrid things lurked in the foul-smelling liquid. The grate was a good ten feet from the ground; magic would have to be used to reach it.

"You ready?" Ferran asked.

Luxon nodded. As he was the most powerful magic user in the team, he would be the one to lift the others up to the grate.

"Ladies first," he said with a smile. Sophia stepped forward and gave him the go ahead.

He closed his eyes and summoned his magic. In his mind's eye, he imagined the Witch Hunter floating high into the air. Sure enough, Sophia was lifted from the ground by an invisible hand. Slowly, she rose higher until she reached the culvert. Once level with the opening, she stepped forward. One down, four to go.

Ferran went up next. Once at the culvert, he drew his tourmaline blade and went to work on cutting the iron bars. After him went Drusilla, then Kaiden.

Levitation was a spell of the Upper Ring, and one of the most challenging that a mage could do. His thought briefly flickered back to the first time he had used such a spell. He smiled at his naivety. He was a lot stronger now compared to what he was like then. Narrowing his eyes, he cast the spell and floated upwards. By the time he reached the others, Ferran had successfully cut them a way inside.

They were now in a pitch black tunnel which stank of putrid water. Drusilla pulled a fire stone out of her tunic pocket and brought it to life. The walls were covered with slimy green algae.

"Hold onto your noses," she said apologetically. "The last time I came through this way I was almost overcome by the stench."

A large metal grate barred access.

Drusilla scratched her head.

"Hmm, this wasn't here last time," she muttered.

"Perhaps an extra security measure after your last visit?" Kaiden said.

"The metal is too thick for my tourmaline blade to cut through," Ferran added.

Luxon stepped forward and rubbed his hands together. The space between the bars was too narrow for a person to squeeze through but not for a small animal. He shrugged his robe from his shoulders and took off his clothes, before handing the bundle to his mother who looked away in embarrassment.

"I'm going to transmute into a rat, squeeze through the bars, turn back into me again and unlock the grate," he said in response to the curious looks the others gave him. He winked at Sophia. He swore she blushed.

He closed his eyes and focused. As during his trials, he felt himself begin to shrink until his companions towered over him. The looks of surprise etched on their faces was hilarious. His senses were magnified and the stench of the sewer was overwhelming; although, as a rat, it also smelt appealing. He scurried over to the grate and ran through the bars with ease. Once on the other side, he concentrated. A flash of light and he was once again himself. There was a latch on the grate which he lifted. The grate swung open.

The others walked through, laughing.

"Mother, my affects if you please," he chuckled.

They moved through the tunnel without incident until they reach a ladder made of rusty iron rings. Drusilla gave the firestone to her son and told him to hold it high. She then pulled a piece of cloth from her tunic and unfolded it. Upon its surface was a crudely drawn map of Stormglade.

"This ladder will take us out here," Drusilla explained, pointing to the map.

"The eastern plaza?" Ferran asked.

"Yes. To the north is the main plaza, which is where I think the sigil stone is. To the west is the citadel and docks – it's there that the Sarpi are keeping their prisoners. We all remember our roles?"

They all nodded.

Luxon and Drusilla would head for the main plaza and seek out the sigil stone. Sophia, meanwhile, would scale one of the tall towers that overlooked the city; from there she would use her bow to provide cover. Kaiden and Ferran had been tasked with freeing the prisoners. If their mission went ill, Luxon would launch a fireball into the sky to signal Faramond and the Keenblade army that had amassed a mile to the east of the city. The tribe's fake assault would hopefully buy them enough time to slip out of the city undetected.

Ferran climbed the ladder and carefully lifted the iron manhole cover that concealed the tunnel. Slowly, he raised his head out of the hole. The street was empty. He waved for the others to follow and climbed out of the tunnel.

Once above ground he sprinted into an alleyway that led off from the plaza. Kaiden was next and headed in the same direction. Sophia followed. She looked around for a few seconds to get her bearings, then slipped off down a side street which led towards the tower she planned to use as a vantage spot. Drusilla and Luxon brought up the rear. Once out of the hole, Luxon used his magic to move the manhole cover back into place.

They were in.

CHAPTER TWENTY ONE.

Ferran and Kaiden moved quickly through the backstreets and alleyways of the city. Whenever they encountered a patrol, they hid in side streets or inside one of the many ruined buildings. Whatever had occurred in the city had left it badly damaged. In one of their hiding spots they were forced to lie next to the skeletal remains of one of Stormglade's deceased citizens.

As they got closer to the tower housing the prisoners, the sound of metal striking stone became louder. They rounded a corner and skidded to a halt at the scene before them. Where a wide open plaza had once stood there now was a scar in the earth. Thousands of people were chipping away at the ground with iron tools. The place looked more like a mine than a city.

"What are they doing?" Kaiden whispered.

Ferran was about to reply when he spotted a tall, cloaked figure striding through the makeshift mine. The Nightblade narrowed his eyes. Something about the way the figure moved reminded him of something, and it was nothing good.

"C'mon, the prison is a few more streets this way," he said, before ducking low and moving off.

They heard the prison before they saw it. Inhumane screams echoed out into the cool night air and sent the hairs on their necks standing on end. Kaiden drew his silver sword, whilst Ferran held the hilt of his tourmaline blade tightly.

As they got closer to the prison, other sounds merged with the screams. Cruel, mocking laughter and savage snarls added to the growing sense of dread. They kept to the shadows until they reached the base of the tower.

A fire flickered angrily, casting long shadows onto the surrounding structures. Around the flames stood a group of armed men dressed in black armour and hoods. All of them were drinking.

"Sarpi," Kaiden muttered as he recognised their attire. Anger surged through him; he longed to unleash his vengeance upon them.

Ferran placed a hand on his friend's chest to calm him. The last thing they needed was to be spotted too soon. A head-on approach would get them killed; they needed to take the enemy by surprise. They ducked back into the darkness when they heard more voices approaching.

Two people dressed in long black cloaks walked over to the fire. They were not Sarpi, but an old man and a woman. Both wore amulets around their necks.

A wave of dizziness washed over Ferran, almost making him stagger. Kaiden caught him before he did so.

"Those two," Ferran whispered pointing to the newcomers. "The amulets their wearing, they're draining my magic."

"When do we get a turn on that blonde witch then?" growled one of the Sarpi to the amulet wearers.

The old man scowled and said nothing. The woman, however, glared at the Sarpi.

"The people that you are guarding are not for the likes of you. Lord Danon needs them to bolster the ranks of his most devoted followers."

The Sarpi laughed at the woman's arrogance.

"No one is more loyal to the master than we Sarpi. You N'gist are nothing but fools seeking to reclaim your lost glories. Hmmm, you're not bad on the eyes, lady. How about we have a go on you?"

The other Sarpi chuckled at their comrade's bravado. The woman scowled.

"I suggest you show us some respect; after all, you and your kind are nothing but freaks – the fools cursed by Zahnia."

The Sarpi stopped their laughing, their hands dropping to their swords.

"Say that name again and I will gut you like a fish, bitch," the Sarpi snarled.

The woman laughed mockingly.

"Have I touched a nerve?" she giggled. She walked through the group of Sarpi, her hand brushing over their bodies seductively. She smiled mischievously before clapping her hands.

"Come now, I was merely pointing out that you are nothing but the dirt under our master's boots; that you are nothing but the pathetic victims of Zahnia. We N'gist are his true children."

The Sarpi trembled with anger. For a brief moment, it appeared as though he would cut down the woman standing in front of him. But then, without another word, he stood aside and allowed the N'gist to pass them.

Ferran and Kaiden waited. Before long, the Sarpi had resumed their drinking.

"Stay here, I need to take a piss," slurred one of the guards.

"Here's our chance," Ferran whispered.

The drunken Sarpi staggered off down the street and passed their hiding spot. Silently, Ferran followed until the drunkard led him down a dark side alley. The Sarpi sighed as he began to relief himself in a ruined doorway. Ferran crept up behind his target.

As the Sarpi was finishing off, the Nightblade pounced. Wrapping his strong arms around the Sarpi's throat, he squeezed with all of his might. The Sarpi gasped for air and clawed weakly at his arms, but Ferran held on tightly until the fight went out of his quarry.

Quickly, he stripped the Sarpi out of his armour and hastily put it on. Next, he dragged the unconscious Sarpi further down the alley and rolled the body into a ruined cellar. After that, he hurried back up the alleyway to where Kaiden was hiding. He gave him a thumbs up before putting on a drunken stagger and walked towards the other Sarpi guards.

"Took you long enough," growled the guard who'd had the run in with the N'gist.

"Yeah, well I needed the time to knock out your friend and steal his clothes," Ferran replied.

The Sarpi's eyes widened, but the alcohol in his veins slowed his reactions. Ferran whipped out his tourmaline sword and summoned the magical weapon to life.

The deadly blade caught the slowed Sarpi in the throat and sending him staggering backwards. With almost casual grace, Ferran pirouetted on his heel to cut down the other drunken guards.

Kaiden emerged from the shadows, his sword in hand.

"Nice work," he praised.

Ferran shrugged. "They were drunk; made it too easy," the Nightblade replied, sounding disappointed. He deactivated the tourmaline blade and tucked it into his belt. "Help me move these. I've got a feeling the N'gist won't be so easy to handle."

Drusilla led Luxon through eerily abandoned streets towards the main plaza. The sound of digging grew louder as they approached. Luxon couldn't shake off an uneasy feeling that had made his skin crawl ever since they exited the sewer. He gripped his staff, Dragasdol, tightly.

No guards had barred their journey and no one had spotted them, despite them moving quickly. But he couldn't shake off the feeling that things were going far too easily. Drusilla slowed to a stop and looked at her son.

"What's the matter?" she asked, a hint of impatience in her tone.

Luxon frowned.

"It's nothing, let's keep moving."

Drusilla smiled softly, before taking his hand in hers and moving off once again.

"How do you know where the stone is?" Luxon asked as they walked.

"I ... I'm guessing that it is with Danon or on someone close to him. The last time I was here, I spotted a small structure in the plaza. It was heavily guarded by N'gist, so I'm guessing there is something inside that they want to protect."

They clambered over a pile of rubble which had once been a part of one of the city's many watch towers. With the tribes being a constant threat, the city had been built with defence firmly in mind. A tattered banner of the merchant kings fluttered in the breeze; the emblem of the sword and scales had been scorched by fire. Once on the other side of the rubble, they found themselves at the top of a narrow cobbled street that led down toward the main plaza.

Cautiously, they crept to the end of the street. Luxon could see the structure that his mother had described. Between them and it were hundreds of miserable-looking prisoners chipping away at the ground with simple iron tools. Stood by the hut was a tall figure, it looked as though it was waiting for something. Of the guards his mother had described, he could see no trace of them.

Drusilla gripped his hand tightly.

"Looks like we're in luck," she whispered. "Come on."

CHAPTER TWENTY ONE.

Something wasn't right. Sophia was in position at the top of a crumbling tower overlooking the main plaza. From her vantage point she could see most of the city. Her journey to the tower had been incredibly easy; only once had she been forced to hide from a patrol of Sarpi . She looked down at the plaza; where were the guards? She looked over towards the prison tower where Ferran and Kaiden had been heading. Even there, there was a lack of defenders.

Her gaze moved around the edge of the plaza.

She gasped and the hairs on the back of her neck stood up.

Thousands of tiny dots of light shone out from the darkness. All around the edge of the plaza were Sarpi, their eyes glinting in the night. They stood absolutely still in the shadows, weapons in hand as though they were waiting for something. Now that she knew what to look for, she could see just as many black-cloaked figures standing amongst the Sarpi. Again, they stood eerily still.

Her stomach sank as the realisation dawned upon her.

They had walked into a trap.

Drusilla pulled Luxon after her as she hurried into the plaza. The working prisoners paid them little attention. Now that they were closer, Luxon could see that the prisoners were comprised from folks from all over the kingdom. To his surprise, he even spotted some dark-skinned Yundols among them. He had thought little about the continent across the sea since Eclin, but now he wondered if that land had suffered from Sarpi raids like Delfinnia had.

Luxon stopped and pulled his mother to a halt. He closed his eyes for a moment. The vision from the sigil stone flashed in his mind's eye. The stone was not in the hut. He opened his eyes again. His vision blurred as he felt a strange power flow through him. At the far end of the plaza, in a spot that had yet to be worked by the digging prisoners, he saw an object under the stone shining brightly.

"Do you see that?" he asked quietly.

Drusilla looked at him before turning her gaze to where he was looking. She shook her head.

"No, I see nothing ..."

"The second stone is over there, buried. I can see it ..." Luxon muttered.

He began to walk towards the light. They made it half way across the plaza when the sound of someone clapping loudly halted their steps. They spun around to see that the tall figure they had seen next to the hut was walking straight towards them. As the figure got closer, they could see that it was a man – the man from Luxon's nightmares. He had long black hair that fell to his shoulders, and even in the dim light they could see that his skin was pale. His most striking feature was his eyes, which glinted red. His skull was skeletal, his skin cracked and marked, as though he was afflicted with some disease. He wore a simple tunic, breaches and boots. Only the black robe around his shoulders gave him away as an N'gist.

"It's been a long time, Luxon," the man said in a deep booming voice. A wicked grin was on his face. "The last time we met, you banished my beloved wife, Cliria, to the Void."

Even though his face was different, Luxon knew that the man was Danon. He stood in front of his mother protectively and pointed his staff at the dark lord.

"Danon. You look different. Not so- skinny" Luxon replied, doing his best to keep the fear he felt out of his voice.

"Yes well, after Eclin I couldn't move around as a skeletal corpse now could I?" Danon explained. "I possessed the general Rason and used his body to escape. Unfortunately, that body could not effectively contain my power, so I had to find a replacement. This one was offered to me by Accadus of Retbit. I think it was one of his wielder friends, if I recall."

He smiled at Luxon. His face straight from a nightmare.

"The young Baron of Retbit is a very good pupil, you know. Far better than you were. With him, I didn't have to hide the fun bits, like necromancy."

Luxon and Drusilla backed away slowly. Luxon glanced over his shoulder, and made sure they moved towards the glowing stone.

"So, it is true. Accadus is your puppet."

Danon threw his head back and laughed.

"He is. And so are you. You have walked right into my trap, just as I had planned. I know that you know where the second sigil stone is." Danon reached into his cloak and pulled out the sigil stone that had been stolen from Sunguard. "The magic in this stone was easy to crack, but alas – the mage who created it was clever. I saw the vision which led me here, but annoyingly it did not reveal where the second stone was hidden exactly.

Only those with the right bloodline can see ... only those with the blood of kings in their veins."

Luxon frowned. His mother had said something similar. He knew the blood of Aljeron, the first wizard, flowed in his veins, but what did he mean by blood of kings?

Danon laughed mockingly at the confusion evident on his face.

"Reunited with your mother after all this time, and she doesn't tell you?" Danon said sarcastically. "How amusing. Shall I give you two a moment before I make you tell me where the stone is?"

Luxon looked at his mother. Tears were in her eyes.

"Mother?" he asked in confusion.

"Oh for goodness sake! For a wizard, you're not very bright are you," Danon sighed, impatience in his tone. "It's simple: your father was the king. Mother dearest had an affair with King Rendall, and you were the result. Oh, and if you're wondering, yes – I always knew."

Luxon staggered under the weight of the revelation. He shook his head angrily. No, his father had been Garrick Edioz, a noble in King Rendall's court. As he looked at his mother, and saw the look of shame in her eyes, he knew deep down that what Danon had said was the truth. His whole life had indeed been a lie.

"The blood of Aljeron allowed me to free Cliria," Danon continued. "Your power allowed me to escape the Void, and now the blood of kings in your veins will lead me to the sigil stones and the resting place of Asphodel. You are just too perfect, Luxon. The culmination of my manipulations and brilliance. It is a shame that you will not join with me,"

Luxon shook. He felt rage, a rage the likes of which he had never felt before. His skin grew hot as his magic grew in power. Before him stood evil incarnate – the one who had toyed with him, and used him.

"I will never join you," he shouted.

With a roar, he channelled his rage into Dragasdol and unleashed his power. A blinding flash of lightning erupted from the tip of the staff and smashed with full force into Danon. The dark lord was hurled backwards by the impact and crashed heavily onto the ground. His cloak smoked from where it had caught fire, and steam emanated from his scorched body. Any normal man would have been slain by the attack, but Danon slowly picked himself off the ground, patted out the flames and dusted himself off. And all the while, he chuckled.

"Such anger! I love it!" he yelled joyously.

Luxon narrowed his eyes. With his free hand, he conjured a fireball into existence.

"Enjoy this," he growled.

Thrusting his hand skyward, he launched the ball of magical fire high into the night sky. He then spun around, and smashed the ground at his feet with his staff. The stone cracked open to reveal the second sigil stone. Quickly, he covered his hand with the sleeve of his cloak, grabbed the stone and tucked it into his pocket. He could ill afford a vision now, not with Danon so near.

Upon seeing the stone, Danon's smile dropped. He glared at Luxon and snarled. Before he could retaliate with his own dark power, an arrow struck him across the face and sent him staggering to the ground once more. Luxon looked up to see Sophia high in a tower; she waved at him frantically.

All hell broke loose.

Faramond stroked his horse's mane. He hated waiting at the best of times, but being made to wait in the dark with Fell Beasts closing in from all sides was the worst. He sat astride his armoured warhorse in his full battle dress. His cuirass of steel scales covered a chainmail shirt and thick cotton undershirt. He was sweating, despite the coldness of the night. His legs were covered in mail greaves and his feet by leather boots inlayed with iron. On his head he wore a steel helmet that covered most of his face. The image of a charging stallion was engraved in the metal. Topping it off was a tall plume of white goose feathers. He looked every bit the warrior prince. Around him were a thousand of his kinsmen. The smell of so many horses was almost overwhelming but it did not bother him. He had grown up around the beasts; his tribe depended on the animals. To his right, sat awkwardly astride a white stallion, was Yepert, his mages cloak covering his nose to ward off the smell.

"You are brave to be here," Faramond said.

Yepert looked over at the prince, who looked like some hero of old in his armour. He didn't feel brave; a part of him wished that he had volunteered to have stayed back at the camp with Hannah to help prepare for the wounded that would no doubt result from the night's events.

"I promised to be there for my friend. I vowed to not let him out of my sight," he replied, frowning.

Luxon was inside the city that dominated the flat plains. Yepert had wanted to go in with him and the others, but had been persuaded to stay by Ferran. His cheeks flushed red. He knew the Nightblade still saw him as a clumsy child; memories of his run-in with the banshee years previously filled his mind.

"I may not be inside the city at his side, but I will do whatever it takes to help him," he added.

Faramond nodded and clapped Yepert on the shoulder.

"Loyalty is the best quality a man can have. Luxon is fortunate to have a friend such as you."

A horn sounded from somewhere to the north. Faramond sighed. To keep the Fell Beasts from swarming towards his force, he had dispatched groups of outriders to fend them off or lure them away. Every time a horn sounded, it meant that another rider had been slain. He had counted twenty horn blasts so far.

He swore as a close blast made him jump.

"My lord! Look," shouted the sheepish-looking horn blower.

Faramond looked towards where the warrior pointed. A dot of light was soaring high into the sky.

"It's magical fire. It's the signal," Yepert cried.

Faramond gripped the reigns of his horse tightly.

"Signal the attack," he shouted to the horn blower, before kicking his heels into his steed's flank.

The horn blower blew a high note, and as one the Keenlance army roared. The thousand riders surged forward in a wave of noise. Hooves thundering on the grassy plain and the war cries of the tribe echoed out over the plain. Yepert, too, spurred on his mount, his heart beating wildly as exhilaration filled him.

He just hoped his friends were alright.

Luxon whirled Dragasdol over his head and sent magical lightning shooting out in a deadly arc of power. Sarpi and N'gist leapt from the walls overlooking the plaza and poured in from the side streets. He stood back to back with his mother, who likewise used her own magical abilities. The lightning struck a pack of charging Sarpi head-on and blasted them into atoms. His mother, meanwhile, cast fireball after fireball. Sweat poured into Luxon's eyes, and his limbs were growing tired from the sustained use of his powers. In his cloak pocket was the sigil stone; he could not allow it to fall into Danon's hands. Panic filled him; they had walked right into the heart of Danon's forces. Thousands of glowing-eyed Sarpi warriors and cloaked N'gist were coming for them. He narrowed his eyes. Danon was standing calmly amongst the charging enemy, his arms crossed across his chest and a sinister smile on his lips. He appeared quite happy to let his followers deal with them.

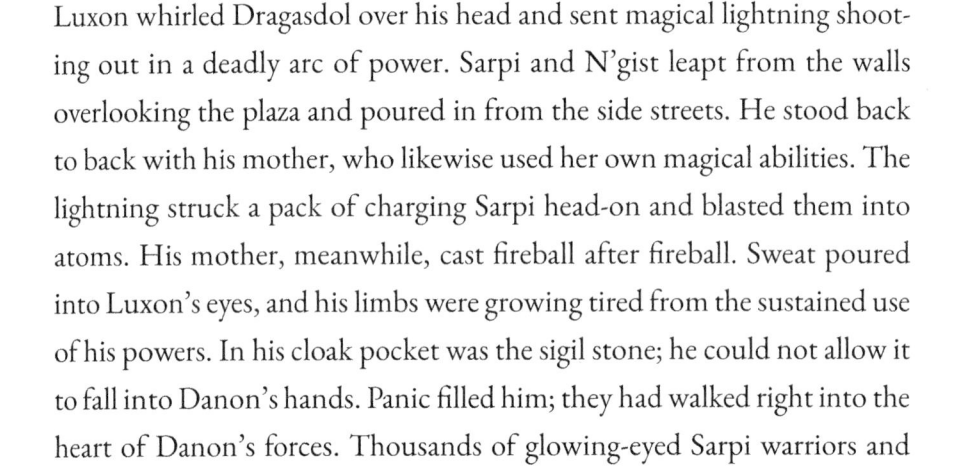

The N'gist advanced behind the Sarpi, familiar amulets held before them. As they stalked closer, Luxon could feel his powers being leeched from him. Behind him, his mother staggered.

CHAPTER TWENTY ONE.

"The amulets, they ... they are draining me," she cried.

With a roar, Luxon unleashed a telekinetic blast which swatted the charging Sarpi aside. The warriors scattered in a tumbling heap of broken bones. The N'gist continued their advance. He launched a fireball, but the intended target summoned a magical shield to deflect it. All the while, Luxon felt himself weakening. He cried out as one of the N'gist staggered and collapsed to the ground, an arrow lodged deep into his back. Another arrow struck, cutting down another of the dark magic wielders. Sophia was moving quickly along the high battlements, shooting arrow after arrow into the enemy's ranks. But it wouldn't be enough. They would soon be overwhelmed, and Danon would claim his prize.

In the prison tower, Kaiden and Ferran moved swiftly. Still dressed as a Sarpi guard, Ferran followed the N'gist through the crumbling structure. Kaiden kept his distance further back. The female N'gist laughed at some joke her elderly companion had made, before unlocking and opening heavy door. Ferran waited a few moments before following them through. To his surprise, he found himself in a wide open courtyard. At one end was another door which led to a tall tower, but it was what was in the courtyard that took him off guard.

He took cover behind a stone column. Bound and tied was a creature. Its long snout was tied so that its jaws were clamped together, and its wings were restrained by iron chains. Its scales were pale grey and its reptilian eyes were flecked with red. Judging by its size, Ferran surmised that the dragon was a juvenile. The woman walked over to the dragon and laughed as she kicked it violently on the nose.

"It won't be long before the master will need to replace you," the woman cackled. "Your dragon magic is running low. What good will you be when we can no longer enhance our amulets with it? No, I think you will be served up to the undead and werewolves."

With a mocking laugh, the N'gist moved off and through the door leading to the tower. Ferran turned to see Kaiden appear at the other doorway. He waved him over.

"You go after the N'gist. My magic won't be much help against them. Here," he said taking a vial from his belt. "This is a Void vial. We Nightblades use them to send Fell Beasts back to the Void. Use it against those bastards if you can't get the jump on them, and remember: make sure no innocent is nearby when you throw it."

Kaiden took the vial and tucked into his pocket.

"What are you going to do?"

Ferran pointed at the dragon.

"I'm going to free this thing. Perhaps it will help us."

Kaiden raised an eyebrow.

"Or, it could eat you. Be careful, my friend."

The Nightblade smirked.

"I always am. Get going," he said, slapping his comrade on the shoulder. "Get your wife and child out of here."

Kaiden nodded and drew his sword. He kissed the hilt before following the N'gist out of the courtyard.

Ferran focused on the dragon. Slowly, he moved towards it. The creature's large eye focused on him, its gaze radiating fury. Ferran held his hands open before him to show that he meant no harm. As he got closer, the great beast growled, and even though its jaws were bound, razor sharp teeth could be seen. Ferran pulled down his hood to show his face. Fighting and hunting Fell Beasts was one thing; trying to calm a dragon another. He took his tourmaline sword from his belt and summoned the glowing magical blade to life. The dragon began to shake, and its front talons raked at the broken stonework.

"Easy, easy," Ferran said nervously. "I am here to set you free. Do you understand what I am saying?"

The Dragon stopped struggling, its large eye fixated upon him. If Ferran knew any better, he would swear it was pleading with him. The pupil narrowed as he raised the blade.

"Remember I saved you," he soothed before setting to work cutting the iron chains around the Dragon's legs. "By Niveren, please don't eat me."

Kaiden kept to the shadows as he followed the N'gist. The woman's mocking laughter echoed down the narrow stairwell. Kaiden crept upwards until he reached an open doorway which led out into a wide corridor. At the far end was a heavy iron door. Down the right hand side were other doors which led to other prison cells. He peered through the bars of one of the cells and gasped. The body of a man wearing a burned mantle of the order of Niveren lay on the ground. It must have been the Knight Vigilant, the warrior had failed in his quest.

"May Niveren guard your soul, brother," he prayed quietly.

On the left hand side were tiny barred windows which were spread out at regular intervals. He tucked himself against the cold stone of the doorway and peeked down the corridor. The two N'gist were stood outside the door at the far end. He tilted his head in an attempt to hear what they were saying, but all he could make out was cruel laughter. The woman unlocked the heavy door and went inside the cell. A scream sounded, making him flinch. The woman stepped back into the hallway, but now she was accompanied by a child. It was Ilene! The N'gist held the crying little girl tightly by the arm and was dragging her roughly back down the corridor.

Kaiden tightened his grip on his sword. He breathed deeply and tensed his muscles; he would only get one shot at surprising the magic users. The old man cackled at the little girl's plight and led the way back towards the stairs. As he reached Kaiden's hiding spot, he spotted the intruder. Too late. With a shout, Kaiden stabbed his sword forward savagely and impaled the N'gist in the guts. The old man's eyes widened in surprise, and blood foamed from his lips. With a kick, Kaiden withdrew his now blood-covered blade and sent the old man's body tumbling down the spiral stairs. He then stepped into the hallway and raised his sword so that its tip was pointed at the woman. Ilene's eyes widened as she recognised her father.

"Let her go, witch," he commanded.

The N'gist stared at him. A moment passed. Before he could react, she shoved Ilene forward, sending the girl crashing to the floor, and raised a hand to unleash a blast of lightning. The magic struck Kaiden in the chest, and he fell backwards; his sword flew from his grasp and clattered loudly onto the stairs. The smell of charred flesh almost made Kaiden gag, and the pain was excruciating. His eyes flooded with tears as his chest steamed.

"Daddy!" Ilene screamed.

The N'gist cackled wickedly.

"Watch, little girl, as I send your daddy to the afterlife."

The woman stalked towards him. Kaiden reached for the vial on his belt that Ferran had given him.

"Ilene … run back down the hallway" he croaked. He could feel the magical lightning burning its way through his body; the pain was excruciating. "Do it, honey. Run away!"

Ilene did as she was told, and ran down the corridor. Kaiden gripped the vial tightly and rolled onto his side. He cried out in pain. The N'gist was only a few paces away; in her closed fist she had created a fireball that would burn him alive. One more step …

He roared as he threw the vial at the ceiling. The glass shattered loudly. For a moment, the N'gist glared at him.

"What was that?" she demanded.

"You'll see, bitch."

The corridor began to shake violently as the magic contained in the vial activated. A crack appeared on the ceiling and spread along its length. The air itself felt different as the magic did its work. The N'gist screamed as the air above her head split open. The Void breach was hungry.

A howling sucking wind began to emanate from the breach. Kaiden crawled to the doorframe and held onto the stonework tightly. The N'gist was not so lucky. With nothing to hold onto, she was lifted from her feet and pulled into the breach. Her screams echoed, before the Void breach closed with a flash of light.

The sound of alarm bells and his daughter's voice drifted into Kaiden's consciousness before darkness took him.

CHAPTER TWENTY TWO.

Ferran cut the dragon's final bond and stepped backwards. The great beast opened its large mouth in a wide yawn and flexed its powerful muscles. It reared up onto its back legs and unfurled its wings. Ferran held his breath as the beast fixed its gaze upon him. He was about to say something when a crash sounded and screams sounded from the nearby tower. The dragon snarled.

"Remember, dragon: I, Ferran of Blackmoor set you free. Help me and you will have repaid your debt to me!"

The dragon growled ominously.

"I owe you nothing, human. Your kind took me from my kind; you tortured me, stole my power ... I should eat you."

More cries came from the tower. Ferran stared hard at the dragon.

"Do you what you wish, but my friend is in danger. If you want to escape this foul place then you are going to have to fight. If you hate men then slay the ones that captured you, for they are my enemies too. Help my friends," he growled dismissively, before sprinting across the courtyard and up the towers staircase.

The dragon watched its saviour go, its emotions torn. A horn sounded in the distance catching the beast's attention. Bells began to ring out over the city, a noise that the dragon hated. Angrily, it raked the ground with its talons and roared; it would have its vengeance. It flapped its leathery wings and launched itself into the sky. If it were a fully grown adult, it would not have been able to squeeze out of the courtyard. It felt good to be free.

As he reached the top of the stairs, Ferran skidded to a halt. Lying on the floor was Kaiden, his clothing still smoking from where the magical lightning had hit him. Quickly, Ferran moved to his friend and checked his pulse. It was still beating.

"Is he okay?" asked a sobbing voice.

He looked up to see a little girl sat on the floor nearby. He gave her a reassuring smile.

"He'll be fine. He's just taking a nap is all," Ferran replied with a smile.

In his heart, though, he knew that he had to get Kaiden to a healer, and soon. Banging was coming from the door down the hallway. His grin dropped as he hurried toward the prison cell. He summoned his tourmaline blade to life and delivered a brutal blow to the door's iron lock. The magical blade cut deeply into the metal, and with a loud crack the lock broke in two and the door swung open.

Alira stood in the doorway. Upon seeing Ferran and Ilene she cried out in relief and scooped her daughter into her arms.

"Oh thank Niveren you're safe," she said happily. Her smile dropped as she looked further down the hallway and spotted Kaiden.

"He lives, Alira, but he needs a healer," Ferran explained. He ushered the other prisoners out of the cell.

"By the gods ... Huin? Grig?" he said in surprise as he recognised the old healer and his companion. The two men at that time had been on the run as the civil war had led to a backlash against magic wielders. The healers had saved Yepert's life when a banshee had attacked the lad.

"The Nightblade from the King's Road! It is good to see you," Grig smiled. Ferran took the old man's hand and hurried him over to Kaiden. The knight's breathing had turned shallow and strained.

"Can you help him?"

Grigg crouched down over Kaiden and assessed his wounds. The old man's brows knotted in concentration as he placed a wrinkled hand onto Kaiden's forehead. He closed his eyes and muttered a spell. A bright light shone from his palm. As the healer worked, Ferran turned to the prisoners.

"We have to get out of here. From the sound of the bells, our diversion has begun. The plan is for us to make our way to a sewer, which will lead to a way out of the city. Can any of you fight?"

All in all there were ten prisoners. No one raised their hands.

"We may have magic, but we aren't fighters," said one of the prisoners, a young woman who wore the clothing of a trader.

"There were more of us," Alira added softly. "There were mages and Nightblades, but they were taken by the N'gist."

Ferran turned back to Kaiden. The old healer sat on his heels beside him.

"I have done what I can for him," Grig explained soberly. "I have stabilised his condition, but I will need to concoct a potion to revive him fully. He will need to be carried."

Ferran ordered two of the male prisoners to carry Kaiden. Each man put one of the knight's arms over their shoulders.

"Right everybody, stay close and follow me."

Yepert turned his horse just in time to avoid the fireball that smashed into the ground. The Keenlance forces were being held at bay by the N'gist on the walls flinging spells.

Where the powerful magic had struck, the field was covered in craters and the charred remains of warriors. Yepert glanced up to see a squadron of Keenlance warriors loose a volley of arrows. The projectiles soared high, but before striking the enemy on the walls they slammed into a magical shield.

Yepert shouted in frustration. How were they supposed to kill the enemy whilst they hid behind magical barriers? The Keenlance tribe had no mages of their own to counter. None ... except for him.

CHAPTER TWENTY TWO.

Arrows rained down from the city's walls and cut down more warriors. Yepert straightened up in his saddle. He spotted the black-cloaked magic users on the battlements and aimed his hand. With a shout, he used his own magic to send a ball of flame of his own shooting at the enemy. Again, the attack was blocked by the barrier.

More arrows and fire rained down onto the Keenlance army.

"C'mon Luxon, get out of there before we're all killed," Yepert muttered through gritted teeth.

The diversion was quickly turning into a suicide mission.

He cried out as his horse was struck by an arrow. The animal whinnied in pain before collapsing mid-gallop. Yepert flew from the saddle and crashed heavily to the ground, unconscious.

Sophia was quickly running out of arrows and time. Sarpi were running up the stairs leading towards her position on the battlements. She loosed another arrow, which took one of the enemy in his neck. The man screamed as he fell from the wall. She reached over her shoulder to draw another arrow from the quiver on her back, but it was empty. Swearing, she put her bow over her shoulder and drew her two short swords. She looked to her left and then to her right. Sarpi were stalking towards her from both directions, their swords drawn. She felt panic rising within her; she was trapped. The ground shook as the battle in the plaza intensified. To her amazement, Luxon and his mother still stood. The wizard was unleashing spell after spell and was surrounded by scores of dead N'gist and Sarpi.

Standing further away was Danon, a cruel smile on his face. Why had he not intervened? Her question was answered when the dark lord stepped forward and raised his hands. Dark tendrils of magical energy flowed from his fingertips to envelope the dead. To Sophia's horror, the bodies began to twitch and writhe until the slain were once again stood upright. Danon's necromancy had resurrected his fallen followers to turn them into snarling undead. Desperately, she looked out over the battlements. Below her were the city's main defensive walls, which were teeming with enemies. Beyond that was the Great Plains and the sight of the Keenlance forces being forced to retreat.

She had no choice. If she stayed, she would surely be killed. She cried out in frustration; she didn't want to leave her friends, but if she did not she would die. Shaking, she muttered a prayer to Niveren and turned. She jumped and hauled herself onto the top of the wall. Carefully she lowered herself down and sought out handholds in the crumbling stonework before climbing downwards. She hoped that the enemy beneath her was too distracted by the tribe's attack to notice her escape.

Luxon sagged to his knees in exhaustion. Seeing Danon revive all those he had slain had taken the fight out of him. It was pointless. No matter how many he slew, they would just return as undead. His head was pounding; he had over exerted himself and he could feel his limbs trembling. The Void sickness was threatening to overwhelm him. Behind him, standing defiantly, was his mother. She, too, was on the verge of collapse. Her magical powers were almost spent; the N'gist amulets had done their job well. Her tanned skin was now a ghostly white and her eyes dim. Yet, still she stood over her son like a mother bear defending her cub.

"Get up Luxon," she said. "Touch the sigil stone; see the vision and destroy the stone. I will protect you."

"You can't hold them off alone," he argued.

"Do it, son ... I love you."

Luxon closed his eyes against the tears forming. His mother stepped forward and held her head high. The snarling undead shambled towards her. Danon laughed.

"Laugh at this, you monster ..." Luxon snarled.

He reached into his robe and gripped the sigil stone tightly. A tingling sensation shot up his arm as the stone reacted to him. Was he really the son of a king? Before he could think further, a vision flashed into his mind.

A dark place that stank of death and damp. Wetlands for as far as the eye can see, and in its heart stands a stone structure. Ancient ruins surround it and a doorway leads down into a dark tunnel, at the end of which was an altar. The resting place of the kings of old.

He gasped as the vision faded, and shook his head to clear the images that had burned themselves into his mind.

"Did you see it?" Drusilla asked. "The location of the final stone?"

He nodded as he staggered to his feet. He threw the stone onto the ground. Upon seeing it, the smile on Danon's face dropped. It was Luxon's turn to smile. Gripping Dragasdol, tightly he raised it high. He focused his power into the staff, making it turn as hard as rock, and smashed it onto the stone. The stone shattered, exploding in a blinding white light as the magical power contained within was unleashed. To his amazement, Luxon and his mother were unharmed as the white light covered them. The undead and Sarpi surrounding them were not so lucky. As the white light shot outwards, it vaporised all that it touched. Danon, however, was spared; he created a barrier to protect himself from the blinding intensity of the magical explosion.

The light faded.

Luxon blinked.

Drusilla grabbed him by the hand.

"Now's our chance!" she cried.

There was now nothing standing between them and the plaza's exit. The hope of escape invigorated them and they broke into a sprint. Behind them, Danon roared.

"Kill them!"

The Sarpi and N'gist that had avoided the blast now surged after them. Hope of escape turned into despair; they would never outrun the pursuing enemy.

"Look!" yelled Drusilla breathlessly.

In the sky and diving towards the ground was the unmistakable shape of a dragon. For a moment, Luxon thought that his old friend Umbaroth had come to save the day, but he realised that the dragon was too small and not silver.

The dragon roared and unleashed its fire. Luxon and Drusilla glanced over their shoulders as they fled. The flames struck the pursuing enemy, turning them to ash.

Ferran was ahead of them. The Nightblade was standing in the alley leading to the plaza and gesturing for them to hurry up. The dragon circled in the sky.

"We are even, Ferran of Blackmoor!" the dragon roared before flying off into the night. Ferran tossed the dragon a salute. He hurried forward and put an arm around Luxon to steady him.

"We're getting out of here," Ferran said. "The Keenlance forces have withdrawn from their attack, and horses should be waiting for us where we got in."

A scream made him spin around. Drusilla's eyes were wide and blood seeped through her dress. A Sarpi arrow had found its mark.

"Get out of here!" she cried. She staggered forward two more steps before collapsing to the ground, the arrow sticking out of her back.

"Mother, we can't leave you!" Luxon yelled. He tried to struggle out of Ferran's grip but he was too weak.

More arrows were striking the stonework around them. Striding towards them was Danon.

"There's nothing we can do. We have to leave, Luxon!" Ferran shouted.

He tightened his grip around the frantic wizard and dragged him away.

CHAPTER TWENTY THREE.

The sunrise in the east cast the plains in light. Craters still smouldered from where the grass had been struck by fireballs and arrows littered the earth. Bodies of hundreds of Keenlance warriors and their horses lay like broken toys, and hungry ravens now greedily feasted upon them. Danon walked through the carnage, savouring the sight of devastation and the smell of charred flesh.

His N'gist followers were spread out over the plain collecting the bodies of the slain. They would serve him in the coming battles. His fury at losing the sigil stone had been terrible to behold; many more undead had been added to his army's ranks after he had vented his frustration upon his followers.

He stopped as he spotted a body lying face down in the tall grass. It wore the cloak of a mage.

Curious, he walked over to it and rolled it onto its back with a foot. A smile split his face as he recognised the young man. He touched Yepert's face, his smile widening. He was alive.

He snapped his fingers and two Sarpi hurried over to him.

"Luxon's friend ... Perhaps the sword is not lost to me," he muttered to himself. "Take this mage to my quarters in the city," he commanded.

The Sarpi bowed deeply before picking Yepert up and carrying him off.

Danon watched the sunrise with contempt. He detested the light; it, like his brother Niveren, had betrayed him long ago, and he would not stop until he had extinguished it from the face of the world. He looked at his hands. They were not his own; his original body was long lost, destroyed by his brother, only his soul remained unchanged. He smirked; Niveren had sacrificed his immortality and that of his descendants to stop him. Danon however retained his.

He would live forever; victory would be his, either way.

CHAPTER TWENTY FOUR.

The weary Keenlance warriors rode back towards the tribe's camp. Of the thousand that had ridden to Stormglade, less than four hundred had returned. The cries of the wounded, and of wives and children now left widowed and fatherless, joined the awful cacophony of despair. Amongst the survivors were Luxon and the others. After escaping the city, the wounded had been put onto carts that had been waiting a few miles away. It had been touch and go if Kaiden would survive the trip, but thanks to Grig and Huin's powers of healing the knight still clung to life. Sat at her husband's side was Alira, her eyes red from tears. She had to be strong for Ilene, who clung to her skirts. The sun had risen in the east and the sight of the broken army was a miserable thing to behold. And yet, despite the losses and injuries, the mission had been a total success. The prisoners had been liberated and the sigil stone destroyed, Danon's hunt for Asphodel had been halted, at least for now.

Luxon slumped in his saddle; despite the success he felt little joy. His mother was dead, their reunion ended by a Sarpi arrow; his best friend was missing and another severely hurt. He rubbed his eyes, the tears leaving them red and sore. Ferran and Sophia rode at his side. The Witch Hunter had done her best to comfort him, but from personal experience she knew that he would need space and time to grieve on his own.

Faramond was at the head of the column. He stared into the horizon, his expression grim.

"We have riled the beehive," he uttered softly.

Ferran, who was at his side, nodded.

"Danon will come," the Nightblade replied soberly. "His army will sweep across the Great Plain like a flood. The tribes cannot stand against such evil alone. Send word to the other tribes, unite them and then march on the Watchers. There we may have a chance of holding him."

Faramond looked at his companion, a haunted look on his normally stern face.

"How can anyone resist such power? His N'gist wiped out more than half my force. Our weapons couldn't even get close to them. Against magic, we are powerless."

Ferran looked down the column at Luxon.

"We have a wizard," he shrugged. "I saw that young lad do the impossible at Eclin. I saw him slay a dragon, I saw him stand toe to toe with Danon and Cliria, and win."

Faramond followed the Nightblade's gaze. "He is a broken man. His mother and friend's deaths have taken the fight out of him. You can see it as plain as day. Look how his shoulders slump. I fear the weight of such responsibility is proving too much to bear for the wizard." The prince sighed heavily. "I will send riders to the other tribes and do as you say. We must unite if we are to stand a chance of surviving."

Ferran nodded. On the horizon they saw the thin plumes of smoke drifting lazily into the sky. The Keenblade camp was not far away. The long grasses of the plains swayed in the cool breeze, and small birds flitted to and fro, eating the insects that lived on the wildflowers covering every patch of earth. Ferran envied the animals, for they were not burdened with the troubles of man.

"I will ride ahead to the Watchers and warn Commander Fritin of the danger heading his way."

Faramond scoffed at the mention of the legion commander. The tribes had no love for the legion, and the feeling was mutual. Centuries of skirmishes had made them enemies.

"Perhaps the threat of Danon will be enough to allow both sides to put aside their differences," Ferran said seriously. "Only together can we hope to stop him."

The Nightblade turned his horse and rode down the column. He trotted over to Sophia and told her of his plan to ride ahead to the Watchers.

"Stay safe," Sophia said to her husband. The two embraced tightly.

"Same to you, my wife. I'll make sure the gates are open for you." He glanced at Luxon, who was staring blankly at the ground.

"Keep an eye on him," he added softly. "We're going to need him."

He kissed Sophia deeply, before spurring his horse into a gallop and riding away from the column.

The ride to the Watchers passed without incident, but Ferran did spot a group of riders from one of the plains tribes riding hard on the far horizon. The massive walls of the fortress stood strong and unbreakable on the thin peninsula that led the way into the heart of the Kingdom of Delfinnia. Banners flew on the high walls. Ferran narrowed his eyes and counted them: twenty two altogether, far more than had been flying on the previous visit. Cautiously, he rode towards the heavy iron gates, his hands at his sides to show he came in peace. High on the ramparts he spotted legionaries taking up positions. A hundred bows were no doubt being trained upon him.

He slowed his horse as the gates creaked open. Six Bloodriders charged out, their lances lowered. With expert skill, the horsemen surrounded Ferran.

"Are you alone?" the Blood Rider captain asked.

The man's clean shaved face was grim and his eyes had dark rings around them.

Ferran nodded.

"I am. My companions are a day's ride behind me. I have to talk to Commander Fritin."

The riders raised their lances.

"That might be a problem. Commander Fritin has been replaced. The Baron of Bison has taken command of the Watchers and Bison soldiers have reinforced the garrison."

Ferran's eyes widened at the news.

"Well, that's a surprise, not unwelcome but a surprise nonetheless. What brought that about?"

The Bloodriders took up formation around his horse and led the way towards the Watchers' gate.

"A lot has happened since you and your friends entered the plains," the Blood rider captain explained, his voice low. "Word reached us a day after you left that Davik, the king's regent, had been murdered. The barons of Balnor and Robinta blame Ricard of Champia for his death, and as a result raised the banner of revolt against Sunguard. King Alderlade remains in the capital; what his condition is we do not know. The Baron of Bison came here to recruit the Watchers' Legion to Ricard's cause."

Ferran slumped in the saddle. Davik had been a good friend and a good man. Now the kingdom's leaders were again at each other's throats, and judging by the grim looks on the warriors around him, civil war was on the horizon.

They passed through the gate and into a wide square which was filled with soldiers milling about. Unlike before, there were now men wearing the yellow and black surcoats of Bison, as well as the troops of the King's Legion. Ferran and the riders dismounted. He was then led over to a group of men who were laughing loudly.

Standing in the centre of the square was a thin, tall man dressed in mail armour and ornately decorated surcoat. His clean shaven long face was offset by a pair of blue eyes and a head of short grey hair. It had been years since Ferran had last met him, but Baltar of Bison was a hard man to forget. The baron was a great horseman and had led his barony for more than forty years. He was a simple man, a man who lived for a women and drink. He was not a man of courage.

"By Niveren's balls is that Ferran of Blackmoor I see before me?" the baron greeted jovially. As per usual, the baron had a tankard of mead in his hand. The redness in his cheeks showed that he'd been drinking.

"It is, Baron," Ferran replied with a bow.

"That fool, Commander Fritin told me that you and a bunch of wielders had passed this way. What on Esperia sent you out onto the Great Plains?"

Before Ferran could answer, the baron downed the contents of his mug and lobbed it across the square. The mug smacked a patrolling legionary on his helmet. Baltar and his men boomed with laughter.

"Baron, why are you here?" Ferran asked after the laughter died down.

Baltar stopped laughing, a dark expression crossing his face.

"I am here to take the garrison and march north to Robinta. I have been tasked by Regent Ricard to force Baron Rusay to reconsider his position. The wretch has halted all food exports from Robinta heading to the capital. If those supply lines are not reopened, then Sunguard will begin to starve by the end of the month."

Ferran stared at the baron, and anger swelled in him.

"Are you mad?" he shouted angrily. "You want to strip the defenders from this fortress? What if I told you that Danon himself and a vast host of Sarpi, N'gist and undead is heading this way? Niveren damn you barons and your power grabs," he added, shaking with rage.

The soldiers stopped what they were doing, and all looked at him. The colour drained from Baltar's face.

"D-Danon you say?" the baron sputtered.

Ferran grabbed the baron by his surcoat and pulled him close.

"The tribes are heading this way, and Danon's army will follow soon after. We must prepare to face him here. Send word to Sunguard. Hells, send word to every corner of the realm and tell the barons and nobles to send every warrior they can here. If we do not hold the Watchers, than Danon's host will march on Bison, then Kingsford and then the rest of the realm."

He turned to face the men that had gathered in the square,

"I have seen this evil with my own two eyes and it is coming."

He released Baltar. The baron stepped backwards, his eyes wide. For a moment it appeared that he would dismiss Ferran, but the stern expression on the Nightblade's face convinced him. The baron was a drunkard and a letch but he was also a pragmatist. For a moment he hesitated.

"If you are lying, Ferran, I will hang you from these walls myself," Baltar muttered.

Ferran shrugged.

"Why would I lie? Send for aid. Send word to Kingsford; we will need the navy. If we do not, there will nothing to stop the Sarpi from bypassing the Watchers entirely. For Niveren's sake, man, the fate of Delfinnia depends upon it."

Accadus stirred from his slumber. Wearily, he opened his eyes and sat up. In the corner of his command tent there was a shadow. For a moment he felt terror, but relaxed as the shade moved into the light.

"Are you ready, my apprentice?" the ghostly apparition of Danon asked softly.

Accadus got up from the uncomfortable travel bed and walked over to a bowl in the corner of the room. With a contented sigh he relieved himself, before turning his attention back to the shadow.

"I have been ready for two weeks, master," he replied irritably. "I trust you found what you were seeking in Stormglade?"

He'd had the border legions right where he had wanted them, but Danon's delay had forced him to withdraw and wait. His forces had destroyed all of the border forts except for the one guarding the Zulus Bridge.

"I did not," Danon said. "The wizard and his friends destroyed the sigil stone. But do not worry; I will get what I want. My forces will march upon the Watchers and you will assault the east. Together we will crush the Delfinnians, and the Sundered Crown will be yours."

Accadus smiled and rubbed his hands together. Finally, the war was about to begin.

CHAPTER TWENTY FOUR.

From his vantage point on a nearby hill, Accadus looked across the valley of Zulus. The slow moving waters of the Zulus River glittered in the noon sunlight. Normally, such a sight would have been considered beautiful. Today, however, the image was spoilt by the hordes of undead that were ambling across the fields.

On the river's far bank, the brave soldiers of the King's Legion were battling desperately to hold the Zulus Bridge, the only crossing point for hundreds of miles.

The bridge was defended by a fort and the legionaries inside. Ballistae bolts crashed into the undead and flaming arrows fell like rain. Scores of the undead collapsed to the ground or fell into the river, but most made it to the fort's walls and began to clamber up. Accadus smirked at the panic of the legion defenders.

Sharp twangs sounded as his army's catapults fired one after the other, the noise reverberating off the foothills. Massive stone projectiles arched high in the air before smashing into the fort's battered walls. Undead and legionaries were sent flying in all directions.

Accadus adjusted his chainmail gauntlets before raising his hand to signal the Sarpi forces to advance. It wouldn't be long before they battered their way inside and the road to Balnor would be open.

A horn sounded, and five thousand black clad Sarpi began to advance on the fort. The undead had done their job of thinning the number of defenders. The number of arrows lancing down from the fort was greatly reduced. The middle rank of Sarpi warriors carried long ladders which they would use to scale the forts walls. Accadus narrowed his eyes as he spotted a legionary leap onto the battlements and bellow a rallying cry to his men. The red plume on his helmet showed that he was a commander. Accadus smiled.

"Let us see how long your men's resolve will last," he muttered to himself. He kicked his heels into his horse's flank and charged down the hill towards the fort. As he drew closer he raised his hand and narrowed his eyes. He muttered an incantation and magic flowed through his body. With a cruel laugh he launched the fireball he had summoned. The deadly projectile shot from his hand and struck the legion commander. The force of the impact sent the man flying backwards out of sight, but his agonised scream could clearly be heard.

The battle raged on. But before the sun had set, the fort surrendered.

CHAPTER TWENTY FIVE.

The bells of warships tolled out over the sound of the waves lapping against the quayside. It was night, and only the small lanterns affixed to sterns indicated that there were indeed ships bobbing on the inky waters. The light of the moons and stars was hidden by thick clouds that drifted lazily in the autumn breeze. The King's Navy was at anchor in Kingsford's harbour; the high tides created by the gravity of Esperia's two moons prevented the fleet from staying out at sea.

The fleet was two hundred strong and every scrap of space in Kingsford's huge harbour was occupied by a wooden war galley. The ships' decks bristled with ballistae, grappling hook launchers and catapults. Some had barrels of fire water strapped down to the decks. The liquid was magical in nature and once it came into contact with the air, it exploded with devastating force. No deadlier weapon was available to the navy. Marines patrolled the ships' decks, but their lanterns only offered feeble light to cast back the night. If any of the soldiers could see in the dark, they would have spotted a dozen small black sailed ships taking up position at the harbour mouth. None of the ships had lanterns lit; the Sarpi sailors had no need for them. Their eyes glinted; to them the night was as clear as day.

Sintinius stood on the bow of his ship with his arms crossed and a smile on his face. Word had finally come from the master and the war had begun. The Delfinnians were unprepared, divided, and weak. He and his small fleet of ships had sailed from Retbit in the east, around the coast, and passed the isle of Zahnia undetected. The Sarpi were the masters of the night and excellent sailors. They had almost been spotted by a small fishing boat from Yundol, but before it could flee his men had sent it to the bottom of the sea.

He gestured to the ship's helmsmen to steer the ship into the harbour. Around them, the other Sarpi ships did the same. Silently, they cut through the water, the autumn winds giving them plenty of momentum. Once the small fleet was lined up and sent sailing towards the anchored fleet, the crews of the other ships jumped overboard. Sintinius held his breath at the sound of the crews hitting water. The splashes were quiet compared to the raucous noises coming from the plethora of brothels and inns that lined the quayside. No one would hear them. Eleven of the twelve ships in the Sarpi fleet had been manned by a skeleton crew of half a dozen each; only Sintinius's vessel had a full complement of sailors. He paced the deck as his men helped the other crews clamber up the hull. Once all were on board, he watched the now empty ships as they sailed on into the heart of the harbour. He waited until the first ship crashed into a much larger legion vessel. One after the other, the rest of the unmanned ships struck. He turned and nodded to the archer who moved to his side. The archer reached into his cloak and took out a firestone. He touched the magical stone to the pitch-covered arrow tip. The arrow flared brightly as the pitch caught light, and he had to look away for a moment. The archer stepped forward and drew back the bow's cord.

"Aim true and a great victory we will have here this night," Sintinius said.

The archer smiled and loosed.

The sailors stumbled out of the Buxom Wench's doors in a fit of laughter. The establishment was renowned for the beauty of its ladies and the potency of the ale it served. The three men had spent most of the evening inside enjoying the delights on offer. After all, what were sailors supposed to do when they couldn't take to the sea? Laughter, music and the sounds of giggling whores made the Kingsford quayside one of the most vibrant nightspots in the city.

"Ere, I think that bloody whore's nicked me amulet!" slurred one of the sailors.

The others laughed at him.

"She probably needed something extra after the poor effort you gave her, Maril, you dozy git."

Maril was about to slur an expletive to his friends but a light moving through the night sky caught his attention. Others quickly followed.

"What the heck is that?" Maril exclaimed, pointing at the object that was now falling towards the anchored ships.

The object landed, and the harbour exploded.

Fire ripped through the fleet as flames carried on the wind. The pitch painted onto the hulls of the Sarpi ships had done its job perfectly. Red hot fire leapt from ship to ship, and then it struck the legion vessels with the fire water tied to their decks.

A devastating explosion shattered ripped through the fleet, capsizing ships and sending the deadly, blazing liquid flying in all directions. Wherever it struck, it burnt like the surface of a thousand suns. Panicked sailors leapt into the sea to escape, but even the water itself burned.

Agonised and anguished screams of men trapped below the decks of the warships could be heard above the roaring of the flames. The fire water struck the buildings along the quayside, instantly setting them ablaze. Men and woman, both drunk and sober tried to flee, but both the sea and the ground itself were on fire. There was no escape from the horror.

The archer's aim had been perfect. Sintinius's eyes glinted in the firelight as he watched the bulk of the King's Navy reduced to splinters. With the Delfinnian fleet sinking to the bottom of the harbour, there was now nothing to stop the bulk of the Sarpi navy assaulting the city from the west.

Danon's plan was going perfectly.

CHAPTER TWENTY SIX.

A great cloud of dust rose into the sky on the westward horizon, the only sign so far that Danon's army had left Stormglade and was advancing across the plains. From the distance of the cloud, Faramond guessed that the host was only two days behind. He patted his horse affectionately and rubbed it behind its ears. The trusty animal had been with him through many battles, and he took comfort that they had both lasted this long. Behind him, and moving far too slowly for his liking, were his people. Their city camp had been dismantled and packed onto the wagons in record timing, and now all ten thousand of the Keenlance tribe were on the move. Men, women and children were all on horseback or in the backs of wagons, and riding in a great arc behind were the warriors.

A horn sounded from somewhere far to the south. Faramond shielded his eyes against the sun's glare and smiled. Another plume of dust rose into the air from that direction, signalling that one or more of the other tribes of the plains had heeded his warnings.

"They must be … what? Half a day away, judging by the speed of the wind and the height of the dust," he mused to himself.

Scouts from other tribes had hailed them earlier in the day. If all ten of the great tribes met and merged, it would mark the first horde seen in over five hundred years. Such a sight would surely bring terror to their enemies, even if that foe was Danon.

Faramond's guess had been correct. It was mid-afternoon when the vanguard of the Sigin and Delfin tribes came into view. There was a wary standoff as the three tribes approached one another, but very soon the peoples of each were all mingling together peacefully. The Sigin were a very different people from the Keenlance. For one, the warriors preferred to wear no armour, and their long curved swords were double the length of a Delfinnian broadsword. Instead of bows, they preferred to use crossbows. Their banners displaying a sword cutting through stone fluttered proudly in the breeze.

The Delfin tribe were different again. Their banners were of a slightly different design to those that flew over the battlements of Sunguard and the kingdom. Markus the Mighty had been king of the Delfin tribe before going on to conquer the Golden Empire and winning the Magic Wars. After that conflict, many of the tribe chose to settle the lands beyond the Watchers and help found the Kingdom of Delfinnia; the rest, meanwhile, had chosen to continue their nomadic existence on the Great Plains.

Luxon rode with Hannah. Normally, the sight of such an impressive gathering would have excited him, but his thoughts were dark. Hannah tried to comfort him as best she could, but the loss of his mother and best friend was still too raw. They rode behind a wagon being pulled by four large and smelly oxen. In the back was Kaiden and his family. The knight had regained consciousness, the delight of having his wife and child at his side beating the pain. The healers Grigg and Huin were also in the wagon. The old healer enthralled Alira with tales of his adventures, whilst Huin kept little Ilene happy with games.

"Do you think it will be enough?" Hannah asked quietly, shaking Luxon out of his daydreaming. He looked at her tiredly and his expression softened. Fear was etched on her face, a fear he knew all too well.

"It has to be," he replied simply. "No word has come from the other seven tribes."

"I am afraid, Luxon … I'm afraid I'll lose you; I'm afraid I'll never get to see my family again. I'm sorry," she said, looking away.

He reached over and squeezed her hand tightly.

"You won't lose me, Hannah," he said with more conviction than he felt. "One day, when all of this is over, we will visit your family in Robinta and you will show me where you grew up. I will not let Danon win. The darkness will not win,"

"Why does Danon do this?" Hannah asked, a hint of despair in her tone. "What does he want? He ruled the world once and was defeated, and yet he keeps coming back to darken everything. Is he mankind's curse?"

Luxon looked at her. What she said had struck him. In all the tomes he had read and the stories he had heard, not one of them said why Danon kept trying to enslave the world.

"The legends all say that he was one of the first men – the brother of Niveren himself. The bishops would say that because Niveren was good, so Danon was his evil counterpoint ... but there must be more to it than that. Perhaps knowing the why could be the key to defeating him?"

"If he was once just a man, than how can he still be around now?" Hannah asked.

Luxon raised an eyebrow at her and chuckled.

"Someone obviously fell asleep in lore class," he chided.

"I was never into studying lore. Dissecting things and putting things back together with my magic was much more my thing." Hannah smiled. 'It's good to see you laugh. So then, mister smartass, tell me: how can Danon still be around? I know that necromancy can extend a user's life for centuries, but not forever ... not like him."

"I remember Master Ri'ges telling us that the first men were different to us," Luxon said. "Taller, stronger and imbued with magic. Every one of them was a powerful wielder. They were also said to have been immortal."

Hannah's eyes widened in disbelief.

"When Danon turned on his brother, there was a terrible war. Neither man could outdo the other. Danon gained the upper hand by using dark magic. In order to stop the world falling to evil, Niveren prayed to the god of balance, Chiaroscuro, for aid. The god answered; horrified that balance would soon be tipped in favour of the darkness, he asked Niveren to prove he was worthy to be the Light's champion. He endured numerous trials to prove that he was worthy, but none of them were enough to convince Chiaroscuro. Eventually, when things seemed grimmest, and probably out of sheer desperation, Niveren offered his immortal soul, the greatest gift bestowed upon man by the gods. Needless to say, the offering pleased Chiaroscuro. The god took Niveren's immortality, ensuring that all of his descendants too would now be mortal. In exchange he forged a mighty weapon to slay Danon …"

Luxon paused as he thought.

"The weapon was Asphodel, wasn't it?" Hannah asked breathlessly.

Luxon smiled. Every time the sword was mentioned, people grew excited. There was a reason every good storyteller had their heroes wielding the weapon; it always got the audience's attention. Virtually every story in the Great Library mentioned the blade in some form or another.

"Yes," he replied finally.

Hannah clapped her hands together.

"See, I knew that," she said, sticking her tongue out at him.

A look of confusion crossed her beautiful face. Her dainty nose wrinkled and her wide blue eyes narrowed.

"Wait a minute … Niveren sacrificed his immortality for Asphodel, so why is Danon still around?"

"The clerics say that Niveren's mercy spared his hand. The two fought in a duel that lasted for ten days and ten nights. By the end of it, Niveren emerged the victor, but he couldn't bring himself to kill his brother. Instead, he banished him to the darkest corner of the world. Danon kept his immortality, his soul endures, and he uses his powers to possess new bodies when required. Even when Zahnia the Great banished him to Void, Danon's soul lived on, bound to this world."

"Imagine if Niveren had killed him," Hannah whispered. "Imagine what the world would be like …"

As the day progressed, more tribes merged with the Keenlancers until the number of people and horses marching east was in the tens of thousands. The sun was beginning to descend in the sky by the time the great host came into view of the Watchers. The legionaries and soldiers manning the walls offered prayers to Niveren at the sight. Commanders bellowed orders at their men to prepare the mighty fortress's defences.

Ferran and Baron Baltar watched the horde from the battlements. Sweat was visible on the baron's brow and he licked his lips nervously.

"You had better be right about this, Ferran. A tribal horde has not marched on the Watchers for over five centuries. If they come seeking war …"

"They are not here to fight, Baron. Look," Ferran replied, pointing to a small group of riders that had broken off from the horde.

Luxon's blue cloak was clearly visible. Riding with him was Faramond and Sophia.

Baltar led the way down towards the gates. The huge iron portcullis was down and hundreds of legionaries stood in formation, spears at the ready. On the battlements were archers and the crews of the ballistae that lined the walls. Further back, on the secondary wall, were the huge trebuchets that were being loaded with massive stones. The two men made their way through the gathered ranks.

"You two are a sight for sore eyes," Ferran said warmly to his wife and Luxon, who were waiting on the other side of the portcullis. Sophia kissed her husband through one of the gaps in the metal.

"I never thought that I would be happy to see this place," Faramond said.

He and the baron glared at one another. The men of Bison had little love for the tribes, for it was their people that had defended the realms' western flank and had suffered from the threat of tribal raids for eons.

"What exactly is the plan here?" the baron asked with barely concealed contempt in his voice. "Do you expect me to open the gates and allow a hundred thousand tribes people through and into the kingdom? With the troubles, there is barely enough food for our own people, let alone theirs."

"There are women and children; wounded, too. At least let them through," Faramond replied through gritted teeth. "The warriors, well, they will be needed here. Danon is coming, and from what my scouts are saying, his army is vast. Sarpi, undead, N'gist and Fell Beasts all are marching under his banner. Face it, Baron, you need us just as much as we need you."

Baltar's face visibly paled at the words. Uncertainty was in his eyes. He stared at Ferran, and then at his men who all were all looking to him for guidance.

"I should never have let you talk me into staying here, Nightblade. I ... I have orders from Ricard. I will not fail them."

Ferran closed his eyes; fear had gotten the best of the baron, he could tell. Baltar faced his men, his voice faltering.

"The men of Bison will follow the regent's orders: pack your gear, we march north ..."

Faramond scoffed. Luxon and Sophia gasped in disbelief. Ferran shook his head.

"You bloody coward. You think Ricard's schemes matter in the face of what is coming?"

Baltar stepped away from the Nightblade. The rage in Ferran's eyes was terrifying to behold.

"Watch your tone, Ferran. A baron's command is final," he stammered. The soldiers watched their leader; some were relieved that they would not be staying; others were ashamed at their lord's cowardice.

"I will not take any legionaries with me, and any of my men can stay if they so wish. I ... I am sorry," Baltar added miserably, before turning and walking away.

CHAPTER TWENTY SEVEN.

As the Bison soldiers left the Watchers through the north gate, the legion opened the southern one to allow the wounded and non-combatants from the tribes in. Commander Fritin had been released from the house arrest that Baltar had placed him under and the man was making his presence felt. The sun was now setting. From the battlements, the defenders of the Watchers looked on as the Baron of Bison fled. Legionaries hurled insults at the shamed soldiers. The sense of betrayal would not fade quickly.

Luxon and the others gathered in the tower where they had first met Faramond. The tribal leader looked grim faced and bleary eyed as he took his place. His father, the king had passed away in the night. Old age and the journey across the plains had no doubt hastened his demise. Faramond was now king of his people. No crowning ceremony had been made to make it official; there had been no time. The other men in the room offered their sympathies.

"I will have time to mourn when this is over," Faramond said. "Let's get to it."

A large round table had been placed in the centre of the central chamber and a large cloth map of the Great Plains was laid out upon it.

"So, no help is coming from that cowardly bastard Bison," Fritin growled, "and it appears that the rest of the realm is too busy ripping itself apart to care thanks to the machinations of bloody Ricard."

"Last time we met Fritin, you were all in favour of carrying out Ricard's orders ..." Ferran chided humourlessly. The commanders face flushed red in anger at the comment.

"I was only following orders," he grumbled.

Faramond gave a mocking laugh and the arguing resumed. Luxon stood at the back of the room, watching the argument unfurl. He sighed in annoyance. Was bickering all they could do? The news of Davik's murder had shocked them all. He wished Yepert was at his side; his friend would have said something to diffuse the tension or at least make him chuckle. His loss was almost too much to bear. Yepert had been at Luxon's side for years, and he knew him better than anyone else, even his mother. He wiped his eyes, angrily brushing away the tears that formed whenever he thought of her. Her loss was so raw, and yet he hadn't the time to mourn either of their deaths.

Quietly, he slipped out of the chamber and went outside. The night was cold. A frost would surely settle; winter was on the air. He tightened his cloak tighter about himself to keep out the chill, and ascended the stone steps leading up to the battlements. The view that greeted him at the top took his breath away. Thousands of campfires and tents had been erected below the Watchers' high walls. He tilted his head; the sound of lutes, drums and other music could be heard. The smell of cooking meat wafted into his nostrils, making his stomach growl. He looked down at the tribesfolk. Then he closed his eyes. If he and his friends failed to defend the fortress then all of those people would die, their bodies turned into monstrosities by the N'gist. Their homeland would be lost and Delfinnia would be open to attack. Word had arrived earlier in the night of the burning of the fleet and the raid at Kingsford. The vision he had seen of the ships and sea aflame had come to pass.

He reached into his pocket, his fingertips brushing the small leather-bound book his mother had given him. Curious, he pulled it out and opened it. Text written in an artistic manner filled the first page. He thumbed through the pages; the same handwriting was throughout. Most of the book appeared to cover the early reign of King Markus, but as he got closer towards the end, the handwriting changed. In place of the artistic style was a more rustic, harsher one. Whoever the new author was, they had written in a hurry. The writer described the death of Markus, the tone clearly showing their fury. A rant rambled on for a few more pages, until the word Asphodel caught his eye. The book described the sigil stones.

"The third stone is the final waypoint and the key to the sword ..." Luxon muttered as he read out loud.

With the second stone destroyed he had an advantage over Danon; the dark one wouldn't know where to look! He read on and frowned as he reached a page which had the word Trials written in large letters. He was about to turn the page when a horn blast sounded from the camp below. Other horns sounded until the legionaries on the battlements added their own calls to the chorus. Luxon tucked the book back into his cloak and ran to the battlements. Far below, the tribes were mustering, and warriors leapt into their saddles or donned their armour. Luxon narrowed his eyes and channelled his magic to allow him to see further. A lone horseman was trotting towards the camp. The man was slumped in the saddle, but the blue mages robe he wore was unmistakable.

"Yepert!" Luxon shouted. He ran down the steps and into the courtyard. With a gesture, he used his magic to raise the portcullis, much to the gate guards' annoyance. More horn calls sounded to signal that no danger was imminent. Luxon ran outside of the fortress; a group of Keenlance riders were leading Yepert in.

The smile on Luxon's face faltered as he saw his friends face. It was deathly pale, and dark rings were around his eyes. As he reached the gate, Yepert slid from the saddle of his mount to fall heavily onto the ground. Luxon cried out for help as he ran forward. He skidded to his knees and helped Yepert sit up. He held him tightly.

"I cannot believe you're alive!" Luxon said. 'You're going to be fine, Yep, you'll see."

He was relieved to see Hannah and Grig hurrying over to them.

"The healers will look after you."

Yepert's eyes flickered open. He smiled faintly.

"Lux ... I'm hungry," he said before falling into unconsciousness.

The Keenblade scout watched in horror at the army appeared before him. Faramond had sent riders back west to keep an eye on Danon's forces. The Great Plain was filled with black-clad warriors, their eyes shining in the darkening sky. Marching behind them were hundreds of cloaked figures, carrying no weapons except for long staffs. They were the N'gist. Behind them were thousands of armoured warriors, and the moans of the undead carried on the cold air. The ground shook, and the scout's horse reared in fright. Lumbering behind the army were four mighty Gargantuans. The massive Fell Beasts were accompanied by a tide of smaller creatures. The scout got his mount under control before raising a small telescope to his eye. His heart sank as the small creatures became clear. Goblins marched and pucks swarmed.

"Niveren save us ... the Void marches against us!" the scout cried before kicking his heels into his horse's flanks. He rode with all haste back towards the Watchers.

Luxon glanced around at the other people in the Watchers command room. Each of them was grim-faced at the news the Keenblade scouts had brought upon their return. Commander Fritin rubbed his eyes tiredly, his expression grim. The room was located at the heart of the fortress and in its centre was a large circular stone table, upon which lay a map of the surrounding area. The map itself was covered in marks and doodles where the legion commander had been trying to formulate a strategy.

"The magic of the N'gist we may have been able to resist, but an army of Fell Beasts ... how is it even possible that Danon can command such a force?"

Luxon sat back in his chair as the others began to debate their next moves. Since Yepert's return, he had divided his time between caring for his friend and reading the books in the ancient fortress's library. He had learned that the walls of the Watchers had been protected by magic runes carved into the stonework by the men who had built them. In the age when the fortress had been constructed, magic users had been far more common and just as dangerous. In those days, even the tribes had skilled war wizards in their ranks. His research had also revealed a potential weakness.

Fritin was now in a heated argument with Faramond, who was arguing that his people should be allowed to flee through the fortress gates. Ferran was slumped in his chair, his eyes staring into an empty wine glass. Luxon sighed. They were all afraid. He, too, was terrified but his fear had now been replaced by a burning anger, an anger that demanded that they fight, that they make a stand against the one who sought to bring so much death to the world. He had already lost his mother; he would not lose anyone else.

He channelled the anger in his heart and slowly stood.

"Enough of this bickering," he growled. Using magic, he enhanced his voice so that it sounded far more powerful and authoritative. The men fell silent and stared at him in surprise.

Luxon pointed at the map on the table.

"To answer your question, Commander, Danon gained mastery of Fell Beasts whilst he was trapped in the Void. He slew and absorbed the god Vectrix's power, giving himself that ability. The attacks made by Fell Beasts across the realm these past few years have no doubt been his doing. Make no mistake, gentlemen, we have been at war with the monster since Eclin – we just didn't realise it."

Fritin looked way, unable to meet the wizard's fierce gaze. Luxon looked at the other two; they, too, could not look him in the eye. He knew that they had thought him broken by the death of his mother. He would show them otherwise; the anger would show them otherwise.

"The walls are still protected by the runes carved into the stone work," he explained, moving his fingers over the map. The others watching closely. "Any magic that the N'gist use should be dispelled before it even reaches them. Which means that we should prepare for a conventional assault. As for the Fell Beasts, they will be kept at bay by the rune stone in the fortress's courtyard, which means that Danon's warriors will have to get over the walls to destroy it. If they succeed, then the Gargantuans can get close enough to bring the walls down."

"There is a flaw in your assessment, wizard," Fritin intervened. He pointed to a section of wall. "This section of wall is not protected by runes. About two-hundred years ago it was brought down by a tribal attack, the first and only time the walls of this fortress have ever been breached. The men who repaired it were not as skilled as those who had come before; there are no runes carved into its surface."

"What's the betting Danon already knows that fact?" Ferran growled.

Luxon thrust his finger at the map and fixed each man with a stern gaze.

"Then this is where he will strike. We have to be ready, or we will all die."

CHAPTER TWENTY EIGHT.

Roiling black clouds filled the sky and a heavy persistent rain began to pour. An eerie silence, which the rain now filled, had descended over the Watchers as its defenders watched in petrified awe. The army of Danon had appeared on the horizon. Luxon, Ferran and Sophia stood on the battlements; they all had their hoods up to ward off the downpour.

The previous night had been one of little rest for all of them. Preparations for the coming battle had kept them from their beds.

"So, this is it then," Ferran said softly. The Nightblade squeezed Sophia's hand tightly.

"Our plan is a good one," Sophia replied. "We will hurt Danon this day,"

Luxon almost snorted. The host before them was far larger than he had feared, and the number of defenders was feeble in comparison. Five thousand legionaries, a few dozen Bison volunteers and the tribes were matched against the might of twenty thousand Sarpi warriors, thousands of magic wielding N'gist and countless scores of undead and Fell Beasts.

Kaiden, Alira and little Ilene had left overnight; the knight's wounds meant that he could play no part in the coming fight. He had protested at leaving his friends to fight without him at their side, but Hannah and Sophia had convinced him to go. The prisoners they had rescued from Stormglade had also fled. They had all said their teary goodbyes, and now Kaiden and his family were heading north to the safety of Caldaria. Huin and Grigg had agreed to accompany them, but Hannah had refused to go despite Luxon's pleading. She was as stubborn as a mule.

Luxon's thoughts returned to the scene before him, as the legion's trumpets opened up in a fanfare of noise. Far below on the plains, the warriors of the tribes leaped into their saddles. Six thousand mounted warriors formed into a massive wedge-shaped formation. The tribal warriors fought best on horseback and their skill with the bow was only matched by those of rangers and Witch Hunters. A horn call blew, and the force of cavalry galloped towards Danon's forces, which were still forming up on the plain before the fortress. Luxon licked his lips in anticipation. Danon's army remained out of range of the Watchers formidable defences but that didn't stop the legionaries loading the trebuchets and ballistae.

Leading the tribes' charge was Faramond, resplendent in his armour. Hundreds of war horns sounded, and the sound of tens of thousands of hooves pounding upon the ground was like thunder. From their vantage point on the walls, the defenders roared encouragement to the tribal warriors. Bursting out of the citadel and riding hard to join the charge were the Bloodriders, the elite unit's blood-red cloaks billowing out behind them. Upon seeing them, the legionaries manning the walls cheered.

The first phase of the battle was about to begin.

CHAPTER TWENTY EIGHT.

Faramond led the charge. The enemy drew closer terrifyingly quickly as the horses thundered forwards. He raised his right hand into the air and balled it into a fist. The rider at his side put a horn to his lips and blew a low mournful tone. Immediately, the horde unshouldered their bows and notched arrows. As one they pulled back their bowstrings and loosed. The sky darkened as the deadly projectiles flew towards the enemy. Faramond watched to see what would happen, all the while charging onwards. As he suspected, the centre of the enemy formation was comprised of the N'Gist. Magical barriers were raised, vaporising the arrows before they even got close. He raised his arm again, but this time he rotated his wrist. The horde of riders broke into three. He led the centre block, whilst the left was commanded by the Delfin King and the right by the Bloodriders.

Narrowing his eyes, he picked a target and lowered his lance. The riders around him loosed another volley of arrows, before they too shouldered their bows and switched to the long deadly spears. The force attacking on the right flank had slowed their charge and had begun to shoot arrow after arrow into the werewolves and undead that were moving quickly towards them. On the left, the Bloodriders smashed into the ranks of Fell Beasts. Goblins astride great war boars clashed with the cavalry, and pucks swarmed trying to drag the warriors from their mounts. The sound of clashing steel and the whistling of thousands of arrows was almost deafening. Directly ahead, ranks of Sarpi had advanced in front of the magic users, long pikes in their hands. Faramond yelled to the riders behind him, with expert skill they lowered their lances and reached for the javelins fixed to their saddles. As they sped closer, they threw the heavy weapons with all of their might. Dozens of Sarpi were felled by the barrage, allowing Faramond and his group to smash with full force into the Sarpi ranks. His lanced impaled a shrieking Sarpi and sent it flying backwards. His lance now useless, Faramond drew his sword and set about hacking at the enemy. His blade cut down two more Sarpi, and then the rest of the tribe struck. The cavalry charge was devastating and for a brief moment it looked as though the Sarpi would break there and then. That hope was soon dashed when a group of N'gist strode forward, raised their staffs and unleashed magical fire at the riders. Faramond cried out as flames engulfed his companions, the heat forcing his horse to rear backwards, almost sending him falling from the saddle. He dug his heels into his mount's side and turned away from the fire. The other horsemen did likewise. With their backs turned, they were now vulnerable to a counter attack. Faramond swore as he watched several riders plucked from their saddles by telekinetic magic. The fallen men crashed to the ground and were then speared to death by the vengeful Sarpi.

As he looked behind, he could see that the charge had made little impact on the massed ranks of the enemy. The Delfin charge on the left was already fleeing in disarray. Snarling werewolves were ripping apart horses and men. The moans of the undead grew louder as they gorged themselves. To the right, the Bloodriders had slain hundreds of Fell Beasts with their silver swords, but it still was nowhere near enough.

With a reluctant sigh, he signalled the general retreat, it was a foolish hope that one great charge would win the day. Horns sounded and the surviving riders fled back to the Watchers. The main gates swung open, and as they did so the werewolves and undead surged forward. Faramond rode for his life. He could hear the wolves bounding after him, he could smell the undead. The safety of the Watchers grew closer, and as it did so the mighty fortress's weapons opened up. Deadly ballistae bolts carved their way through the ranks of undead, silver tipped arrows fell like rain to cut down scores of werewolves, and the great trebuchets launched massive boulders which crushed anything they landed upon.

Faramond sighed in relief as his horse passed under the gates. The portcullis was dropped and legionaries ran forward to slam the huge doors closed after him.

He looked around the courtyard to see the other survivors. A few hundred had made it back to the safety of the fortress: a few hundred out of thousands. He slide from his saddle and angrily removed his helmet. His anger softened when he saw the burns his horse had suffered. He whispered soothingly into the beast's ear and rubbed its snout reassuringly. The animal snickered and stamped its feet.

"If you're telling me that was a really stupid thing to do, I agree," he said softly. He waved over one of the legion stable hands. "Take care of his wounds and then get out of here; the evacuation of non-combatants will start very soon."

All the while, the fortress's defences continued to fire. The deafening crack of the trebuchets and the twanging of the ballistae continued.

Then a war horn blared; a horn that belonged to the enemy.

Luxon stood alongside Sophia and Ferran on the battlements of the Watchers' outer wall. The cavalry charge had achieved its purpose of slowing down the enemy advance. Behind them, hurrying out of the main gates, were the non-combatants and wounded. Messengers had been dispatched to Sunguard and the baronies to warn them that Danon's army had launched its war. Due to the Watchers' remote location, the battle would likely be over before any of the riders reached their destinations. The warriors that had survived the charge were now hurrying to positions on the walls, Faramond among them. The tribal prince held his sword high, shouting words of encouragement to his people.

Ferran gripped his wife's hand tightly as the first wave of undead charged the walls. Siege engines were being pulled through the ranks of Sarpi. Tall towers made of wood and steel rumbled forward on massive wheels. The towers were being pulled forward by what appeared to be slaves. Ferran watched the attack through his spyglass. Sure enough the rope pullers were chained together, the unfortunate former citizens of Stormglade. Those who had been killed and brought back as undead had been turned into Danon's slaves.

"Danon must know that the walls are protected by runes," Luxon said, pointing to the catapults that were being moved into position. The Watchers' defences continued to fire into the advancing undead hordes, the moans of the zombies was growing louder by the second.

Anger filled Luxon. So much death had been caused because of the evil that filled the plains before them. He tightened his grip on Dragasdol and began to walk along the battlements. Ferran and Sophia hurried after him.

"Luxon, you know the plan," Ferran called from behind him. "We cannot risk you overexerting yourself too soon, if you suffer from another attack of the Void sickness …"

Luxon slowed and sighed; the Nightblade was right.

The undead had reached the base of the walls and had now begun to clamber over each other to try and reach the terrified soldiers manning the battlements. Volleys of flaming arrows slammed into the shambling horde, cutting down hundreds. Panicked shouts caught their attention. Werewolves had successfully scaled the walls of the western flank. Legionaries drew their silver swords and rushed to counter the threat. Luxon winced as he watched a werewolf lunge over the crenulations, grab a terrified legionary and hurl him over the side. More wolves were cresting the battlements; more legionaries fell to claws and fangs.

"I have to help them," Ferran growled. He turned to Sophia and kissed her deeply. "Stay safe, stay alive ... I love you," he said before summoning his tourmaline blade to life and leaping over the battlements. As he fell, he used his magic to slow his descent. He landed safely and sprinted towards the fight, his blade slashing as he went.

The stone beneath their feet shook as the first of the enemy catapults launched a boulder the size of a small hut against the walls. Debris and dust exploded outwards from the impact site. More boulders smashed against the fortress, leaving scars upon the once pristine stonework. Hand to hand fighting had now broken out on the outer walls as the undead climbed. Silver swords glinted in the sunlight, blood sprayed, zombies moaned, men screamed and shouted. It was carnage. Over the noise came another horn blast. This time the black-armoured Sarpi began to move forwards. Some of the warriors carried long ladders which they could use to scale the walls.

"Look!' Luxon shouted. "The Sarpi are advancing on the weak spot. Danon is betting that the undead and his other horrors will weaken the defences there."

"It seems to be working," Sophia replied. Sure enough, the defenders were already being stretched thin. The undead were attacking all along the outer wall.

"C'mon, we have to do something."

They hurried down the stone steps and pushed their way through the soldiers manning the inner wall. Luxon shouted at them to follow him. The legionaries hesitated, but the tribal warriors immediately hurried after him. They would follow the wizard anywhere and they were eager to take the fight to the enemy. As they moved through the inner gate and passed the rune stone which was keeping the Fell Beasts at bay, more soldiers joined them. Commander Fritin had ordered several hundred men to hold the inner wall, but what use were they if the enemy breached the outer defences so soon?

They reached the wall just as the first Sarpi ladders appeared. Already, black-clad warriors were rapidly climbing. Luxon ran forward and, using Dragasdol, shoved the ladder off the wall. He leaned over the crenulations and smiled as the ladder crashed into the advancing enemy. Sophia began to shoot arrows into the Sarpi ranks, her arrows quickly being joined by those of the tribesmen that had accompanied them. Luxon glanced to his left. He spotted Ferran's tourmaline blade flashing; the undead were slowly being pushed back. All the while, the Watchers' Ballistae continued to fire. A cheer sounded from one of the weapon crews as a bolt decapitated one of the siege towers that was drawing ever closer. A shout of warning prompted Luxon to duck. A Sarpi had appeared at the wall, his sword narrowly missing Luxon's head. Luxon raised his hand and blasted his attacker backwards with telekinesis. The Sarpi screamed as he went flying off the wall. Another Sarpi appeared and leapt at him. Luxon raised his staff to deflect the sword blow that was aimed at his heart. The blade clanged loudly as it struck the dragon-fire-enchanted wood. An arrow whistled past Luxon's ear and hit the Sarpi in the face. Sophia nodded to him; Luxon thanked her. More and more Sarpi were beginning to crest the battlements, as over a dozen ladders successfully latched themselves to the wall. Luxon moved from ladder to ladder, using his staff and his power to send them tumbling from the wall. Fireballs, lightning, wind – he used all of the destruction spells he could think of as he went. He could feel the power surging within him as he fought. His staff whirled around him as he gave into his instincts. He parried and lashed out with his staff; the fight was a blur, and he moved by instinct, letting the magic and the anger flow through him. Thanos had always told him to keep control. Why? He could feel himself losing control, and it felt glorious. He was aware of the soldiers battling around him, but it felt like a blur. As he fought, he felt invincible. He brought his staff upwards and roared. Lightning split the sky and thunder blew men off of their feet.

"Luxon!"

Someone yelled his name. It sounded like Sophia; there was fear in her tone. He ignored it.

He continued to fight. He could feel himself laughing manically as he slaughtered his way through his enemies. His mother's face flashed into his mind's eye and his rage was renewed. It felt like molten hot lava coursing through his veins; it was painful, but it was glorious. He felt himself leap onto the battlements and then jump. With power coursing through him, he landed right in the middle of the Sarpi ranks. He could sense their surprise, their fear. He moved at impossible speed, his staff whirling. He sensed the staff connecting with the enemy, he felt the flames that poured from its end to engulf and incinerate. He bellowed with laughter as the Sarpi fled from his wrath.

If he could see himself he would not have been laughing. His skin had turned deathly pale, his eyes had turned black and his sandy blond hair was now white as snow. Black tendrils emanated from his body and thick black veins ran up his neck. Behind him, he could hear screams. Was someone calling to him? Calling for him to stop?

CHAPTER TWENTY NINE.

Yepert could hear the sounds of battle, and he was afraid. He still felt weak, but he couldn't just sit by and let his friends fight without him. Ferran had told him to wait inside the fortress's main keep and be ready to run if the battle went ill. Running to and fro around him were the boys of the legion. Most were no older than ten; all looked afraid but at the same time they were determined not to fail in their duty. Yepert apologised as a lad shoved past him carrying quivers full of arrows. Other boys hauled buckets of water, satchels of food or swords; all were hurrying to the frontline. Without the boys resupplying them, the legionaries would quickly run out of ammunition, or collapse from hunger and exhaustion.

"Do something useful or get out the way!" yelled one of the boys.

Yepert apologised again and ducked back into the small room where he had been recuperating. Dust fell from the rafters as a stone hurled by one of the enemy catapults struck the keep. Some of the boys cried out, but most carried on with their tasks in nervous silence.

He closed the door and sat heavily on the bed. A wave of weariness almost overwhelmed him. His head hadn't been right since that night outside Stormglade. He had wracked his brain trying to remember what had happened, how he had made it back to the Watchers, but it was all a blur.

Yepert!

He jump in fright at a whispering voice.

"Who's there?" he stammered.

I have a task for you, Yepert, the eerie voice rasped.

Yepert stood up. He looked wildly around the room, desperate to find the source of the voice.

He cried out as a sharp stabbing pain lanced his brain. He staggered and fell onto the floor with a thud. The pain grew worse.

Do not fight me, boy. It is useless to resist.

Yepert tried to move, but couldn't. Terror gripped him as a familiar shadow appeared in the corner of the room. He tried to scream as a black hand reached for him.

The battle raged all around. On the walls, the men of the legion and the tribes fought with desperate determination to hold off the enemy. The sounds of clashing steel, the cries of the wounded and dying, and the thunder of siege weapons firing was near deafening. Yepert staggered out of the keep, his head spinning. He moved clumsily as though drunk, but the reality was far worse. In his mind, he was screaming. He couldn't control his movements; a malevolent power was using him like a puppet. He tried to resist, but it was hopeless; the dark power that was controlling him was far too strong. It was as though he were looking out through the eyes of a stranger as he moved. The body of a tribesman crashed onto the ground in front of him, a Sarpi arrow sticking out of his torso. Yepert wanted to turn and run back to the safety but his legs would not do as he wanted. He staggered down the stone steps which led from the outer walls and into the central courtyard. Wounded men covered every scrap of ground, and healers moved amongst them doing their best to ease their suffering. The boys of the legion ran back and forth as they did their best to resupply the archers on the battlements. Yepert's head jerked around against his will until his gaze settled upon the tall black stone that stood in the centre of the courtyard. It was the sigil stone. Panic filled Yepert as he realised what the dark power intended to do. He tried to shout a warning, but no one paid him any heed. The stone was defenceless; no one expected an attack from inside the citadel. His legs began to move him towards the stone. To anyone watching, he would have looked comical, like a drunk who was passed the point of no return. He pushed his way through the wounded until he reached the base of the stone. A heat began to build inside him. He knew it was magic, but it was a magic far greater than he had ever felt before. Desperately, he tried to stop his arms from rising. Sweat poured from his head and his limbs quivered.

I will not let you do this! he shouted in his mind.

A mocking laughter replied.

You are nothing boy. You are my tool, my weapon, my agent, my slave, a harsh voice roared.

Yepert felt a fear the likes of which he had never felt before. The voice was full of rage and scorn. It was full of an ancient and bitter hatred. It was the voice of Danon himself.

Watch as you bring ruin to your friends and your world, the voiced mocked.

Yepert screamed as his hands touched the stone. The heat he had felt now surged through his body and into the stone. It was a dark power, a terrible ancient magic. The sigils etched onto the stone began to glow red. The glow grew and grew until the whole stone began to shine like a beacon. Around him, Yepert could hear shouts of alarm from the soldiers nearby.

The stone shattered in a blinding flash.

The world went black.

CHAPTER THIRTY.

Ferran was sent flying forwards by the force of the magical explosion. He fell against the battlements, and only the strong grip of a legionary keeping him from tumbling over the side and into the swarm of undead below. He shook his head to clear it; the deafening sound of the blast was ringing in his ears. All along the wall, soldiers were staggering to their feet or lying unconscious on the ground. Panic gripped him as clawed hands began to grab at his leather armour, trying to pull him over the wall. The foul breath of a zombie filled his nostrils as it moved to take a bite of his shoulder. The legionary tried to hold on, but unless Ferran could free himself from the foul creatures grasp he would lose his grip. The Nightblade looked around desperately, his tourmaline sword had been torn from his grasp by the explosion. With the wall's defenders temporarily stunned, the undead swarmed over the crenulations. Further along the wall, they breached the line. The cries of the defenders carried on the wind as the undead began to devour them. Ferran cried out as he spotted his sword. He raised his hand and used his magic to call the weapon to it. The hilt landed in his palm. He reached behind him and placed it against the snarling zombies head. With a snap-hiss, the magical blade sprung to life and went straight through the beast's skull. Immediately, the strong grip that had threatened to pull him over the battlements eased. The zombie tumbled backwards into the mass of other undead.

With the pressure gone, he stumbled to his feet, his ears still ringing. He gasped as his eyes settled on the carnage in the courtyard below. The sigil stone was gone, replaced by a huge crater. His eyes grew wide, there was now nothing to stop the Fell Beasts from attacking. He spun around: sure enough goblins and pucks began to advance upon the Watchers. Horns sounded warnings along the walls as the defenders spotted the new threat. The soldiers on Ferran's stretch of wall rallied and returned to their grim task of holding the walls. From the panic in their eyes, he knew it would not be long before they broke and fled.

He swore as the ground began to tremble. On the horizon, and approaching fast, were three Gargantuans. The massive Fell Beasts would soon reach the walls and smash them to pieces.

"Ferran!"

Faramond was moving quickly towards him. The king of the Keenlance tribe was smeared with dirt and blood. His armour was covered in scratches and his helmet was battered.

"Ferran. Thank Niveren you're still alive," the king panted. "The sigil stone is gone. I know not how, but there is nothing to stop the Fell Beasts from attacking. That coward Fritin is calling for a retreat to the inner keep ..."

The king stopped talking, his jaw dropping as he spotted the three massive monsters lumbering towards them. His eyes grew wide with fear before he regained control of his emotions. He was a king; he could not show weakness in front of his people.

"The rune stone is destroyed; it won't be long before the outer wall is completely overrun," Ferran replied. "A fighting retreat to the inner wall may be for the best."

He pointed to the inner wall. "That wall is taller and narrower. Its height could give us an advantage over the Gargantuans and will be easier to defend then the outer wall. Tell your warriors to heed Fritin's command. Danon has won this round," he added bitterly.

Another blast of lightning split the sky, and both men turned to face the western side of the wall.

"Luxon ..."

"By Niveren, what is the fool doing?" Faramond shouted as he spotted the young wizard. "He's gone mad!"

Sure enough, Luxon was at the base of the wall and facing down the Sarpi army. Fire, lightning and other deadly magic poured from his staff and fingers.

"Even with his powers, he can't keep that up forever," shouted Ferran.

The Nightblade broke into a run, with Faramond close behind. They pushed their way past struggling defenders and foes. As they hurried through the melee, Faramond shouted the retreat to his warriors. Legion horns blared to signal the same.

Ferran glanced to his left as he ran. The eastern wall was lost, of that there was no doubt. The plains before the fortress were teeming with snarling goblins and pucks, which began to clamber up the stonework. The undead and werewolves were now climbing over the battlements. What defenders were left turned tail and fled as they fast as they could towards the Watchers' inner wall. Archers now took up positions on the higher wall. The ballistae in the towers that ran along its length were re-aimed to fire down into the ward which lay between the fortress's two curtain walls. The ward quickly became a killing ground.

Finally, Ferran and Faramond reached the west wall. Rallying the walls defenders was Sophia, a look of panic on her blood-stained face. A great sense of relief filled Ferran as he saw that his wife was unharmed. She spotted him and hurried into his arms.

"Praise Niveren you're safe," she whispered into his ear.

Ferran eased the embrace and looked into his wife's eyes.

"The outer wall will soon be overrun. Get these men to safety."

"What about Luxon? He ... he jumped over the wall. I've never seen anything like it. Such rage."

The stone beneath their feet shook violently as a volley of fireballs launched by the advancing N'gist struck the vulnerable part of the wall. Danon was now free to bring his own magic users into the fray. Against such odds, Luxon could not win.

"He's lost control. I'll get him," Ferran yelled over the din.

Sophia kissed him deeply. She then turned and joined Faramond in shouting orders at the outer wall's remaining defenders.

Ferran's mind raced. Somehow he had to make a thirty foot drop, grab Luxon and get to safety. He looked around desperately before his gaze settled upon a nearby ballistae tower. The weapons crew was preparing to abandon their position. He broke into a run and sprinted up the tower's curved staircase to the summit. The ballistae crew cried out in surprise as he burst out onto the weapon's platform. His black armour and stern expression gave him an imposing appearance.

Ferran smiled as he spotted the long coiled rope that lay next to the ballistae.

"Attach the rope to the ballistae," he ordered.

The guards hesitated; their desire to flee was obvious.

"Do it and then go."

The soldiers nodded and began to hastily attach the rope. In the event of a conventional siege, the ballistae crews would attach thick ropes to specially designed heavy iron-tipped bolts and fire them at approaching siege towers. The crews would then hit a lever that would attempt to pull the rope back in. The weight of the bolt and the momentum of the rope being withdrawn would then hopefully cause the siege tower to wobble, and in some cases pull it over entirely. The broken remains of a Sarpi tower further down the wall was a testament to the success of the strategy.

"Rope attached, sir," the ballistae crew's captain said after a few moments.

"Good. Get out of here; fall back to the inner wall."

The crew hurried off down the tower's curved staircase.

Ferran looked out over the battlefield. It was utter carnage. To his right, the tribal warriors were engaged in a vicious fighting retreat against Sarpi who were now pouring over the walls. To his left, the legion had formed a shield wall and was fending off swarming Fell Beasts and undead. Their bravery was allowing their comrades to flee to the safety of the inner wall. Below him he could see Luxon. The wizard was out of control. He had erected a magical shield that the N'gist were now hammering at with volleys of their own deadly power. It wouldn't be long before Luxon exhausted himself; rage can only sustain a man for so long, after all.

Ferran gripped the ballistae and swung the heavy weapon around so that it was aimed at the next stone tower over. He drew his tourmaline blade and summoned it to life. Narrowing his eyes, he estimated distances. If he was going to pull off this mad idea, he couldn't afford to make any mistakes.

Satisfied that the ballistae was aimed correctly, he pulled the firing lever. The weapon kicked like a mule as it fired out the heavy bolt, the rope unfurling behind it. The bolt pierced the stonework of the targeted tower and embedded itself securely. The rope was now taught behind it.

"Here goes," Ferran muttered. He climbed onto the edge of the tower and carefully grabbed hold off the rope. Uttering a prayer to Niveren, he cut the rope free of the ballista.

Below him, Luxon was being forced backwards by the N'gist. The wizard was staggering under the assault. If Ferran didn't act soon, he would surely perish. Ferran jumped.

At first he fell straight downwards. For a moment he felt panic, but then the rope snagged and he began to swing. In one great arc he went, the ground approaching at an alarming rate. Wind whistled in his ears as he fell, drowning out the sounds of battle.

"Luxon!" Ferran roared.

The wizard glanced up in surprise. His skin was deathly pale and his hair was once again sandy blond; fear had replaced the rage in his eyes. With his right hand, Ferran gripped the rope tighter, and with his left he reached for Luxon. The two came together with a thud, but the momentum of the swing was enough to lift them back into the air. Ferran's left arm wrapped tightly about Luxon's waist. Sarpi arrows whistled passed them and he could feel the heat of the N'gist magical attacks passing close by.

Ferran had calculated correctly.

The rope's momentum carried them higher until they reached the top of the other tower. At the height of the arc, he pulled on the rope to swing them about the tower's peak. Then he let go. For a brief moment they flew like birds, before crashing onto the top of the tower in a tangle of limbs. The wind was knocked out of them both by the impact.

Ferran sat up and laughed. He'd done it!

His joy was replaced by concern as he looked at Luxon. The wizard was shivering and his eyes were full of tears. Ferran helped his friend up.

"Can you walk?" he asked.

Now that Luxon was no longer a barrier to their advance, the bulk of the Sarpi army surged forward. The N'gist concentrated their magic, and within moments a huge hole was blasted into the citadel's outer wall. Frantic legion horns blared to signal the retreat. If they didn't hurry, they would be trapped. Luxon nodded to indicate that he could walk. Ferran threw one of the wizard's arms over his shoulder and hurried down the tower's curved staircase. At the bottom, he peered out into the courtyard. So far, the enemy hadn't overrun the area. They hurried as quickly as they could across the courtyard and up a flight of stone steps. A metal door was built into the base of the inner wall. He banged on the door with a fist. A few seconds went by before the door opened with a screeching of metal. Sophia stood in the doorway.

"You crazy bastard," she said.

"Yeah, well it worked didn't it?" Ferran replied with a smirk.

Sophia helped him with Luxon, before slamming the heavy door shut and bolting it closed.

Together they moved down a passageway, before once again ascending a tall curving staircase. At the top they came to another door which led out into keep of the fortress. Soldiers hurried to and fro to help the wounded arriving from the outer wall.

Commander Fritin was at the centre of the chaos. A bloodied bandage was wrapped about his head, but the commander was still bellowing orders to his men.

"Close the bloody gates!" he roared.

Legionaries ran forward to carry out his orders.

"Sir, we still have people out there," called one of the soldiers.

Fritin strode over to the solider.

"If we don't shut the gates we all die. Do as I command. We will just have to beg for Niveren's forgiveness ... if we survive this."

CHAPTER THIRTY ONE.

Danon watched the battle unfolding with a smirk on his face. The defenders had fought bravely, just like they always did. He had to give it to the mortals, they fought for every moment of time that they could get. He had seen it thousands of years ago and he was witnessing it again now. Some things never change.

Standing next to him was a Sarpi general. They were loyal subjects; they had never wavered in their devotion to him, despite the punishments suffered for doing so. Whilst the other civilisations of man had favoured his brother Niveren as a god, the Sarpi had remained loyal to Danon. In some ways they shared a lot in common. Both had been cast out; both had been abandoned by the light.

"Send my men in, my lord," the general hissed. "Let us show you our devotion,"

Danon smiled wickedly. Yes, they were truly his. His one success. He would not stop until the world of men were as loyal to him as they. When that happened, Niveren's failure would be complete. They would fall to their knees before him or they would die. He would show them that Niveren's great sacrifice had been for nothing.

"No. I know how devoted you and your kin are to me. I will send in the gargantuans. Let the Delfinnians see the power at my command."

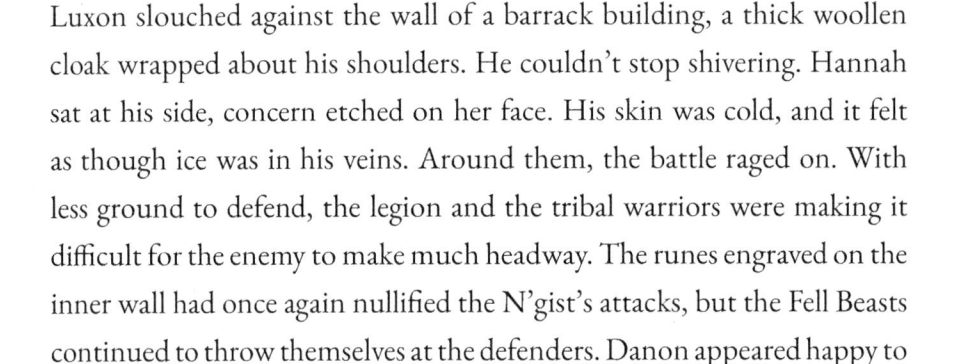

Luxon slouched against the wall of a barrack building, a thick woollen cloak wrapped about his shoulders. He couldn't stop shivering. Hannah sat at his side, concern etched on her face. His skin was cold, and it felt as though ice was in his veins. Around them, the battle raged on. With less ground to defend, the legion and the tribal warriors were making it difficult for the enemy to make much headway. The runes engraved on the inner wall had once again nullified the N'gist's attacks, but the Fell Beasts continued to throw themselves at the defenders. Danon appeared happy to keep the Sarpi and N'gist in reserve and let his monsters do the bulk of the fighting. If the Watchers fell, he would have more than enough warriors to launch a full scale invasion of Delfinnia.

Hannah looked up as Ferran approached them.

"I've tried everything I know," Hannah said despairingly. "My magic is not having any effect on him."

Ferran knelt down before Luxon, removed one of his gloves and placed his now bare hand to the wizard's forehead. It was icy cold. He closed his eyes and sighed.

"It is the Void sickness. By losing control like he did, the sickness has intensified. It is like a poison that needs to be drained. This is far beyond our powers to heal."

Hannah wiped the tears from her eyes.

"There must be something we can do, some way to help him," she said, her voice quivering.

Ferran swore under his breath. Their entire strategy had depended on Luxon's power. Without him able to fight, there was nothing to match Danon. Hannah cried out as the ground shook violently. It shook again and again; it sounded like a giant's footsteps.

"What is that?" Hannah asked, fear in her voice.

Ferran looked to walls. Panicked shouts came from the defenders and a horn sounded in warning, its note low and ominous.

Running footsteps approached. It was Faramond and Sophia.

"So Danon has sent in the gargantuans," Faramond said softly. "Three gargantuans."

The moment Ferran had dreaded had arrived. He stood up slowly, loosened his limbs and took the tourmaline blade off his belt.

"This is a fight that only a Nightblade has a chance of winning," he said darkly.

He reached into his tunic and fingered the three vials that were securely tucked inside. Kaiden had used one in Stormglade. If Ferran had known that he would be facing so many Fell Beasts, he would have packed a lot more.

"I won't let you face them alone," Sophia said sternly. Ferran smiled at his wife.

"I wasn't going to stop you. I'm going to need all the help I can get. One would be bad enough, but three?"

Faramond looked at them both as though they were mad, before laughing.

"You are crazy. I will do what I can to help you bring down those monsters," he chuckled.

Luxon tried to talk, but his words came out slurred. Hannah gripped his hand tightly.

Ferran crouched down in front of his friend.

"Hannah will look after you, Luxon. Don't worry about us, we've been in tighter spots than this." He looked at Hannah. "Get him inside. If the walls fall, flee and do not look back."

Hannah wiped her eyes again and nodded.

"We will," she promised.

The ground shook again and a deafening roar split the sky. The sound was so loud that they had to clamp their hands over their ears. On the walls, the men of the legion cried out in fear; only the stern shouts of their commanders stopped them from fleeing. Ferran nodded to his companions before turning and running towards the walls. His tourmaline blade was lit and ready. Close behind him, Faramond drew his sword and Sophia unsheathed the deadly curved daggers at her belt. They ran up the steps and shouldered their way through the soldiers manning the battlements. Sophia gasped as the view before her took her breath away.

Fell Beasts swarmed like ants in the Watchers' ward as they sought a way to attack the men defending the inner wall. Arrows rained down upon them, cutting down scores at a time. Huge chunks of the outer wall had collapsed where the Sarpi siege weapons and N'gist magic had done their work. Sarpi archers had scaled the outer wall and were now exchanging fire with the defenders on the inner wall. Sophia ducked as a Sarpi arrow whistled passed. Another part of the outer wall exploded outwards as one of the gargantuans smashed through it. The beast was massive; its armoured head shook violently from side to side and, again, a deafening roar filled the air.

Sophia, Ferran and Faramond skidded to halt and ducked behind the crenulations. This was the first time Sophia had even seen one of the monsters. She peaked over the side. The creature was now lumbering into the ward on four tree-trunk-sized legs. Armoured plates covered the entirety of its body and spiny growths grew through the gaps. Its huge head was the shape of a hammer's head and covered in red plates. Its eyes were yellow, and its vast mouth was full of razor sharp teeth. A long barbed tongue like that of a snake flicked out like a whip.

Ballistae bolts lanced towards the beast, the heavy iron bolts bouncing harmlessly off of its armour. Cries came from behind. Sophia turned just as another of the behemoths smashed through the outer wall. Debris flew in all directions and a cloud of dust enveloped the ward between walls.

Ferran pointed to the first of the gargantuans.

"We take this one first," he yelled over the din. The others nodded in agreement.

The monster had reached the base of the inner wall and began to claw at it. It pulled back its head before slamming it against the stone. Sophia cried out as the wall shook. Some of the legionaries lost their footing and fell backwards into the courtyard far below.

Ferran broke out into a sprint. Another strike like that and the wall would fall. Already, after just one impact, there was massive crack. The three of them reached the top of the wall; the beast was right below them.

"What's the plan?" Faramond shouted.

"I've only ever fought one of these things before," Ferran said. "That time I was with my brother Nightblades. Out of the twenty of us that started the hunt, only three of us made it back alive. The only weakness they have is a small gap in the armour between their skull and neck. If we can strike a blow there, we might be able to bring it down." He touched the vials in his pocket again. "We have to weaken it enough so that the vials will be able to send it back to the Void."

"Let's get to it then," Faramond replied, determination on his face.

The Nightblade turned to the king and held his hand out. Faramond smiled and gripped it tightly. "May Niveren protect us," he said before climbing up onto the battlements. Ferran climbed up, too, and pulled up Sophia.

"This is crazy," she muttered.

The gargantuan began to rear back in preparation for another blow against the wall. Arrows lanced down at the creature, but all bounced harmlessly off of its armour.

Ferran shouted at the nearby legion archers to stop shooting, then jumped. For the second time that day he was falling towards danger. The gargantuan roared as it spotted the black-clad figure hurtling towards it. With its huge bulk, the creature had little room to manoeuvre, being in between the shattered remains of the outer wall and the still-standing inner wall. As he got closer, Ferran channelled his magic to slow his descent. He landed with a thud onto the gargantuan's back, wind-milling his arms to keep his balance. He looked up to the wall and waved to Faramond and Sophia. They, too, jumped. Steadying himself, Ferran used his magic once again, this time to slow the falls of his comrades. He was nowhere near as powerful as Luxon, and the strain of using such magic caused his arms to quiver with fatigue. The gargantuan rocked side to side, knocking him off of his feet. With a cry he began to slide off the beasts back. Quickly he raised his tourmaline blade and stabbed downwards. The magical blade bit deeply into the creature's armour, slowing his descent. Eventually he came to a stop, his feet dangling over open air.

Below, he could see goblins and pucks massing close to the gargantuan. The Fell Beasts were waiting for the walls to be breached. He hauled himself back up and clambered back onto the gargantuan's back. Faramond had landed safely and was carefully making his way towards the beast's neck and the chink in its armour. He heard Sophia shouting.

Spinning around, he spotted his wife close to the gargantuan's tail which was now resting against the ruined remains of the outer wall. Sarpi warriors were running down its length and onto the gargantuan's back; their aim, to stop Ferran and the others. Sophia drew the daggers from their sheaths on her belt. She flipped one so that she held it by the blade, and then pulled back her arm. With deadly accuracy, she threw the dagger at the lead Sarpi. With a scream, the warrior fell from the gargantuan's tail. Sophia threw the second dagger, taking down another Sarpi, before drawing the sword at her hip.

"Help Faramond. I'll hold them off!" she shouted over her shoulder.

Ferran turned and swore. Faramond had made it close to the monster's neck, but just as he was about to thrust his sword downward he was swatted by the beast's tongue, which now moved like a threatened snake.

Faramond staggered back to his feet. The tongue snapped at him again, but this time the king ducked under it. He swung his blade in a wide arc and sliced deeply into the salivating organ. As the blade struck, the gargantuan roared in pain. It reared backwards, almost making Ferran lose his footing once again. Using magic, he regained his balance and ran towards the neck. Faramond was now engaged in a deadly ballet with the whipping tongue.

"I've got this thing distracted!" he called.

Ferran pressed on. He ducked under the tongue and reached his target. Sure enough, there was a thin patch of bare flesh between the plates of the creature's neck and armoured skull.

He placed the tip of his tourmaline blade at the point. Muttering a prayer to Niveren, he gripped the hilt with both hands and thrust downwards. The magical blade pierced the flesh like a knife cutting through butter. The beast roared in agony, and then its legs gave out.

"Hold on!" Ferran shouted, before grabbing the wound he had made.

Cheers sounded from the walls as the defenders watched the gargantuan collapse with an impact that shook the ground like an earthquake.

As the dust cleared, Ferran reached into his tunic and pulled out one of the vials. He spotted Faramond running towards him.

"Get Sophia and get out of here," Ferran shouted. "I have to banish this wretched creature."

He plunged the vial into the wound and focused his magic. Using a telekinesis spell, he broke the vial. For a moment, nothing happened, giving him time to leap off of the gargantuan's crippled body. He landed in a crouch, only to find himself surrounded by snarling goblins. Looking around, he spotted Faramond and Sophia slide from the body and fall into a similar predicament. Slowly, he stood up and readied his sword. A goblin lunged at him with an iron-tipped spear, Ferran easily batted it aside and countered with a thrust of his own.

Then the vial broke, unleashing the magic that had been contained within.

A portal to the Void ripped open, sucking the gargantuan in from the inside. The beast roared again as it was pulled into the vortex. Ferran planted his sword into the ground to anchor himself in place. He pulled out another vial and hurled it at the goblins. Again, he used his magic to shatter the vial. Instantly, another portal opened and sucked the goblins towards it. The Fell Beasts tried to flee, but the magic was too powerful. Dozens were sucked back into the Void from whence they came. Once the magic had been spent, the two portals imploded in a flash of blinding light. Ferran lowered the arm he had been shielding his eyes with. The goblins had gone, and the way back to the wall was now clear. Looking to his right, he saw Faramond engaged in a sword fight with a Sarpi. Sophia ran over and skidded to a halt next to her husband, and helped him back onto his feet.

"One down. Two to go," she said breathlessly.

The other gargantuans had now fully breached the outer wall and were taking up position to begin smashing the inner wall. The defenders rained arrows, stones and whatever else they could find upon the beasts.

"We'll never stop them all," Ferran replied tiredly. "We need to get back to the wall. Fritin needs to order a retreat whilst he still can."

Sophia called to Faramond who had just finished impaling the Sarpi warrior on the end of his sword.

"Go! I'm right behind you," he bellowed.

Sophia reached the base of the wall first. The stonework had been damaged by the gargantuan's attack, but legionaries still manned it. She called up to them and a rope was thrown down. Behind her, Sarpi warriors were swarming through the breached outer wall and gaining fast. Only the sharp shooting of the legion archers was keeping them at bay.

Quickly, one after the other they began the arduous climb to the battlements. Sarpi arrows clattered off of the stonework, shredding their nerves as they climbed. Finally, Sophia reached the top and strong legion arms helped her over the side. Ferran was next and finally Faramond.

Once they were all back on the battlements, Ferran led the way towards the second gargantuan. As they ran the defenders cheered them. The slaying of one of the great beasts had restored to them some courage. As he ran, Ferran knew that the odds of succeeding in taking down another were slim. Unlike the first, the second gargantuan was being protected by goblins which were riding upon its back. Undead swarmed around its massive feet and N'gist mages were covering it with a magical shield. The beast raised its huge head and slammed it against the wall with devastating force.

A large crack appeared in the stonework. Another blow and the wall would fall. A horn sounded from the spot where the third beast was, its mournful tone warning that it too was battering at the wall.

Ferran slowed his run and stopped. Sweat dripped into his eyes and his limbs felt rubbery.

"It's no use," he muttered under his breath.

The scene before him filled him with dread. The enemy was too many, the defenders too few. Goblins were scaling ladders that they had managed to latch onto the walls. Legion swords flashed in the fading sunlight as they cut into the monsters. Bodies of men, legionary and tribesman alike, lined the walls, the courtyard below, and every spare scrap of ground.

A loud crash came from the wall ahead, and the panicked screams of men carried on the air. The enemy was through.

Ferran closed his eyes. The Watchers would fall. And along with it, the realm.

CHAPTER THIRTY TWO.

Yepert wandered in a daze. His face was covered in dirt and grime. All around him was death. The cries of wounded men filled the air, and blood covered the stones of the courtyard. A man in plate armour pushed passed him, sending him crashing onto the ground. The world spun. Where was he? How did he get outside? His mind reeled with confusion. The legionary ran on without a backwards glance. Other soldiers were now running past him; panic was all around.

He cried out as someone grabbed hold of his cloak and pulled him out of harm's way. Bleary eyed, he looked up to see Hannah, a look of determination on her tear-streaked face. She dragged him around a corner and into an alley that ran between two barracks buildings. Another cloaked figure was sat there.

"Luxon?" Yepert croaked.

Hannah moved him so that he lay next to his friend.

"Where have you been, Yepert?" Hannah sobbed. "Why are you outside? You were supposed to stay in the keep until we came for you." She hugged him tightly.

"I don't know. I ... I ... don't know how I got outside ... Last thing I remember, I was inside and then ..."

He cried out and held his head as a sharp pain lanced through his skull.

Say another word and you die, whispered a voice in his head.

Yepert cried out again and shut his mouth. The pain was too much to bear.

"The walls have fallen! Run for your lives!" cried a fleeing soldier.

Hannah hurried to the end of the alley and peeked around the corner. A huge hole was in the wall, and a massive creature was in the breach. Goblins, pucks and undead swarmed through. A cohort of legionaries formed a shield wall before them, and the bloodletting continued with a new desperate savagery. More warriors rushed into the fray whilst others fled for their lives. At the front of those running and riding to save his own skin was Commander Fritin. He bellowed at his men to get out of the way.

"Coward," Hannah snarled.

She hesitated. The fortress would soon be lost, but how could she get them all out? Luxon was still drifting in and out of consciousness, and Yepert was a babbling mess. She longed to see a friendly face.

Suddenly, the sky filled with a deafening roar. It was a roar that shook the very foundations of the fortress, a roar so loud that attackers and defenders alike paused the slaughter.

Hannah gripped the stone tightly and cried out.

Coming fast out of the sky were three massive creatures. Their wings were held tight against their castle-sized bodies as they dove through the clouds. Each of the creatures was a different size. One was smaller than the others, another bigger, and both were dark coloured. The one leading them, however, was massive, its silver scales glinting in the fading light of day.

"Umbaroth," she whispered in awe. Luxon had told her tales of the king of the dragons. She hurried over to Luxon and knelt before him.

"Luxon, wake up! Umbaroth has come, he is here to save us," she cried, tears of hope streaming from her tired eyes.

Upon hearing the name of his old friend Luxon stirred.

"Impossible …" he muttered before closing his eyes again.

Hannah laughed with joy. Perhaps all was not lost.

Ferran grunted as his tourmaline blade cleaved a goblin's head from its shoulders. Sophia ducked a spear point, before stabbing with her daggers, and Faramond roared as he brought his sword down in a two-handed thrust into the foe before him. The three of them had managed to get off the wall, but now they and a few dozen legionaries and tribal warriors were surrounded by enemies. Fighting back to back, they were making some progress through the snarling goblins.

A roar boomed from the sky above, making both men and monsters alike flinch. For a brief moment, the battle seemed to pause as every combatant stared in awe at the three dragons diving towards the fortress.

"It cannot be ..." Ferran uttered in stunned disbelief.

He recognised the powerful visage of Umbaroth, but it was the smallest of the three dragons that took him most by surprise. It was the dragon he had liberated from Stormglade.

As one, the dragons opened their cavernous mouths and poured fire upon Danon's ranks. In an instant, the dragon fire swept over the goblins that were swarming around them. The fire vaporised the beasts and carved a hole through which Ferran and the other survivors could flee. Faramond held his sword high into the air in salute to the dragons and whooped.

"Let's move!" Ferran ordered.

They broke into a sprint towards the keep, the last line of defence. The dragons circled high overhead and delivered another deadly salvo of fire, this time concentrated on one of the gargantuans. The gargantuan roared in pain as the fire struck and melted the mighty beast's armour. Ferran watched as the dragons were forced to shy away from their attack as the N'gist launched a volley of magical attacks.

He caught up with Sophia and Faramond.

"They are buying us time to escape. Even with three of them, it won't be enough to stop the enemy. Danon seems to have learnt his lesson from his defeat at Eclin."

"Damn the N'gist to the Void," Faramond spat.

"Let's get to the keep. We need to get Hannah and the others before we leave," Sophia said.

CHAPTER THIRTY TWO.

Ferran nodded in agreement.

Danon watched the dragons fall from the sky. The Sarpi general at his side cowered upon seeing them. Danon snarled.

"So, Umbaroth returns from his exile. Drakis has failed me," he muttered darkly.

He clenched his hands into fists, before striding towards the battle raging before him. Looking up, he tracked the movements of the dragons. His N'gist followers were doing well to stave off the flying serpents, but whilst they were distracted in doing so, too many of the enemy were escaping. He had wanted to crush the men of the tribes and the legion utterly.

Not taking his eyes off of the dragons, he clambered over the rubble of the outer wall. He narrowed his eyes at one of the black dragons. He would show the king of dragons that to challenge him would cost the lives of his kin. He shouted to his N'gist, who gathered around their master. Raising his hands high into the air he channelled his dark power. The air around him became icy cold and a dark shadow seemed to engulf him. Uttering a foul incantation, the shadow spread from his body to envelope his followers. He could feel their power feeding his own.

Far above the world, a piece of rock that had orbited the planet below for millennia changed direction. The rock began to fall. It struck Esperia's atmosphere, turning a brilliant fiery white. It fell at supersonic speed, towards the battle raging far below.

A sound like thunder signalled the rock's arrival. Ferran looked up just in time to see the meteor smash with full force into the bigger of the two black dragons. The impact sheared the mighty beast in two, sending its two halves tumbling to the ground. Fear gripped his Ferran's heart.

The once mighty beast's carcass smashed into the ground, creating a small earthquake as it did do. Witnessing the slaying of the dragon broke the defenders' resolve. What discipline there had been was now replaced with abject terror as everyman fought for their own survival.

As the defenders turned and fled, many were cut down by the now charging Sarpi, or ripped apart by the monsters at Danon's dark command. Umbaroth and the other dragon broke off their attacks and flew back into the clouds.

Ferran, Sophia and Faramond fled down the main road to the gate leading to the lands of Delfinnia. Halfway up the road, Sophia slowed and called for the others to stop. The Witch Hunter pointed to a narrow alley which lay close to the keep. Some of the legionaries had ran inside the stone tower, thinking that they could mount one last defence. Ferran knew better. Against the numbers they faced, they didn't stand a chance.

"It's Hannah and the boys," Sophia said. They ran over to the alley. Hannah cried out in relief.

"Praise Niveren you're still alive," she sobbed, hugging Sophia tightly.

"Are they alright?" Faramond asked as he watched the approaching slaughter.

"No. Luxon is barely conscious. The Void sickness ... I cannot heal it. Yepert is hurt too, I think he has a concussion."

"We need to leave. Now. Faramond help me," Ferran said reaching down and hauling Luxon to his feet.

He draped one of the wizard's arms over his shoulder. Faramond did the same with Yepert. Together, they moved back out onto the main street. Behind them, the enemy had set about setting fire to the legion's barracks. Acrid black smoke began to obscure their vision as they headed towards the gate. Rounding a corner, the gatehouse came into view. A small group of legionaries was ushering survivors through it and urging them to scatter into the countryside. If they all fled together it would be easy for Danon's forces to hunt them down like rabbits.

"Are there any more survivors?" asked a bloodied legionary, the captain of the small group. The desire to flee and save his own skin was evident in his eyes.

"We saw some men run to the keep," Sophia replied.

The legionary shook his head. "Crazy fools. They are only prolonging their deaths."

"Aren't we all?" muttered Faramond.

Dark rings of exhaustion were under the king's eyes. Ferran pitied him. He had been a king for only a few hours and yet he had ruled over the doom of his people. How many Keenlance warriors had survived? A thousand? A hundred? None?

The captain ushered them through the gate before ordering his men to seal it behind them. The heavy iron portcullis slammed shut with a thud.

"It won't hold them for long," the captain said, "but it should buy us a few moments. Good luck." He then joined his men in taking off their steel cuirasses and helmets. The armour would only slow them down.

Sophia and Hannah led the way up the road, whilst Ferran and Faramond brought up the rear. Luxon's feet dragged on the ground and Yepert was barely able to walk.

"We'll never get away fast enough," Hannah said.

As if in answer to her statement a shadow covered them. Umbaroth flew low above them and landed on the road ahead. The smaller dragon, meanwhile, circled above.

"Do not be afraid. Come. We will take you to safety," the silver dragon said, its powerful voice shaking the very air.

They hurried over to the huge dragon, who carefully picked them up one by one and placed them onto its back. When it was Luxon's turn to be lifted, the dragon hesitated. It lowered its head closer to the barely conscious young man.

"Forgive me, my friend," Umbaroth said softly. "I should never have left you." He raised his head and focused his huge eyes on Ferran and the others.

"What is wrong with him?"

"Void sickness," Ferran replied. "The worst case I have ever witnessed. If he doesn't get help soon he will die."

Umbaroth nodded his head in understanding. With surprising gentleness, he scooped Luxon up with his talons.

An explosion came from down the road. The gate, the final obstacle to Danon, had been destroyed. Pouring through the breach came the Fell Beasts, and close behind them marched the Sarpi. Upon seeing the dragon, the enemy broke into a charge, but Umbaroth flapped his massive wings and took to the sky.

Climbing high, Ferran was able to see carnage unfolding in the Watchers from above. The enemy looked like ants swarming over a carcass. At the sight he uttered a silent prayer to Niveren. A wave of tiredness came over him. His arms trembled and his head ached. He rolled onto his back and closed his eyes. The rhythm of the mighty dragon's wings flapping was soothing. It wasn't long before sleep took him.

CHAPTER THIRTY THREE.

A familiar smell stirred Ferran from his slumber. Groggily, he opened his eyes and found himself sat on grass underneath a tall birch tree. With the approaching winter, the trees leaves were turning a darkish red and falling softly like rain onto the ground below. He looked up at the sound of feet crunching through dead leaves. Sophia approached, a tired smile on her face. Her long dark hair was tousled, but the dirt and grime that had covered her face was gone. In her hands she carried a bowl of steaming hot soup.

"I didn't have the heart to wake you," she said gently. She knelt down in front of her husband and stroked his cheek softly before handing him the bowl.

"Where are we?" Ferran asked. He sniffed the soup: mutton and onions. His stomach growled in anticipation of its hunger being sated.

"Somewhere in the Westerlands, I think. I saw a river to the east. We can't be far from Ridderford."

Ferran whistled in surprise. They had travelled over four hundred miles in less than a day. Having a dragon as a friend certainly cut down on travelling time. He sipped the soup, savouring its taste as it touched his tongue, and the warm sensation as it moved to his stomach.

"Is everyone alright?" he asked, suddenly remembering Luxon and his perilous predicament.

Sophia frowned.

"What is it?" Ferran asked, concern in his voice.

"Umbaroth says that he can help Luxon. But to do so means taking him somewhere far away. A place where magic has left its mark on the world."

"Caldaria? That's not a bad thing."

Sophia shook her head.

"Not Caldaria. Where this place Umbaroth speaks of is, he would not say, just that it is far from here. He said he would also take Yepert with him."

Ferran got to his feet, all thoughts of food now replaced with worry. Together they walked to where the others were resting in a large open glade hidden amongst the birch forest.

Faramond sat on a fallen tree branch and was prodding at a campfire. He stared into the flames, his expression fierce. He waved at them weakly as they approached. Ferran clapped the king on the shoulder as he walked past. His attention was fixed on Hannah who was trying to feed Luxon soup with a wooden spoon. With one hand she held his head, while the other held the spoon to his mouth.

"He won't eat," she said, her lips trembling and her eyes threatening tears. Ferran squeezed her shoulder. The girl loved Luxon with all of her being, that much was clear. The sight of him lying there, his skin deathly pale and his eyes open – but not seeing – was a terrible thing to behold.

Yepert sat nearby. The lad was sat on the grass, his cloak wrapped tightly about his shoulders. Some of his vitality had returned, and with Hannah's healing magic he had regained most of his strength. His eyes were full of worry for his friend.

Lying at the back of the glade was Umbaroth and the smaller black dragon. The two massive creatures were locked deep in conversation. Ferran squeezed Sophia's hand, and together they approached the dragons. At their approach, Umbaroth raised his huge head.

"Greetings, Ferran of Blackmoor, Sophia Cunning," the dragon greeted in his deep, rumbling voice.

"It's been a long time, Umbaroth," Ferran said. "Where have you been all this time? Not that I'm ungrateful for you showing up when you did, but why did you?"

Umbaroth pointed a clawed talon at the smaller dragon.

"You can thank Tratos here for that."

The smaller dragon lowered its head close to Ferran. It nuzzled its nose against the Nightblade. The move took Ferran by surprise, and Sophia laughed at his expression.

"You saved me from the N'gist," Tratos explained. "You set me free. After I left Stormglade, I sought out help. I found Sarkin. He had been looking for me for months. I told him everything that had happened, and it was he who called to Umbaroth. Sarkin was my friend."

Ferran nodded in understanding. Sarkin had been the dragon cut down by Danon. He remembered Luxon telling the tale of his and Yepert's encounter with the dragon on the King's Road.

"I heard the call from my kin," Umbaroth interjected. "The first call since ... my exile"

Ferran looked back to where Luxon lay. He had promised to protect him, but the Void sickness was beyond his ability to heal. Time was running out; with every passing moment Luxon was getting weaker.

"Where do you want to take him?" Ferran asked Umbaroth.

The dragon rested his head on the grass so that his enormous eye was at the same level as Ferran. The iris alone was as tall as the Nightblade. It blinked once before the dragon replied:

"Danon planned for this to happen. He knew what time in the Void would do to someone as powerful as Luxon. The magic that gives him his strength is tainted by the corruption of the Void. Every time he uses it, the Void sickness tightens its grip. His losing control of his anger and his power allowed the sickness to overwhelm him. He needs to be purified of the taint. To do that, he must go to the place where magic itself was born. Only then may he have a chance of surviving."

Ferran stared hard at the dragon.

"The birth place of magic? You can't mean ..."

The dragon lifted his head and raised his body from the ground so that he now towered above the tree tops. His mighty wings spread out behind him, creating a breeze which shook leaves from the surrounding trees.

"Fear not, Nightblade, I will protect Luxon and his friend," Umbaroth said striding over to where Luxon lay. Hannah cried out as the dragon carefully picked him up with his talons and placed him on the spiny ridge just behind his scaled head.

Yepert looked up at the dragon, then at his friends. He couldn't leave Luxon. Whatever perils awaited them, they would face them together, and the dark voice in his head insisted that he go. He hugged Hannah tightly.

"We will be fine. I'll get him back to you, I promise," he said with more confidence than he felt. For a moment he considered telling her of the voice, but a lancing pain caused him to wince and hold his tongue. He clambered onto the claw offered to him by Umbaroth, and soon he was sat on the dragon's back.

Ferran, Sophia, Hannah and Faramond stood together to watch them go.

"Luxon will return, I promise you," Umbaroth said solemnly before taking to the sky.

EPILOGUE

Ricard knelt before his nephew. His face was red with shame and his eyes were dark and tired. All he had wanted to do was to protect the realm; he wasn't the monster his enemies made him out to be. The assassination of Davik had taken a heavy toll upon him. The arrogant confidence he felt in the days leading up to that dark deed was long gone; instead, guilt and fear reigned supreme. The realm was in chaos. Accadus of Retbit had marched his army across the Zulus River and advanced to the walls of Balnor. Ricard's knuckles went white as he pressed them against the marble floor. The reports he had read had made his blood run cold with horror. The bloodletting had been horrific; tens of thousands had been slain, and the city had been sacked with a savagery not seen since the Magic Wars. Worse of all had been the fate of the city's young baron. As an example to the rest of the realm, Accadus had flayed the boy alive and strung his corpse from the city walls.

Now, Ricard had more bad news to deliver to his king. The Watchers had fallen, thousands of tribespeople had poured into the Westerlands and Bison unchecked, and Danon had returned. His huge army was on the move, defeating any force that tried to oppose it. The city of Bison was crying out for aid. In his heart, Ricard knew the city would fall.

"Do you have news of Luxon Edioz, uncle?" Alderlade asked.

The boy king's voice was full of hope. He was sitting on a throne that was far too big for him; his feet didn't even reach the ground.

Ricard shook his head. "I have heard nothing of the wizard Luxon Edioz, sire. It is presumed that he perished at the Battle of the Watchers."

Alderlade banged his fist on the side of his throne.

"I commanded him to find my stone!" the boy whined. "Where is it? I want it?"

Ricard frowned at his nephew. His kingdom was falling apart all around him and yet he was on the verge of tears because of a stupid stone.

The thought had crossed his mind before, but this time a resolve firmed inside him. Slowly, Ricard stood. He turned to the guards stood nearby and caught their eye. They were his men. His hand drifted to the hilt of his sword. He was already accused of murdering Davik. Of that he was innocent. Would the people forgive him for what he was now thinking of doing? Surely they would. The realm was on the verge of destruction at the hands of the enemy. Now was the time for leadership: a true king, not some snot-nosed child. Nephew or not, it was for the good of Delfinnia.

He gestured to his guards to seal the doors that led into the throne room. The king ... no, not the king, the boy was still whining about the stone. Ricard drew his sword, stood before the king and gestured to the guards.

"Long live the king," Ricard whispered as his men roughly grabbed the screaming boy and dragged him out of the throne room.

The End

ALSO BY M.S. OLNEY

Other Books By M.S. OLNEY

The Sundered Crown Saga-

Heir to the Sundered Crown

War for the Sundered Crown

Quest for the Sundered Crown

Voyage for the Sundered Crown

Heroes of the Sundered Crown

Master of the Sundered Crown

The Sundered Crown Boxset 1

Sundered Crown Tales -

Danon

The Crimson Blade

The Nightblade

The Empowered Ones-

The First Fear

The Temple of Arrival

The Empowered Ones boxset

Myths of Aldara-

The Awakening Light

Unconquered

Blood of kings

Terran Defenders

Genesis

ALSO BY M.S. OLNEY

Rebirth